MAYHEM AT SEA

LUKE RYDER
BOOK 3

JOHN G. BLUCK

ROUGH
EDGES
PRESS

Mayhem at Sea
Paperback Edition
Copyright © 2023 John G. Bluck

Rough Edges Press
An Imprint of Wolfpack Publishing
9850 S. Maryland Parkway, Suite A-5 #323
Las Vegas, Nevada 89183

roughedgespress.com

Paperback ISBN 978-1-68549-311-0
eBook ISBN 978-1-68549-310-3
LCCN 2023941934

MAYHEM AT SEA

ONE

FLOODLIGHTS LIT a Vietnam War-era Huey UH-1 helicopter nestled in a remote clearing near Mendocino and Ft. Bragg in Northern California.

The chopper's pilot, a man of many aliases, preferred to be called "Pilot." A seasoned drug runner, he watched while two comrades loaded the storied warbird with two tons of American, Russian, and Chinese weapons; scuba equipment; and two folded black canvas tarps.

The men finished stowing the cargo and leaned back on the chopper's fuselage.

"All done, Pilot," the taller one said.

The men stood straight and retreated to their rented truck, where one of them opened the driver's door.

"Thanks for helping," said Pilot, a gray-haired man in his fifties. He walked to the aircraft and waved. "Bye."

"Best of luck," the taller man said.

Pilot started the sixty-year-old whirlybird, a reliable, easy-to-fly machine. Because it had auxiliary fuel tanks, its range was six hundred eighty statute miles. The surplus Army helicopter had cost Pilot a hundred fifty thousand, although its original price in 1970 had been three million bucks.

The chopper was his mechanical pet. He considered it a defanged dragon because the company which had sold the helicopter to him had removed its weapons. He'd named it Fafnir after a mythical Scandinavian dragon.

While Pilot guided his craft upward, he wondered if he'd made the right choice to take this job. Yep, Tony Franco would pay him at least a hundred thousand to fly the Huey a dozen miles. But Pilot didn't like Tony's plan because Pilot was to stay two or three days with Tony and his men to evacuate some of them in exchange for another five hundred thousand. Tony said he'd been planning his operation for most of a year and had considered all possibilities. But Pilot figured no one could foresee everything. If it were possible to peek into the future, Tony would have won the daily double when betting on the horses. Better yet, he would have bought himself a winning lottery ticket.

All the same, Pilot had chosen to ignore the warnings his guts had been sending to him. Pilot guided the chopper west and headed out over the Pacific Ocean, a dozen feet above the water, below radar, and into the thick blanket of fog. The flying machine's vibrations were familiar, even relaxing to him.

He turned up the soothing music flowing into his head-set. It was Ludwig van Beethoven's Eroica Symphony. Still, he had to take a deep breath while his flying machine gained altitude and briefly popped above the fog. He searched for a large ship's distant lights in the bright moonlight, which lit the top of the fog bank. From more than half of its surface, the moon was reflecting sunlight to Earth. Luckily, the air was clear above the layer of fog except for a rare cloud. The stars were pinpricks in the black sky, and the ocean air was refreshing though it smelled of brine and algae.

TWO

AT 2:55 AM on calm Pacific waters ten miles west of the California coast, the luxury cruise ship *Sea Trek* sailed north toward Alaska at twelve knots through the night. Recently, the moon had been brightening. It would become full in two days. The ocean smelled slightly salty. The temperature was fifty-six degrees. These pleasant conditions forebode a relaxing, waterborne, fourteen-day vacation. Yet, thirty-eight-year-old passenger Luke Ryder was in his bed in his cabin, unable to keep his eyes closed. In contrast, his African American girlfriend, Layla Taylor, a woman in her twenties, lay next to him in a deep sleep.

Ryder, a six-foot-two Kentucky deputy sheriff, had never been at sea before, nor had he ever walked along an ocean shore. The excitement of traveling on a cruise ship with Layla, enjoying the ship's live shows, and touring Alaska kept his mind busy. More at home in the Kentucky woods than any place crowded with people, he especially wanted to see bald eagles, bears, and whales. These thoughts fired up his brain while he considered what he'd do first after the sun rose.

There was another reason for his sleeplessness, too. Less

than a week ago, he'd been on an undercover assignment in California. He'd been a member of an FBI task force investigating a cold case murder at a NASA research center in the Golden State. Though he wouldn't admit it, his healing throat still hurt where the murderer had throttled him during a struggle.

Ryder was happy the dark bruise on his neck had faded enough so he could stop wearing a turtleneck sweater to hide the injury. Because he'd solved the murder and caught a North Korean spy to boot, FBI officials had asked him to become a full-time FBI employee. Ryder had told the FBI task force agent in charge, Rita Reynolds, he wouldn't quit his deputy sheriff job and leave Kentucky. But he was having second thoughts.

* * *

MEANWHILE, in the fresh air on the stern of the *Sea Trek*, one of the ship's crew heard the distant sound of a helicopter. Its distinctive whup-whup-whup sound was barely audible over the noise of the ship's engines and wake. He wondered why a chopper would fly over the ocean at this wee hour of the morning.

The mammoth ship was a floating hotel, three hundred fifty feet from bow to stern and twenty stories high. Fourteen decks were accessible to its thirty-six hundred passengers. A crew of thirteen hundred served the guests and operated the two hundred fifty thousand ton vessel. Painted bright white, except for decorative streaks of blue on its bow to represent waves, the vessel was state of the art, having been built in 2029 for nearly two billion dollars. Bright red lifeboats hung along its sides, though the ship's designers bragged it would take an atomic bomb to sink it.

Balconies lined Decks Eight through Fourteen, where ocean-view passenger cabins dotted the two vertical sides of the ship. At this early hour, most of the lights in these cabins were out while the vast majority of the vessel's guests slept.

A small number gambled in the ship's casino or drank in one of the onboard bars which remained open.

The ship had departed San Francisco at 4:00 PM the previous day. The vessel was a hundred fifty miles into its trip. Sailing at a leisurely pace, it was as far north as Mendocino, California. A speed of twelve knots—roughly fourteen miles per hour—was ideal because it saved fuel and made the journey comfortable for passengers. The huge watercraft stayed ten miles offshore because its captain wanted to avoid the shipping lanes, where big cargo ships plied the water farther out to sea.

* * *

RYDER STIRRED when he first heard the loud racket of helicopter blades while a whirlybird flew toward the ship. He opened his eyes wider and stared out of his cabin window at the moonlit ocean's fog bank. He tried to spot the chopper. Something undefinable about the sound bothered him. Next to him, Layla remained in a deep, restful sleep. Her ebony skin blended into the darkness of the cabin.

Ryder wondered if someone on the ship had become ill, and a medevac helicopter was about to land on the stern helipad to take an ailing person to shore for medical care. Though Ryder's mind was busy guessing about the approaching chopper, his body was so tired his eyelids felt heavy. He relaxed. Soon, he softly snored, and he was fully at rest, his uncombed, black hair splayed across his white pillowcase. In his dreams, he at last felt at peace. It was time to clear his mind and heal his body and soul.

THREE

A NATIVE OF BROOKLYN, New York, Tony Franco stood in the shadows near the helipad on the stern of the *Sea Trek* cruise ship. Thick fog swirled around the vessel.

Tony thought himself a modern buccaneer, and he believed, in time, he would become more famous than the notorious pirate, Blackbeard. Thirty-one-year-old Tony had curly, black hair pulled back into a short ponytail. He also sported a neatly cut black beard in contrast to Blackbeard's large beard, which contemporary accounts said came up to his eyes. Tony had learned Blackbeard sought to terrify his enemies so they would surrender without a fight. Tony planned to do the same.

The sounds of the approaching Huey UH-1 helicopter became louder. The main rotor's twin blades whirled at close to the speed of sound—about seven hundred seventy miles per hour—producing a signature whup-whup-whup sound. This chopper could carry a dozen men plus their weapons, and it had a normal range of two hundred eighty-five miles. But Tony had ordered just one person was to ride aboard the Huey, the pilot. Hence, the aircraft was able to carry four thousand five hundred pounds of cargo—including AK-47 automatic rifles, ammunition, shoulder-fired antiaircraft Stinger missiles, rocket-propelled grenade launchers with their ammunition, and three hundred pounds of C-4 explosives.

Veteran pilots claimed Huey choppers were reliable and easy to fly compared to other types of whirlybirds. But then again, to fly a helicopter took skill and lots of practice.

Two days earlier, two men had painted one large red cross on each side of the Huey's olive-drab fuselage using vivid, crimson latex house paint. The helicopter's sides were also scarred with three patched war wounds, where Viet Cong bullets had slammed through the chopper. While the flying machine neared the sleeping *Sea Trek*, the chopper was again going to war, for she carried arms and explosives, not medicine and bandages.

Tony saw the helicopter when it emerged from the fog. He glanced at the darkened recesses near the helipad. He could hardly make out the outlines of twenty of the twenty-six men he'd hired to help him take control of the ship. He'd promised them each five hundred thousand dollars minimum to take part in an act of modern piracy. They'd get more if they were to collect a bigger ransom for the release of the ship than Tony had anticipated, or if some of the men died. These were hard men who had either been soldiers with combat experience or drug smugglers who'd lived through rough encounters with the US Coast Guard.

The downwash, wind generated by the helicopter's spinning rotor blades, blew the fog aside and scoured Tony's face while the chopper gently settled onto the deck of the helipad. At the same time as the blades slowed, the pilot exited the craft. From the foggy shadows along the stern deck, Tony's handpicked men ran onto the helipad and opened the sliding side doors of the aircraft. The men removed two heavy, blanket-covered stretchers from the chopper. Carrying them, they scampered back into the shadows. In the darkness, the men threw the blankets aside, revealing twenty fully locked and loaded AK-47 rifles paired with Ka-Bar combat knives.

Tony handed index cards to his five team leaders on which he'd written numerical codes needed to open certain cipher door locks. "They changed the codes yesterday," Tony said in his New York accent. He'd bribed one of the ship's crew to obtain the new codes.

The men grabbed the AKs and knives while Tony watched. He said, "Synchronize watches. Everybody ready?"

"Yes, sir," said the leaders, each of whom was part of a four-man team.

"Remember, do not fire unless truly necessary. Use the Ka-Bars instead." Tony scanned the men's eyes.

Some men grinned. Others were grim.

"Move out," Tony said. He patted each leader's back when the five groups departed for their assignments. They were to take the vessel's bridge, engine room, communications center, the ship's chief and deputy chief of security, and last and best of all, Heather Falcon. She was the Silicon Valley heiress of the CEO and founder of Hacienda Computer Systems, a multibillion-dollar corporation. The twenty-year-old blond woman was the icing on the cake. Tony would partake of her until her daddy paid a one hundred fifty million dollar ransom. Tony's heartbeat galloped when he remembered pictures he'd seen of Heather. Yes, he'd doubtless enjoy her company. He would demand another three hundred fifty million dollars for the release of the ship and its five thousand passengers and crew.

Tony was in his element. Taking a ship was a sport. He wished to defeat his enemies as if he were playing a board game with them. It would be a competition for which he'd make up the rules and change them to win. He would never admit defeat, because he thought he was invincible.

He couldn't wait to bring a bunch of oligarchs to their knees. He'd show them all. And he'd get away with it. "They'll be sorry," he said aloud.

Why did Tony feel like he did? A secret he had never revealed, even to his best friends, was that when he was young, he had had a girlfriend whom he'd loved, and she had loved him. But her father—a banker who had millions of dollars in stocks and bonds—had threatened to disown his daughter if she didn't break off her relationship with Tony. The banker hired a private investigator and learned young Tony, then a college student at Stanford, was dealing drugs and cavorting with prostitutes. Armed with this information, the banker had finally convinced his daughter to leave Tony. Ever since then, Tony had done what he could to wound the ultrarich.

FOUR

AT 3:20 AM, five pirate assault teams of four men each approached key places across the ship—the engine room, the communications center, the security officers' cabins, Silicon Valley heiress Heather Falcon's suite, and the bridge.

At 3:21 AM, the teams acted.

The Team One leader, Pelz, eased up to one of the doors of the ship's bridge. He focused on the door's cipher lock. With a thick, tough finger, he typed four numbers on its programmable keypad. The door's lock clicked open. Holding his AK-47 automatic rifle in his right hand, he pulled the door toward him with his free hand. He propped the steel door open with a heavy-duty waste can. He and his three men then rushed into the ultramodern bridge, aiming their weapons at the four crewmen who controlled the ship.

"Don't do anything stupid," Pelz said in a gravelly voice. "We're taking command. Continue with your routine duties."

A skinny, pale, youthful man at the helm controls was shaking like an aspen tree in a stiff breeze. He nervously glanced at the intruders and then noticed the calm eyes of the older officer in charge of the bridge, a man of fifty.

The officer nodded at the young man and then scanned his skeleton crew of three. "Do what the man says."

"Wisely spoken," Pelz said.

His three colleagues took positions around the bridge, their rifles at the ready.

The cruise ship officer addressed the pirate. "I take it the chopper with the red crosses isn't for a real medevac?"

The pirate leader stared at the officer and then grinned, showing stained teeth. "Your new captain will arrive shortly. Address him as Captain, but he prefers Tony. Follow his every instruction, and you won't be harmed." The buccaneer inhaled. "The engine room and communications center have already been taken by our men."

Pelz saw movement at the door when the pirate in command, Tony, entered. He sported two custom leather pistol belts draped across his chest like bandoliers. They had two holstered Glock pistols and pouches for magazines. His left pistol belt also held a sheathed Ka-Bar combat knife. Tony had earlier bragged to his team he would use Blackbeard's fear tactics to prod the crew to surrender. One way to encourage dread was to be armed to the teeth. Blackbeard had also sported two braces of pistols crisscrossed on his chest in bandolier fashion.

Tony strutted to the center of the bridge, glanced through the forward windows, posed like an actor on stage, and said, "I'm Tony, your new captain. If you and other crew members follow my commands without question, I will reward you with untraceable cryptocurrency in special overseas bank accounts. Depending upon how you comply, and the complexity of your jobs, you will be paid a fair share of the booty I will take."

Each of the three young crew members ventured a glimpse at their senior officer.

Tony pulled a folded black cloth from the backpack he wore. He unfolded the cloth. It was the Jolly Roger flag. "Young helmsman, run this flag up the mast after I'm assured our teams have taken the entire ship. Come forward, lad."

The elder officer took the helm. "Go ahead, Reggie."

Reggie, a pale, pole-thin man, briskly walked to Tony, who handed him the pirate flag. "On my command, you'll hoist this banner."

He gulped. "Yes, Captain."

Tony patted the young man's back. "See how easy it is to follow orders? You'll be the first person for whom we will open a special account. Being the first man on the new crew to take an order and complete it, you'll receive a bonus of ten thousand dollars in crypto." Tony turned to the other three cruise ship sailors. "Of course, if someone disobeys an order, the penalty is death."

* * *

MEANWHILE, when Team One was securing the bridge, the Team Two pirate leader guided his three men into the engine room far below the ship's stern. When they entered the cavernous space, they smelled oil and heard the loud sounds of the roaring engines. The noise hurt the leader's ears, and the vibrations of the machinery penetrated his entire body.

The men held their AK-47s at high port, close to their chests, with the weapons' muzzles angled up. While they clambered down a steel staircase, their footfalls caused a clanking noise that mixed with the rumble of the ship's engines.

The room was at least forty feet high. Metal stairways, pathways, ramps, and catwalks crisscrossed the large space. Each of these had railings and handholds. In a rough sea, they would be a godsend.

High-pressure sodium lamps lit everything in a dull, dark-yellow glow, giving the room an otherworldly appearance. The buccaneer leader imagined he was invading an alien spaceship, not a seagoing vessel. He spotted fancy, computerized controls near some of the machinery, which packed the voluminous room. The heat of the place warmed his body.

Lots of big pipes snaked from place to place, forming a confusing jumble. They ran every which way and at different, odd angles. The buccaneer figured the engines and the ancillary equipment were a nightmare to maintain.

The Team Two leader caught sight of two rows of engines, each array composed of eight identical motors. They were encased in steel covers shaped like huge upright laundromat washing machines. A curved one-foot-diameter pipe ran upward from each machine into the maze of pipes overhead.

A middle-aged, stocky man in blue overalls approached. He wore ear-protection headgear similar to a headset. "Who the hell are you?" he yelled over the din of the engines.

The pirate pointed his weapon at the man and screamed, "Sit on the chair, and you won't get hurt."

With bright, intelligent eyes, the man glared at the intruder. "What do you want?"

"The ship. You in charge here?"

"Yep."

"How many guys you got workin' here besides yourself?"

The man waited long enough to irritate the pirate. "Three."

The Team Two leader turned to his men and bellowed, "Spread out. Find the other three. Bring 'em here."

One pirate nodded and began to search. His two companions went in separate directions.

The pirate leader again directed his attention to the engineer-in-charge, leaning close to him. "Mister, we've taken the whole ship. There's a new captain, Tony Franco. You will call him Captain, but he prefers Tony, and you will follow his every order, or you will be severely punished. The penalty is death."

The stocky man stared defiantly, but he'd begun to sweat. "How long do you intend to be on this ship?"

"'Til we get paid a big ransom. Cooperate, and everything will be okay." The ruffian smiled in an effort to calm the situation. Had he been too harsh?

A pirate came around the corner of a row of machinery. He pushed a pale white man in front of him.

The Team Two leader yelled, "What's your name, young man?"

"Jeff Brooks, apprentice engineer."

The older engineer-in-charge turned toward Jeff. "Do whatever they tell you, Jeff."

"Okay." Jeff took a quick glance at two wooden crates he'd stored in a corner under boxes of spare parts. He hoped the pirates wouldn't search the area.

* * *

AT THE SAME time the engine room was overtaken by Team Two, Pirate First Mate Arlo Ahern led his three armed men along a passageway in the crew's cabin area on Deck Two near midship. The passage was well-lit. The white walls, or bulkheads; the polished, light tan floor tiles; and the off-white acoustical panels above his head reminded Arlo of a hospital corridor.

While Arlo and his small group strode along, they met no crew members. Those who weren't at work were asleep. This was a good thing. Arlo didn't relish the thought of dealing with even one or two additional sailors. They would delay achieving his goal: to imprison both the *Sea Trek*'s chief of security and his deputy chief.

When the armed party passed a cluttered employee bulletin board that displayed company notices and personal postings, Arlo noticed the cabin numbers changed to another series of digits on the far side of a cross passageway. On his left, he saw Cabin 2205's door. It was Security Chief Jay Bullock's room. The next cabin was 2207, where Deputy Security Chief Bill Honeycutt was staying.

Arlo had planned that Tex Curtis and he would take Jay. The other two pirates on his team would arrest Bill.

Arlo stopped near Jay's door, poised, ready to open it. At the same moment, another pirate neared Bill's cabin. Arlo nodded. Then he and the other pirate tapped in codes on the door locks to open them.

Arlo heard Jay's cabin lock faintly click, and he cracked open the door. A sliver of light from the cabin beamed onto the hallway tiles. He swung the door open and saw Jay, a husky man, sitting at his maple-stained hutch desk typing on a laptop computer. A double bed, a mini-refrigerator, and a TV also crowded the small, cramped room.

Jay turned. "What the hell?"

Because Arlo had unlocked the door and pushed it open with his left hand, he held his rifle in his right hand. The muzzle pointed down, though he'd begun to lift it upward.

Jay saw Arlo's weapon. In the blink of an eye Jay wrested open a desk drawer, grabbed a pistol, and began to raise it.

A chill of fear raced through Arlo's body. He instinctively dove into the tiny cabin with his AK-47 rifle in an awkward position. While he began to move his weapon to a firing position, an object whizzed by him.

Tex's Ka-Bar knife struck Jay in his torso with a thud. Jay dropped his pistol, and peered down at the combat knife stuck in his chest. He collapsed and shuddered. Then he was still.

Arlo rushed forward and checked Jay's neck for a pulse. "He's dead." Unable to speak for a moment, Arlo finally said, "Thanks, Tex."

Tex approached the body. "Tony said no shootin' if possible." He spoke in a strong Southern drawl.

Jay's blood spread across the carpet, soaking into it.

Arlo felt his pulse rate start to slow, though he knew his heart was still thumping like he was running at full speed. He took a deep breath. "Check to see if they took Bill."

"Aye, Aye." Tex left.

Arlo examined the dead man's laptop screen. Jay had been composing an email to his wife. Regret hit Arlo like a surge of nausea. Was it worth a promised half-million dollars to forever see Jay's eyes staring into nothingness?

Arlo wiped away a tear when Tex pushed Bill into the

cabin. The prisoner's hands were bound behind him with heavy-duty plastic tie wraps, and he wore pajamas.

Bill gagged when he peered at Jay's body. "Shit," he said.

Tex walked around Bill toward the corpse, leaned over it, and yanked the knife from the dead man's chest.

Tex then approached Bill and placed the combat knife against his captive's throat, blood dribbling down the blade onto the man's exposed chest. "You'll get the same unless you tell us where the ship's armory is and open it."

Tex pressed his prisoner's skin down with the flat side of the razor-sharp blade.

Bill whispered, "It's down the passageway in Cabin 2210."

Tex moved the blade away from the man's throat.

Arlo glanced past the unmade bed and the clothes scattered across the floor toward Jay's open cabin door. "Leave the body. Let's go."

* * *

WHILE ARLO WAS DEALING with Jay and Bill, the Team Four pirate leader was leading his men toward the ship's communications room.

The leader sidled up to the comms room glass bulkhead bordering the passageway. The floor-to-ceiling window enabled passengers walking along the passage to see the ship's communications staff at work. He peered through the glass door. The uncluttered area was brightly lit and had tan bulkheads and a burgundy carpet. Three young men sat in front of computers and electronic equipment, absorbed in their tasks.

His rifle hidden by his trousers leg, the lead pirate typed a four-digit number on the entry door's cipher lock keypad. After jerking the door open, he rushed into the room with his three armed men, who brandished their AK-47 automatic rifles.

"Hands up. Move away from your consoles," the top buccaneer said in a calm voice.

The three communications men held up their quivering hands, stood, and backed away from their long, beige countertop. It held monitors, keyboards, and eight computers arranged in two back-to-back rows. On the periphery of the room, there were racks of electronic equipment, TV switching gear, and a radio transmitter.

The Team Four leader nodded at his man, Joe Clarke, a.k.a. Tokyo Joe. "Turn it all off, Tokyo."

An electronics, computer, and explosives expert, Tokyo Joe swiftly switched off the power to a myriad of machines and unplugged critical cables. He disabled the ship's pagers, the vessel's telephones, the closed circuit TV system, the cellular sea phones, and the wireless computer services.

"All done," Tokyo Joe said.

The team leader turned to the ship's three communications men. "Relax. Put your hands down. If you haven't guessed, we and others have taken over this vessel, which is being held for ransom."

One of the comms crew, a man with carrot-red hair, shook his head and sighed.

The Team Four leader shifted his attention to the redhead. "Hang loose, Red. Everybody's gonna be okay. Do what we ask, and this will be over in hours, or a couple of days at most. Your company will pay."

The tallest technician who'd been in front of a desktop microphone asked, "Can we go? Your guy knows how to run the systems."

The leader said, "You'll stay in case we have questions." He ceased talking for a second and caught sight of one of his men and Tokyo Joe. "Tokyo, go to the engine room. James, stay here, and stand guard."

The Team Four leader made a mock salute and left with the fourth pirate. They were off to patrol the decks, the bars, and the casino to find passengers, search them, and send them to their cabins.

* * *

WHILE TWENTY-YEAR-OLD HEATHER FALCON slept in her splendid fifteen hundred square foot suite, the Team Five leader and his three buccaneer partners searched for the passageway that would lead them to her cabin.

In sleep, Heather felt at ease, dreaming of a warm, friendly land of her own invention.

Outside her door, Lester Shapiro, Heather's bodyguard, sat on a wooden chair propped against the bulkhead. Engrossed in a paperback Western novel, he, too, was imagining a fictional place and time. He kept close tabs on Heather, whose father, Howard, had founded a multibillion-dollar company, Hacienda Computer Systems, based in Silicon Valley.

The gentle rocking of the mammoth vessel while it sailed at twelve knots toward Alaska eased Heather awake. She got up, exited her bedroom, and went into the common area of the suite, where a piano, a large-screen TV, a bar, and leather furniture stood. She opened an inlaid wooden box and withdrew a top-quality marijuana cigarette. She grabbed her silver lighter, flicked it open, and held its flame under the reefer. Taking a deep drag, she sucked the pungent smoke inward.

Heather was easygoing. She didn't act like a spoiled, rich brat. Instead, she was agreeable and friendly. Modest and bashful, she didn't try to steal the limelight. For these and other reasons, she was well-liked.

With the face and body of a supermodel, she resembled a movie star and could have become one if she had so desired. Her long, thin, blond hair was always well-brushed. She normally wore little makeup except a touch of powder and tasteful red lipstick to accent her pearly teeth. Taller than the average woman, she was thin and athletic.

She would do anything to avoid conflict and live in joyful peace. And so, she prided herself on being a peacemaker, bringing feuding friends together to heal their relationships.

Though Heather was well-adjusted, despite having lived a protected life, she was not used to being on her own. Hence, she often fantasized about living in the freer world of the common citizen. She considered herself a survivor of her lonely but stressful life.

She sat on a leather easy chair, puffed at her reefer, and blew musky smoke from her lips. To her, it smelled like weak skunk spray with the added aroma of lemons, pine wood, and rich soil.

Heather jumped at the click of her cipher lock unbolting. The door opened. Wearing heavy, brown leather boots, a man in khaki cargo pants—with a holster and a pistol strapped to one leg—stomped into the room. Ammunition magazines were stuffed in the pockets of a canvas vest he wore over his black shirt. A large knife also hung from his pistol belt.

"Stay calm, Heather," the brown-bearded man said in a baritone voice.

Heather noticed his curly hair was of average length. He was attractive in a rough sort of way. She felt fear mixed with curiosity and a smidgen of adventure.

When the pirate began to walk toward Heather, she snuffed her reefer in a glass ashtray. Her attention captured by the weird entry of the strange man, she'd forgotten she was clad in a negligee. At once, she felt exposed and ashamed.

"You need to come with us," the rugged man said.

"Did Mr. Shapiro send you in?"

"Who?"

"My bodyguard."

"He's out of action."

"Is he okay?"

"You need to leave."

"Who said?"

"Your father."

"Are you sure?"

"Yes. There's a helicopter on the deck which will take you to him."

Heather was skeptical. "I need to dress." She planned to go into her bedroom and call her dad, Howard, using her satellite phone.

"Sorry, there's no time to waste."

A second man attired in combat clothes, who also wore a holster and pistol, entered the suite.

The Team Five leader nodded to the man.

The second buccaneer moved behind Heather and secured her hands with plastic tie wraps.

"Stop it. Who the hell are you?"

The Team Five pirate leader was silent. He smiled a subtle smile.

She needed to pee, but she held it. She drew in air and meant to scream, but when she opened her mouth, the second pirate tied a gag on her.

Heather grunted.

The pirate who'd gagged her said, "Don't fight it." He tied a black blindfold over her eyes.

Heather envisioned her father's face, his costly suit, and the silk ties he wore. She could virtually feel his strong hug, his nervous energy. Her dad was charming, attractive, ambitious, and highly driven. Though he wasn't a person known to express his emotions, she knew he loved her the way only a father could love a daughter. He would do everything in his power to free her. But would it be enough? She hoped she'd live to see him again.

When the team leader's partner guided her out of the door, her bare feet stepped in a wet and sticky substance. Her left foot brushed what felt like a paperback book.

"Be careful," the team leader said to the other pirate. "Keep her from bumping into stuff. Remember, hands off."

The second buccaneer led Heather to the suite next to the captain's quarters, which Tony had taken for himself.

Heather wondered what had become of her bodyguard. She felt like she was stepping into a movie, or experiencing a drug-induced dream.

Meanwhile, the Team Five leader began to search Heather's suite, hoping to find her satellite phone and expensive jewelry.

* * *

MAY 16, 4:30 AM

Confident the ship was secure, pirate and self-proclaimed captain, Tony Franco, entered the captain's suite, strode to the bar, and chose a bottle of whiskey. Still standing, he poured two ounces of booze into a glass and sipped the light brown liquid.

Tony turned to his second-in-command, Waylen. The thirty-two-year-old man was six-foot-one and built like a heavyweight boxer. "You want a shot?" Tony held up the whiskey bottle.

"Thanks, Cap, but I'd prefer a beer and a hot dog with mustard." Waylen's blue eyes and pale skin hinted he was of Northern European descent, unlike most of his drug-smuggler pals, who were from Latin America or had roots there.

Tony nodded at a small refrigerator behind the bar. "Check in the fridge. Could be a beer in there. But it's too early for a hot dog."

"I was joking, Skipper." He reached into the refrigerator, pulled out a brown bottle, and twisted off its cap, which he set on the bar.

"Where'd you put the blond bitch's satellite phone?" Tony asked.

"On the desk." Waylen pointed toward a far corner of the suite.

Tony walked to the desk and picked up the phone. "I'll call her father. He'll know it's no joke if the call comes from her phone."

"Good idea."

Tony set his whiskey glass on a coffee table in front of a brown leather couch. He sat. "But first, I'll call the offices of the *Sea Trek*'s owners in New York City. They'll check this number and find it's from Heather's phone. Then they'll know it's not bullshit."

Tony walked to the window so he could get a satellite signal and punched in the number for Free Spirit Ship Lines.

"Free Spirit Ship Lines. Mary speaking. How may I help?"

Tony cleared his throat. "This is Captain Tony Franco. My men and I have taken over your ship, the *Sea Trek*. This isn't a joke." Tony heard Mary gulp.

"Sir, I don't believe you."

"Miss, I appreciate your skepticism. However, I assure you I am serious. I know it's too early for your management to be at work. Please write down the information I'm going to give to you."

Tony heard Mary take a deep breath. "I'll take a message, but I still don't believe you." Her voice was unsteady, and she sounded like her throat had tightened. The noise of rustling papers came through the sat phone Tony held.

"I'm ready, sir."

"I demand three hundred fifty million dollars in cryptocurrency. I will call back to check if we have a deal. If we do, I'll provide wiring instructions. If I do not receive the money by 11:59 PM, Pacific Time, Friday, May 17, I will sink the *Sea Trek*. I have placed C-4 explosives in the engine room and elsewhere on the vessel. Did you write this down?"

Mary struggled to speak and then said, "I'm writing the quickest I can. Please slow down."

"Of course, dear. When you've caught up, please let me know. After I'm done, you can read it back to me."

"Okay, go on, sir."

"I am using Ms. Heather Falcon's satellite phone. Do you see the number listed on your desk phone's display?"

"Yes."

"Please note it. This will verify I'm not a prankster."

"I wrote it down." She took a breath. "Could you repeat the name?"

"Heather Falcon. She's a passenger on this ship and the daughter of the CEO of a company by the name of Hacienda Computer Systems. They're a big Silicon Valley company."

"I've heard of it."

Tony took a breath. "After this call, I will phone Heather's father. I will require he pay a hundred fifty million in cryptocurrency for her release. Also pass this information on to your people. Have you got it all down?"

"Give me a minute. I prefer to write neatly."

Tony heard Mary's pen scratching. The sound ceased. "We'll radio your office from the bridge of the *Sea Trek*, which will doubly prove this is not a prank."

"I've noted everything you said."

He smiled at Waylen, who stood nearby. "Read back the message."

Mary did so.

"Excellent, Mary. Goodbye."

He set the phone on the coffee table, took a sip of whiskey, and caught Waylen's attention. "Please escort Heather in here. I'd like her to call her father."

"It'll be a pleasure, Cap."

* * *

MAY 16, 4:45 AM

Her hands still bound behind her back with plastic ties, Heather sat on a brown leather chair in the luxury suite next to the captain's cabin, which was reserved for members of Free Spirit Ship Lines' board of directors. Her long, blond hair was disheveled, and her eyes were red. She'd stopped crying a half hour ago.

She was afraid she'd soon be raped. The memory of how the second pirate had tightened the ties around her wrists still haunted her. She felt herself shiver, though sitting on the leather chair had warmed her. Every so often, her teeth chattered.

Lots of times, she'd yearned to be a normal young woman, not a billionaire's heiress. What she'd give to be an average Jane, struggling to pay tuition. It would be a great problem. She'd work, if she were in need of money. She thought about her classmates at Stanford, where she was a senior majoring in liberal arts. To become rich, the majority of her acquaintances would change places with her in an instant, even knowing her current status.

She sat taller in the chair and thought of what she could

do to stay alive. She resolved to surmount her fears and brace herself for worse events to come. Losing her dignity for minutes, hours, or even days was doable. She could view her situation as an adventure, though a scary one. She intended to be a survivor. She would steel herself. She stuck out her chin.

How would she act? She'd be complacent. After all, she was naturally easygoing. She would be agreeable even if she were raped. She had to get on the good side of the kidnappers—if there was a good side? She shuddered and then took a deep breath.

She began to tune out reality and started to daydream. She'd heard a pirate say most of the buccaneers were from Bogotá, Colombia. She decided she'd survive this ordeal even if she had to live the life of a sex slave in a drug lord's Bogotá mansion. Life was better than death. She might be favored by the drug lord. She could have servants and learn Spanish. A soft, slight noise at the cabin door startled her out of her reverie.

All of a sudden, the suite's door creaked and opened. A tall, muscular blond man entered. "Stand up, young lady. Yer gonna meet the captain. I advise you to be polite."

Heather felt shivers course through her body. She stood.

The man's light blue eyes studied her. He grabbed her arm and led her out of the cabin and into the captain's suite.

A handsome man with a pointed black beard stood up from his seat on a brown leather couch. "You're Heather, I believe. Welcome. Waylen, please cut those tie wraps off her."

"Yes, Cap." Waylen used his Ka-Bar knife to slice off the plastic bonds, which fell onto the carpet. He picked them up and threw them into a waste can.

Heather rubbed her wrists and felt the numbness in her hands subside.

"Call me Tony, please." He paused. "Would you like a drink to steady your nerves, Heather?"

Heather brushed her long blond hair aside and forced herself to smile. She thought smiling would help. "No, thank you. It's too early to drink." She glanced at the clock on the bulkhead. The time was 4:50 AM.

Tony took her hand lightly in his. "Don't be afraid." She did not resist. "Let's sit on the couch."

She sat down. "This is your phone, Heather. My men found it in your suite. I understand you wish to phone your father. Correct?"

"Yes."

"You have courage, young lady." He rubbed his chin. "Before you call your daddy, I need to tell you what to say."

Heather nodded, but she could not stop herself from shivering. "Of course."

"Inform him I'm Tony Franco, the new captain of this vessel. Tell him I'm holding you for a ransom of a hundred fifty million. Convince him to pay for your release, or you'll never see him again. Capisce? I will take over the call after you greet him."

Heather's pale white skin flushed deep red. "I understand."

"Your father will pay. If not, you will live, but you'll be my guest." Tony handed her the phone. "Call your father. Use speakerphone."

Heather selected her father's cell number. She knew he kept his phone in his pocket all day and at his bedside at night.

On the third ring, a man with a baritone voice said, "Heather, what's up? It's early."

"I'm in trouble."

There was a noise, which could've been the elder Falcon's bedcovers being tossed aside. "I'm listening."

"Kidnappers took me for ransom. There's a Captain Tony Franco next to me. He wants a hundred fifty million for my release."

The sound of a gasp came through the speaker.

Tony grabbed the phone. "This is Tony. We have taken your daughter, and the ship, the *Sea Trek*, too. We're also demanding Free Spirit Ship Lines pay another three hundred fifty million for the release of the vessel and its five thousand passengers and crew."

"You bastards better not harm my daughter, or I'll get people to kill you."

Tony sighed. "I admire your passion." He grinned. "But you aren't in a position to bargain. My deadline is 11:59 PM, Pacific Time, Friday, May 17. If I haven't received a hundred fifty million dollars in cryptocurrency by then, you'll never see Heather again. Plus, I will sink the *Sea Trek* if Free Spirit Ship Lines hasn't paid me three hundred fifty million dollars by then. I have placed C-4 explosives in the engine room."

"What if Free Spirit doesn't pay the ransom for the ship, and I've paid one hundred fifty million?"

"I'll get Heather off the ship before I blow it up."

"How?"

"You'll learn after the fact."

"How do I pay?"

"I'll give you wiring instructions once you are ready to send the money. How long will it take you to scare up the cash?"

"I have to check with my accountant. But I will pay."

"You'd better get cracking, Howard. I'll call you at noon Pacific Time today for an update." Tony disconnected the phone.

Heather tried to keep a straight face. She felt like smiling because her father hadn't hesitated to pay for her release, but then again, she knew her ordeal had not yet ended. Her troubles could become even worse. She still had to stay on this black-bearded pirate's favorable side.

Tony smiled. "Young lady, your father is concerned and generous. Be proud." He gazed at her for a moment. "And you, miss, are a worthy and brave soul. I salute you both."

"Thank you, Tony."

Tony turned to Waylen. "Take Heather back to her new suite. Then please have Tex bring this lady a suitcase of her clothes, her makeup, and whatever else she needs, except, of course, a weapon."

Waylen smiled. "With pleasure, Cap."

FIVE

THOUGH HE'D HAD a mere three hours of sleep, Luke Ryder opened his eyes when the rising sun's morning rays woke him a minute before six. His girlfriend, Layla, was asleep, her eyelids moving while she dreamed. She was a classic beauty. Her face was a narrow oval, and her lips were thin but sensual. They matched her sleek body, though her breasts and hips were womanly.

Ryder eased out of bed and put on sweatpants, a sweatshirt, and white socks. He laced up his worn jogging shoes, moved toward the cabin's door, and softly opened and closed it. He set off to find the jogging track which circled the upper deck of the ship.

A recovering alcoholic, he'd not taken a drink for many months. From the start of his fight to become sober, jogging and exercise had been his strong allies. Physical activity helped him cope with stress.

He relished solitude. A former game warden, Ryder enjoyed hunting and fishing, breathing fresh air, and soaking in sunshine. He reckoned he never would become a true city person, happy in the hustle and bustle of large groups of people.

Even when he interacted with his neighbors in the small wooded Kentucky valley, the "holler" where he had been born, he'd felt like an outsider. Though his father was from the holler, his mother was a native of Naples, Italy. She had spoken with an accent and was a Roman Catholic, unlike most of the residents of the valley. They had viewed her with suspicion. Now his parents were dead, and he'd made a close connection with his new girlfriend, Layla.

Layla planned to dine with him in the finest onboard restaurants. She'd also set her heart on seeing live entertainment in the *Sea Trek*'s lounges and visiting the ship's shops, shows, swimming pool, spa, art galleries, and naturalist lectures.

On the other hand, Ryder mostly wished to attend the lectures about Alaska's wildlife and plants. He wasn't enthusiastic about most of the other attractions on the vessel. But to please Layla, he had resolved to attend all the activities on the *Sea Trek* with her.

While he thought about what Layla would want to do first, he neared steps leading to the top deck. Ryder chose to take them instead of riding one of the vessel's elevators.

He viewed the rising sun lighting the ocean with horizontal rays while he climbed higher. The tips of the small, steel-gray waves sparkled with a yellow glow. The sky was clear, and he felt a cool breeze beginning to blow stronger from the west. The vastness and power of the sea made him feel at home on the water, close to nature, the same way he felt in a forest searching for deer at dawn.

When Ryder reached the top of the ship, he noticed the sun was rising on the vessel's left, the port side. He could also see the distant shore of California off to his left side. It suddenly dawned on him the *Sea Trek* was sailing south toward Mexico, not north toward Alaska. He wondered if the captain had decided to swing south in a big arc and then steer north again to get farther from shore. It seemed odd.

Ryder stepped onto the oval track, which followed the edge of the upper deck. The jogging course circled the ship's tall, wide funnel, or smokestack.

He first stretched and then began to jog. When he neared the stern of the ship, he saw a helicopter painted olive drab, which also had a large red cross on its fuselage. A man stood near the aircraft's open sliding door.

Ryder slowed and watched the man remove a wooden box from the whirlybird. Straining his eyes, Ryder saw "C-4 EXPLOSIVES" stenciled on the side of the box. Ryder's guts sent a warning to his brain. The chopper was an ancient machine, not a modern medevac aircraft.

Another man, with dark chocolate-colored skin, scampered to the helicopter and took out a second box. Ryder was closer. He didn't need to squint to see the second box was also labeled C-4 EXPLOSIVES. The man caught sight of Ryder, set the small wooden crate back in the chopper, and started toward a stairway leading up to the top deck. Silhouetted by the rising sun, the man climbed the stairs, which ended near Ryder.

Ryder stopped running. He saw the man had khaki trousers with a pistol strapped to his right leg, and wore a military-style canvas vest with snap-shut pouches. He had a tall, muscular build.

"Go back to yer cabin." His black afro tousled in the wind. "We got an emergency on board."

Ryder cocked his head. "What emergency?"

"I ain't allowed to say, but the captain is gonna broadcast a statement on the ship's TVs at eight this mornin'."

Ryder shrugged. "Could you give me a hint?"

"No." The man came closer. "You got ID?"

"Nope. I'm joggin'."

"I gotta pat you down."

"Why?"

The man rested his right hand on his pistol. "It's best you do what I say."

"Okay," Ryder said, raising his hands to belt level with his palms facing out.

The man searched Ryder. "You's clean. What's yer line of work?" he asked while he assessed Ryder.

Figuring the man was an armed criminal, Ryder didn't

want him to learn he was a deputy sheriff. "I'm a high school English teacher."

"You's in tip-top shape fer a teacher."

"I'm coachin' the football team."

The man was mute for a minute, as if he were analyzing Ryder's answers, and then said, "Okay, get to yer cabin."

At first, Ryder wondered if there had been a mutiny. But the men had been unloading explosives. Were they terrorists?

While Ryder descended the stairs toward the deck where his cabin was, he caught sight of a flagpole. A Jolly Roger banner was blowing in the stiff breeze, snapping in the wind.

* * *

MAY 16, 6:22 AM

Layla was buttoning her blouse when she heard the cabin door click, and she saw the doorknob begin to turn. She figured Ryder had returned after exploring the ship.

Ryder entered the cabin and walked toward her. He appeared out of sorts, not his normal self. His whiskery face was troubled, and he seemed more distressed than she'd seen him since he'd first tried to stop boozing.

"Terrorists or pirates may be on the ship." He sat on the unmade bed and patted it.

She eased down on the mattress. "What happened?"

"I saw two men unloadin' C-4 explosives from a helicopter parked on the helipad. One was armed, and he came up to me. Said the captain would make an announcement about the situation at eight and told me to go back to my cabin. Then I saw the Jolly Roger flag flying on the ship's mast."

Layla was silent for a second. "Pirates? You serious?"

"Serious as a slap in the face. Those guys are pirates or terrorists. There's no tellin' how many there are, but to take a ship this big with lots of crew and thousands of passengers, there's gotta be a lot of bad guys on board."

"Your satellite phone's been ringing." She pointed across the bed at the portable phone on the sheet near the pillows and the window.

"I bet Rita called."

"The FBI Rita?"

"Yep."

Rita Reynolds had been the agent in charge of the NASA cold case murder task force Ryder had been a member of until the past week.

Ryder grabbed the phone.

Despite her calm appearance, Layla felt jittery. She began to focus on her inner thoughts. Taut with worry, she knew she had to act fearlessly. She automatically projected the image of a strong lady. It was one of her survival tactics. To those who'd seen her when she had faced trouble, she seemed to be a tough woman because of her word choices, facial expressions, and aggressive actions.

Still, underneath, she was a caring person. Though she fought the urge to cry, she often would do so on the sly.

She disliked most men, but she loved Ryder. He treated her with respect and was not demanding. Was she at last in love forever? She had a deep yearning for him, and felt she could not live without him. She had told Ryder everything about herself, except for one secret. She didn't know who her daughter's father was. Recently her four-year-old had begun calling Ryder Daddy.

No matter what might happen on the *Sea Trek*, she knew she must stay alive so she could return home to care for her daughter, Angela.

Layla had a gut feeling the FBI's Rita Reynolds would reveal something during her phone call with Ryder, which could help him deal with the pirates.

Layla snapped out of her reverie when Ryder said, "I gotta get near the window to get a strong satellite signal."

SIX

RYDER STOOD near his cabin's large window. He tapped Rita Reynolds' number on his satellite phone's contact list.

Rita answered on the second ring. "Luke, I tried to call three times. The FBI's recording this, and others are listening, too. Pirates or terrorists have taken over your ship."

"I know."

"I'm your FBI contact," Rita spoke rapidly. "Duke Duncan, the commander of the FBI's Hostage Rescue Team, the HRT, is running the *Sea Trek* operation. I'm not sure if the SEALs or the Army's Delta Force will get involved. They've trained and worked with the HRT before. We'd like you to scope out the pirates and report back to us periodically. Duke must decide if and when his teams should assault the ship."

"Here's what I know. Twenty minutes ago, I was joggin' on the upper deck. Guys were unloadin' crates marked C-4 explosives from an old helicopter on the helipad. There's a skull-and-crossbones flag flying on the ship, too."

"Oh boy." Rita inhaled. "The FBI has confirmed a drug smuggler, Tony Franco, and at least a dozen men posed as passengers and took the ship. The Coast Guard launched a drone and took pictures of the *Sea Trek* when the fog cleared. We asked the Coast Guard not to confront the pirates." Rita caught her breath. "Franco demanded the ship's owner, Free Spirit Ship Lines, send him three hundred fifty million dollars in cryptocurrency, or he'll blow up the vessel. He also took a rich young lady hostage, Heather Falcon. Franco wants her father to pay another one hundred fifty million in digital currency for her release. His deadline for the ship owners and Mr. Falcon is 11:59 PM tomorrow night."

"Anything I should do besides keep an eye on the pirates?"

"No. Just monitor the bad guys. Anything else you remember about them?"

"The man who stopped me was armed with a pistol, searched me, and asked what I do for a livin'. I said I'm a school teacher. Lucky I left my badge in the cabin."

Rita sighed. "I know you're not on the task force anymore, but you're the sole person aboard we know of who has a direct connection with the Bureau. The FBI still would like you to accept a full-time position with us."

"I don't want to switch jobs. I'm a Kentucky deputy sheriff, and I'm gonna help even if I'm not in the Bureau."

Rita exhaled. "Thanks, Luke. Keep assessing the threat. How many pirates are there? What are they armed with? Where did they place their C-4 explosives?" She took another breath. "We have three FBI HRT teams. In three hours, they'll be deployed on the California coast in Black Hawk helicopters. The HRT has maritime capabilities, too. But frankly, our options are not good. We're most worried about the thousands of passengers and crew if a bomb blast sinks the ship."

Ryder said, "According to the guy who frisked me, the new, so-called captain's gonna make a statement at eight this morning on the ship's TV channel." Ryder scratched his nose. "Even if he has fifty pirates aboard, he'll have a tough time watchin' over five thousand people."

Rita cleared her throat. "I have suggestions. Get rid of your badge. Hide your satellite phone."

"Will do. No tellin' what the pirate would've done if he'd known I was a deputy."

"In case the Hostage Rescue Team attacks, you should identify yourself with this password, Mr. Bear. Layla's password is Miss Bear."

"Got it. I'll call after the pirate captain gives his talk."

"Okay. No macho guy stuff. Stay alive." Rita disconnected the phone.

Layla moved closer to Ryder on the bed. "So, what do we do?"

Ryder told Layla her password and then asked, "Don't you have a roll of tape in your luggage?"

"Yes."

"I gotta throw my badge overboard. I'll tape it to the coffee mug I bought yesterday and toss it in the water from the balcony."

Layla unsnapped her case and handed the tape to Ryder. After taping the badge to the mug, he unlatched the sliding door and inspected the balconies and decks below and above him. He saw a pirate armed with an AK-47 on a higher deck where the swimming pool was located.

When the guard turned his back, Ryder hurled his mug into the sea. The splash blended in with the sounds of the waves and the ship, which was traveling south at twelve knots.

Ryder scanned his cabin and saw a vent on the bulkhead above the double bed. He stood on the mattress. Using Layla's fingernail file, he removed two screws from the vent cover.

"Can you give me your flashlight?"

Using the flashlight, he peered into the vent and wondered how he could lower the phone inside the sheet metal enclosure and still be able to retrieve the device. He thought a string and a piece of wood could do the trick. He stepped down from the bed and grabbed a roll of dental floss and a short black pencil. He removed the rubberized cover from the phone, tied the floss around it, and replaced the protective cover. Next, he cut a groove around the pencil with Layla's nail file. He tied the floss to the pencil.

"Let's see if this works."

Ryder lowered the phone into the vent and lodged the pencil into an unused bolt hole. The phone was securely in place. It was unlikely anyone would spot the black pencil nub in the shadows of the venting.

Layla asked, "What'll we do next?"

"Think and plan," Ryder said.

"Like what we should do or say if a pirate comes up to us?"

"Yeah. For example, I won't say I'm a deputy. Remember, I'm a high school English teacher in Lexington. You're a preschool teacher."

"Okay."

"We'll lay low. If you see anything important, tell me. I'll relay it to Rita. Let's study the deck plan brochure. We gotta know how to get to the lifeboats and life jackets."

Layla opened her suitcase. "Here it is."

SEVEN

TONY SAT in a leather chair in the captain's suite and stroked his short, black beard. In contrast, the real captain of the *Sea Trek*, Julius Johnson, was locked in the brig, deep in the lower bowels of the ship. He reclined on a small prison cot.

Tony's second-in-command, Pirate Quartermaster Waylen Devor, entered the captain's suite. "Cap, you wanted to talk?"

Tony smiled. "I'd like an update," he said in his strong New York accent.

Waylen lit a cigarette, took a puff, and sat on the leather couch. He flicked ashes onto the carpet. "Tokyo Joe finished wiring the C-4 explosives in the engine room. He put the radio antenna on a mast on the top deck and hard-wired it to the ship's phone system, which is hooked to the C-4. You can be miles away when you push the detonate button on the two-way radio trigger. Tokyo Joe assures me the setup's complete. He sent a test signal through the ship's phone wires, and it worked."

Tony fiddled with his Ka-Bar knife and shifted his two bandolier pistol belts across his chest. "Tokyo Joe knows his stuff. His nickname stuck like gum on a carpet after he set up the bomb that took down the Tokyo high-rise."

"Yep. But he's sorry because now everybody knows he did it."

Tony nodded and stared out of his window at the ocean. "We'll get additional C-4 after the narco sub arrives."

"When?"

"Tonight at eleven. I wanted a nighttime rendezvous. Less likely the Coast Guard will see them."

Tony's close friend, Gino Gonzales, was piloting the drug smuggler submarine. It had been built in the Colombian jungle, dismantled, and then reassembled in a warehouse in Buenaventura, Colombia, a port on the Pacific Ocean. The seaport was a crime-ridden, drug-smuggling mecca. There were many revolutionary groups there, too.

The sub had cost millions to make, and it was sophisticated. A diesel-electric system powered it, and it could sail three thousand miles to deliver drugs. A hundred feet long, the submersible had a cylindrical, fiberglass hull, a ten-foot conning tower, a periscope, and even air conditioning. It could dive eighty feet into the water, stay there for a long time, and transport twelve tons of drugs and seven people.

Because it traveled twelve feet below the water's surface and was made of fiberglass, sonar and radar could rarely detect it. Also, the heat of its diesel engines was vented downward into the water below its hull, making the craft hard to spot with infrared sensors. The vessel was even difficult to see with binoculars because it was painted blue, and there was not much of a wake visible behind it.

Tony smiled while he envisioned leaving the *Sea Trek* a multimillionaire in the comfort of the narco sub. The fiberglass sub had slipped past the Coast Guard's vigilant eyes a dozen times in the past year.

Waylen took a long drag on his cigarette and broke the silence. "We have a guard watching the scuba equipment, which we've pre-positioned by the port shell door. The guard is topping off the charges on the DPV batteries, too."

Each DPV, or diver propulsion vehicle, was a low-cost,

one-by-two-foot, battery-powered, fanlike unit. It could pull a diver holding its handlebars more than four miles per hour for ninety minutes underwater. Tony had recruited men who knew how to scuba dive. His plan was for most of his men to escape underwater after the ransoms were paid. With its engines off, the *Sea Trek* would drift in the ocean about two miles from shore. The men would drop into the water from the shell doors. They could reach shore in a half hour with plenty of charge left in their DPV batteries. The shell doors were on Deck Two, several feet above the waterline at midship on both sides of the vessel. These were the same doors where harbor pilots entered and left the ship to help the captain guide it in and out of seaports.

Tony nodded. "How about the eighteen-wheelers and light planes?"

"We have three semis parked near beaches up and down the coast around San Diego. There are four light planes parked on a farmer's landing strip. Everybody's ready." The plan was for the pirates to land on the beach after midnight, meet at one of the nondescript semis, enter its trailer, and ride to where the light planes stood on a dirt airstrip. These small aircraft would fly under the radar into Mexico.

"We paid the pilots and drivers plenty," Tony said.

All of a sudden, doubts began to plague Tony. Why was he so hellbent on hijacking a cruise ship when he could make a hundred million dollars on one drug-smuggling run? He told himself he was doing it for a half billion at once. Also, it was advertising. He'd become the number one go-to guy to ship drugs to the US. Plus, yeah, he wanted notoriety. He admitted it. Yep. They'd remember him, the modern Blackbeard.

Waylen interrupted Tony's thoughts. "Oh yeah, we set up three M-60 machine guns to take care of Coast Guard divers if they try to board the ship. Two guns cover the sides, and one is forward on top of the bridge."

"Are the guys griping because they have to guard the bridge, the comms room, the engine room, the shell doors, and man three machine guns, plus patrol the passenger decks?"

"They'll have to make do," Waylen said.

"Let's hope so."

"Cap, there's something else."

"What?"

"Arlo is out of sorts about Tex killing the ship's security chief." Arlo, the Pirate First Mate, was third in charge after Tony and Waylen.

Tony sat up straight. "Has Arlo gone soft? It had to be done. The security guy had grabbed a pistol."

"Arlo isn't weak. He's angry. It'll pass."

"Killing isn't easy for fearful men with weak knees." Tony stood. "We need to instill fear into the passengers and crew. We have five thousand people to control. We can't easily do it with twenty-eight of us, including good old Pilot and his Huey."

"How are we gonna scare all those people?"

"Blackbeard terrified people so much, they'd surrender without a fight." Tony rubbed his beard. "Get Tokyo Joe. He needs to set up a TV feed from the helipad for my 8:00 AM address to the passengers and crew. My broadcast will scare the shit out of them."

Waylen stood. "I'll get him here ASAP."

EIGHT

THE SKY HAD TURNED gray and gloomy. The wind was brisk on the helipad, where the Vietnam War-era Huey helicopter was tied down. Near it, Tokyo Joe, an electronics and explosives expert, stood behind a TV camera. He had pulled a coaxial cable to the camera across the deck and was connecting the cable to the camera's output. He'd already set up a microphone near the railing overlooking the wake behind the ship.

Tony shifted on his feet next to a Colombian man who was an enforcer for *Los Hermanos* Drug Cartel. Thin and agile, this man moved like a panther. He was a marksman, martial arts expert, and a cold-blooded killer. The enforcer turned to Tony. "Why you have to do this, Cap?"

Tony glanced backward at an elderly man cowering near the railing, his hands bound behind him. Tony shrugged. "Even if we had fifty men, we would be hard-pressed to control thousands of passengers and crew. The way to subjugate them is to make them fear us."

"*Amigo*, I have had much experience in killing. Most will shake in fear. But among five thousand, there are enough brave men to challenge you. You sure you wanna do this for all to see?"

"Yes. We won't be on this ship for long. In the short term, they will fear us. If we were going to be here for a longer time, I would agree with you."

The enforcer blinked. "It's lucky this is not the 1700s, because then pirates elected their captains. They also voted on important questions."

Tony nodded and picked up the handheld microphone. "Tokyo, we ready to go?"

"Yes, Cap. I'll cue you when to start."

"Remember, after it's over, take the camera off the tripod. Be ready to follow the action."

"Yep, I'll zoom out to a wide-angle to keep the shot steady."

"Whatever. You're the expert."

"Standby, Cap. We're about to go live."

Tony positioned the microphone under his lips. "I'm ready."

"After your speech, place the mike to the side on the deck before you do your thing."

Tony winked and then stared at the camera lens.

Tokyo Joe pointed at Tony, who was live on camera, seen by all who watched the many monitors scattered across the huge ship.

* * *

MAY 16, 8:06 AM

Ryder sat in a chair next to Layla and peered at his cabin's wall-mounted TV set. A simple message on the screen read, "The captain will address passengers and crew shortly."

Ryder saw Layla was nervous. He leaned against her, felt her softness, held her shoulder, and gave it a gentle squeeze. "Let's see what we can learn from this guy," Ryder said. "We could use it against him."

The TV picture dissolved into an image of a man with a short, black beard standing near the olive-drab Huey helicopter. He held a microphone. Two brown leather bandoliers, which held two holstered pistols and a large, dangerous-looking knife, crossed his chest. "Ladies and gentlemen, I am your new captain. I prefer to be called Tony." He stepped closer to the camera.

In the background of the TV image, Ryder noticed an old man with medium-length white hair standing near the railing. His hands were bound behind him, and the wind whipped his hair back and forth. Sternward, the white, turbulent wake of the ship churned the sea.

"My people and I have taken this ship for ransom. I am certain its owners will pay me millions for its return because the *Sea Trek* cost them two billion. It will be simple for them to deliver these funds to me electronically in cryptocurrency." He waited and then took a step forward.

Layla said, "He speaks well for a criminal."

Tony brought the microphone closer to his lips. "I am a man of my word, so if the owners pay, you all will go free. Meanwhile, we've changed course and are heading toward Mexico. Enjoy yourselves. All drinks are on the house until I release this ship. Also, I've asked the casino to provide each passenger with two thousand dollars in chips so you can test your luck." Tony smiled pleasantly.

Ryder said, "He's tryin' to git on our good side."

Tony stared coldly at the camera. "Although I'm generous, I urge you all to obey me and my men without question, and everything will be all right. Don't try to stop us. The rich oligarchs who own this ship can afford to pay. Like Robin Hood, I shall take from the rich and give to the poor. I pledge to you that I am a man to be trusted."

Layla scoffed. "Yeah, sure."

Tony took three steps toward the railing, where a thin, catlike man, the enforcer, pushed the old man down onto his knees.

Tony turned again to face the camera. "However, I must caution you, there will be consequences if you do not obey."

Tony unsheathed his Ka-Bar knife, held it up, and pointed it at the elderly man near the railing. "Here we have a man who retired from the US Drug Enforcement Administration, the DEA. He is an enemy of us pirates who have provided drugs to citizens. Who is to say a person can't enjoy recreational drugs? We should decide for ourselves what to do with our bodies. If drugs were legal, they would be the cost of popcorn. I wonder, was this DEA agent really an ally of us pirates since we made huge profits because his law enforcement activities caused drug prices to drastically inflate? No, he's not a friend. He's responsible for the deaths of many of my friends. Because of him, others are rotting in US prisons. So…"

Tony set his microphone on the deck, stepped behind the man, and swiftly slit his throat. Blood gushed onto the deck. The old man fell forward. His body vibrated in a spasm.

Tony turned to two pirates. "Bury him at sea."

Tokyo Joe disconnected his camera from the tripod and walked toward the body with his lens zoomed out to an extreme wide-angle. Tokyo was careful to avoid stepping in the puddle of blood.

Ryder watched the shaky TV picture while two stocky pirates grasped the elderly man's limp body and flipped it over the rail. There was a splash, and the body slipped out of sight beneath the white foam. Ryder felt his face turn red. "What a son of a bitch."

Tony picked up the microphone. Tiny droplets of blood dotted it. "I assure you this man's ghost will not return to this ship to haunt it, but his spirit will live forever in the depths of the sea in Davy Jones' locker."

Ryder stared into Layla's eyes. "I gotta do somethin' to stop this bastard before he kills anybody else, but I'm not sure what."

Layla was shaking.

Tony leaned into the camera until his face filled the picture. "There will be waste cans set up on each deck where you can deposit your portable phones on the way to breakfast. Please do so, friends. If not, the penalty is death."

Ryder knew he wouldn't be able to update Rita just yet. He stood and noticed Layla was quivering. "When you toss your phone in, I'll pretend to do the same. You ready to leave for breakfast?"

"I'm not hungry anymore, but let's go."

NINE

AN ELDERLY WOMAN was leaving her cabin. She saw a pirate walking along the Deck Twelve passageway and pounding on passengers' cabin doors. He yelled, "Come out. Put your phones in the waste can."

A second pirate stood near a barrel, watching passengers line up and toss their mobile phones into the container. The man glared at the woman while he rested a hand on his holstered pistol.

As she approached the second pirate near the barrel of phones, the old woman felt faint. As her world went black, an alert young man next to her caught her before she fell. In seconds, she came to. "Thank you, sir."

"It's nothing, ma'am."

Near the container, already brimming with phones, she felt her body shake. She awkwardly threw her phone at the barrel. The device hit the rim and tumbled to the blue carpet.

The pirate stationed at the barrel glared at her, and he grabbed her phone from the deck.

She felt an urge to pee and scurried toward the women's room. On her way, she saw a third pirate carrying a mannequin. What was the criminal up to?

* * *

MAY 16, 8:57 AM

In the fresh sea air on Deck Twelve, Pirate Tex Curtis set a male mannequin at the rail and positioned the dummy's arms so they appeared to hold an imaginary firearm. He turned to a second buccaneer who dragged another mannequin, this one a female, behind him. The men had taken the first two of a dozen figures from the ship's clothes and fashion store, Ellie's. "Hey, Russ, you think Cap has gone bonkers, or does this make sense?"

Russ stopped pulling his replica human and set it near the railing so it appeared to survey the horizon. "Cap is squirrelly, but he's crazy like a fox. If the Coast Guard sees these fake pirates, it'll seem like there's more of us." He took a breath. "Let's go see if any of the bogus rifles are ready."

"Where?"

"The craft center. Cap is paying passengers to paint cardboard AK-47s." Russ cocked his head. "Ever see the TV documentary about how the Brits made a bunch of decoy airfields during World War II? The Germans bombed 'em instead of the real ones."

Tex smiled. "I hope the Coast Guard shoots this fake person instead of me." He patted the mannequin's head.

"Me, I can't wait 'til the owners of this boat pay off," Russ said. "The sooner we get off this ship, the better. I don't want my ass shot."

"Arlo told me Cap called the ship company this morning. Could be we can swim for shore tonight."

TEN

HOWARD FALCON, CEO and principal stockholder of the multibillion-dollar firm, Hacienda Computer Systems, sat behind his highly polished, dark walnut desk in his company's ornate home office in Palo Alto, California.

Lingering distress showed on Howard's face. At 4:50 AM, Tony had called Howard's unlisted phone number to report Howard's twenty-year-old daughter, Heather, was his prisoner aboard the *Sea Trek*. Tony had demanded one hundred fifty million dollars in cryptocurrency for her safe release.

Howard at once had called the local San Jose FBI Field Office. He awaited the arrival of Special Agent Rita Reynolds. He tapped one of his spit-shined black shoes on the thick carpet under his desk. His butler had brushed Howard's shoes at 7:00 AM, what he'd done every workday for years.

Howard was forty-eight years old, bony, tall and thin, and had a flat stomach. He prided himself on his appearance and his confidence. Today, he wore an expensive blue suit that matched his deep-set, dark blue eyes. The typical workaholic, he was also handsome and charming, besides being energetic and driven. His face normally did not broadcast his true emotions and feelings. But today was different. He lacked his usual moxie.

His secretary tapped on his closed office door and then peeked in. Her face showed great concern. She was aware of the situation and also knew Heather. "Rita Reynolds and Mr. Alcott are here to see you, sir."

"Thank you. Please send them in."

FBI Special Agent Rita Reynolds wore a business suit. Howard estimated she stood five foot six and was in her mid-thirties. She was attractive, of medium build, with black hair and brown eyes.

In contrast, her companion, Roger Alcott, was chubby and dressed casually in a green sweater and dark slacks. He carried a large, metal-clad equipment case.

Howard stood. "Thank you for coming, Agent Reynolds and Mr. Alcott."

"Fortunately, our field office is close by." Rita took a second to gather her thoughts. "I'm sorry we had to meet under these circumstances. Let me assure you, the FBI has immediately started working hard to secure the release of Heather."

Howard motioned to a small round table surrounded by three comfortable office chairs. "Thank you. Please have a seat."

While Rita sat, she said, "Mr. Alcott has come with me because he's an expert in setting up phone-tracing and recording equipment. Could we have permission to monitor and record your phone calls?"

"Of course. I suppose it can be set up while we speak?"

"Yes." She turned to Alcott and nodded.

Alcott unsnapped his case and began to tinker with the telephone equipment in the office.

Rita turned her attention to Howard. "Agent Henry Dunbar, a colleague of mine, will be here shortly to monitor the phone and take any required actions."

"I appreciate it." Howard gazed at Rita. "But let me be clear." He gulped. "I'll pay a hundred fifty million for my daughter as soon as possible. Track my transactions, but I forbid you to put Heather in further danger."

Rita nodded. "I'm told the plan is to wait for her release before we take overt action against Tony Franco and his bunch."

Howard exhaled. "Catch them if you can after she's free. I've already taken steps to buy crypto money. I'll transfer the funds to the bastard by late tomorrow afternoon."

Rita scribbled in a small notebook. She focused on Howard. "We've been working with the National Security Agency to see if they can track your transactions while they travel back and forth across worldwide networks."

"Isn't tracking money transfers impossible?"

"We'll have to wait and see if the NSA can do it." Rita glanced at the office door, then back at Howard. "I have to go back to my office. Mr. Alcott will stay with you to monitor his equipment. Agent Dunbar should be here soon."

"Thank you, Agent Reynolds."

Rita smiled. "We'll do our utmost to help you and Heather. Take care." She rose to leave.

Howard stood and watched the attractive woman depart. He liked eye-catching ladies, but he often sold them short. He worried whether or not Rita—even with the aid of others in the FBI—could rescue Heather.

ELEVEN

RYDER AND LAYLA entered their cabin on Deck Nine. They carried their to-go breakfast—egg sandwiches and coffee.

Ryder studied Layla's face. She was upset and nervous, though she tried to hide it. Ryder asked, "How you doin', hon?"

Layla frowned. "I'm not sure I can eat after watching the man die." She set the sandwiches down and pulled the top off her paper cup of coffee. "Caffeine will help, though."

Ryder relished the smell of his coffee's steam. He pulled a chair toward Layla. "You can sit here while I fish the phone outta the vent. I gotta call Rita."

Ryder took his shoes off and stepped up onto the mattress. He twisted off the loose vent screws with his fingertips, grabbed the black pencil lodged in the hole in the sheet metal, and pulled his satellite phone up and out. The floss and pencil dangled from the device. He caught Layla's attention. "Could you watch through the peephole to make sure nobody's outside?"

"Yep." Layla set her paper cup of coffee on the hutch's

desktop. She moved close to the peephole. "I don't see anybody."

"Good." Ryder stepped down from the mattress and sat on the bed near the cabin's window, where he could get a signal. He tapped Rita's number on the phone's contact list.

"Hi, Luke. I'm worried about you and Layla. A Coast Guard drone saw a man being executed on the helipad."

"Franco broadcast the killing throughout the ship. He said the guy was a retired DEA agent."

Rita was silent for a moment. "Did you hide your badge?"

"I threw it overboard." He took a breath. "If I get a chance to take out Mr. Franco when he's about to kill again, I won't feel bad about it."

"We're recording this, Luke." Rita took a moment to think. "Because you're a law enforcement officer, you're justified in using deadly force if an innocent person's life is in danger." She sighed. "How many bad guys did you see on board?"

"There's one patrolling each open-air deck every twenty minutes—four pirates for those decks. And there's Franco and whoever flew in the Huey. So far, I estimate six. There's gotta be at least one guy guarding the engine room, one in the comms center, and another on the bridge."

Rita sighed. "I count a potential of nine."

"Did the Coast Guard drone see the three machine guns?"

"No."

"Two of 'em are set up under overhangs along both sides of the ship. The third one is high up on top of the bridge."

Rita said, "Three machine gunners, which add up to twelve perps."

"They gotta sleep, eat, and have backup. Add ten." Ryder scratched his stubble.

"So, at least twenty-two pirates."

"It's a lot of people, but these guys are after a half-billion bucks, so they can afford a bunch of hired guns."

Rita cleared her throat. "We've been debating whether to

assault soon or not. Three hostage rescue teams are ready to go from Black Hawk choppers and speedboats." She paused. "But we're sitting tight. After watching Franco kill the retired DEA agent, our analysts believe Franco's so unstable, he'd set off the C-4 and sink the ship if we attack immediately. The machine guns are a game changer, too. There's ongoing debate about whether or not he has even more firepower."

"Like what?"

"Rocket-propelled grenade launchers, which are shoulder-fired anti-tank weapons." Rita sucked air into her lungs. "We've studied the ship's passenger roster, searching for people with military or law enforcement backgrounds. Retired US Army Colonel Rick Casa stands out." She took a breath. "I can't send you a picture. Most satellite phone systems are designed solely for voice use. I have Rick's cabin number, H499, on Deck Eight at midship."

"I'll knock on his door. Our cabin's above him on Deck Nine, F497."

She coughed. "Everybody else who's a vet or in law enforcement is elderly. It'll be only you and Colonel Casa, if you can recruit him. You still all in?"

"You bet, 'specially after Franco killed the old man."

"We'll put you on the FBI payroll temporarily. Okay?"

"Fine, but I'm only a temp employee. Agreed?"

"Okay. Let's talk about where we stand. Setting off C-4 explosives would be suicidal for the pirates. They haven't asked for safe passage away from the ship after they get their ransom. They may be terrorists. Still, they must have a plan. The Huey helicopter's on the ship, but it can hold just thirteen men max. Even if they flew low under the radar, we or the Mexicans would intercept them."

"I can cause havoc with the pirates."

"No. We need you to be undercover and our eyes and ears on the ship." She hesitated. "Hold on. I'm getting further info."

A minute later, she continued, "I'm told there's a slim chance we'll assault the ship before the ransom deadline at

11:59 PM tomorrow night. But the machine guns would devastate divers trying to board. Assault by parachute is also iffy." She exhaled loudly. "Our shrinks say Franco's unstable. He needs to control people and his situation, and he'll try to prove he's strong."

"Cutting a DEA agent's throat is personal, and he scared the shit out of people."

"The psychologists say he's felt rejected from an early age and doesn't connect with people. He's blocked his ability to love because it would give a lover control over him. I'm reading this from Franco's psych profile."

Ryder shifted on the bed. "So what?"

"He has taken the billionaire's heiress, Heather Falcon, hostage. We're afraid he'll rape her. His profile shows he wants sex, not love. And rapists want to show their power over women."

"I'll try to find out where he's holding her." Ryder gathered his thoughts and then added, "There's a strange thing he did. Right before cutting the old man's throat, Franco said all drinks are on the house, and he's giving each passenger two thousand dollars in chips to gamble in the casino."

"Weird, but he does want to get on the passengers' favorable side." Rita took a deep breath. "Want to hear about Colonel Casa?"

"Yep."

"He's five foot eleven. Must spend time in the sun because he has swarthy skin. He has high cheekbones and hairy arms. His mustache is gray, and he has bushy black eyebrows. He has deep-set brown eyes. In the picture I have, he needs a haircut. His hair's black but graying on the sides. He appears to be in superb shape for a man older than fifty."

Ryder smiled. "I could spot him in a minute from yer description."

"There's other detail in this snapshot. He's wearing jeans, a polo shirt, and a straw cowboy hat—if there is such a thing." Rita took a breath. "We heard he's way over his head in credit card debt."

Layla waved her hand and made a cut sign across her throat.

Ryder whispered, "I gotta go. Layla saw somethin' through the peephole." Ryder ended the call.

Layla backed away from the door. "A pirate walked by."

Ryder exhaled. "Must be 'cuz our cabins are close to the steps and the elevator. I'll wait a while, then I'm gonna search for a retired Army colonel who has a cabin below ours."

TWELVE

ON THE THIRTY-THIRD floor of a New York City skyscraper, Richard Carver sat at the head of the table during an emergency meeting of the Maritime World Insurance Company's board of directors. He glanced at six other troubled board members. "We cover the *Sea Trek* with hull insurance, protection, and indemnity insurance. This includes piracy, kidnap, and ransom coverage."

Richard noticed his fellow board members' faces appeared increasingly downcast the longer he spoke. He glanced at the documents in front of him. "Tony Franco, who's also a drug smuggler, wants three hundred fifty million dollars for the release of the ship and its five thousand passengers and crew. He's demanding another hundred fifty million from billionaire Howard Falcon for the release of his daughter, Heather."

Lucas Levin raised his hand. "Excuse me, but our legal council needs to analyze what we should and should not cover for various types of loss."

Richard zeroed in on Lucas' eyes. "We don't have time. The pirates could destroy the ship in the next five minutes, for all we know. We need to act fast."

Lucas rolled his eyes. "Yeah, you're right."

Richard scratched his head. "The ship is new and is valued at almost two billion dollars. Let's say half of the passengers and crew die if the ship sinks or burns. Payout to relatives averages a half million for each loss of life. Multiply two thousand five hundred deceased people by a half-million bucks. I get a rough total of a billion-and-a-half dollars. And it could be worse." Richard sighed. "We're facing a potential total loss of more than three billion. Paying the pirates three hundred fifty million in crypto is our best option. Mr. Falcon said he's ready to pay a hundred fifty million dollars for his daughter's release. We'll be in court later if he opts to sue us to recover his hundred fifty million."

Dario Beckus leaned forward in his chair. "You think the worst case scenario is we'd pay five hundred million. Correct?"

Richard nodded. "Yes. It's less than roughly three billion dollars. We should send the money ASAP."

THIRTEEN

RYDER LOITERED on the balcony outside his midship cabin on Deck Nine. Forty minutes earlier, he'd stood in front of retired Colonel Rick Casa's cabin on Deck Eight and rapped on the man's door. No one had answered Ryder's knock. He then decided to wait to search for Rick during the lunch hour when passengers would crowd the ship's restaurants and other eateries.

Ryder scanned the seascape. The fresh ocean air vanquished his slight headache, which had begun after he'd witnessed the execution of the retired DEA agent. Ryder decided he needed to better assess the situation on board. How many pirates could he identify? Also, where was the heiress Heather Falcon being held? He recalled having seen her picture in a magazine in his dentist's office. She'd be easy to recognize if she still had long, straight blond hair.

Ryder peered back through his sliding balcony door and spotted Layla applying cosmetics to her cheeks. With pirates roaming the ship, what were her priorities? He figured touching up her makeup made her feel better, though she didn't need any, in his opinion. An unrelated thought hit him. "Layla, didn't you bring a pair of binoculars to watch whales?"

"Yes, hon. You want them?" Layla set her small mirror aside on the hutch top.

"Yep. I don't think the pirates would care if I'm lookin' at them from the balcony. I bet a bunch of folk are searching the horizon for whales to try to forget the situation."

Layla handed him the binoculars. "Are you going to update Rita after you scan the ship? The FBI must be planning something."

"Depends on what I learn." He peered through the field glasses, examining the upper decks. He turned toward the *Sea Trek*'s stern, and he spotted the pirate and self-proclaimed captain who preferred to be called Tony. He was crossing the helipad near the Huey helicopter, his pointed black beard bordering the bottom of his face. His two leather pistol belts crossed his chest like bandoliers. The Ka-Bar knife, a murder weapon, dangled from a sheath attached to one of his pistol belts.

Ryder watched Tony as the man climbed a ladder going up to the sundeck. Ryder then trained Layla's binoculars on the southern horizon. He barely made out a vessel. He later learned it was the four hundred-foot-long Coast Guard cutter, *San Diego*.

* * *

MAY 16, 11:05 AM

With field glasses pressed over his eyes, US Coast Guard Captain Chuck Stone stood on the bridge of the large cutter, *San Diego*, which he commanded. He studied the *Sea Trek* cruise ship on the northeastern horizon, its upper decks visible above a layer of thick fog. "She appears so peaceful from this distance. Hard to believe pirates took her."

Lieutenant Commander Ralph Essex nodded. "Yep, who'd ever think pirates would try something like this off the Pacific coast? Somalia's another story, but here?"

Stone lowered his binoculars and turned to face Essex. "We were caught with our pants down."

"Cap, what's our next step?"

"Hang back, and keep pace with the *Sea Trek*. Observe. But be ready to take action at a moment's notice."

Essex shook his head. "Can't we get the SEALs to swim up and surprise them or rappel onto the deck from choppers?"

"The FBI could do it," Stone said. "They have helicopters standing by. But assaulting the *Sea Trek*'s too risky because five thousand passengers and crew are aboard." Stone recalled having seen video footage taken by a drone when it circled high above the cruise ship. During a break in the fog, the tiny unmanned aircraft had spotted two M-60 machine gun nests and floodlights, which covered the sides of the vessel. Another gun on the top deck aimed over the stern. "The pirates have three machine guns. They can kill boarders like they're shooting balloons at a county fair," Stone added.

Essex said, "They have plenty of firepower."

Stone continued, "Another problem is the SEALs are deployed on the other side of the planet. They can't be here for a week." He fingered the satellite phone in his pocket. "I got a call from an FBI agent on the *Sea Trek* Task Force five minutes ago. She has contact with a man on board. He saw cases of C-4 explosives being unloaded from a Vietnam War-era Huey chopper the pirates used to ferry in arms."

"A woman is working on the joint operation?"

"Yes, Special Agent Rita Reynolds. I'm told she's competent." Stone wondered if Essex, second-in-command of the cutter, was prejudiced against women. "She's a rising star in the Bureau. The FBI director himself told me so."

Essex flushed and forced a smile. "What's your gut telling you about this situation?"

"I wonder if the pirates are terrorists," Stone said. "Nobody on the joint operation team has been able to figure out how in hell they'll try to get away after they get paid. Best guess is they'll ask for safe passage."

Essex rubbed his chin. "They've executed one man. What if they start killing people one by one until their demands are met?"

"We'd grant them safe passage, but we'd lie," Stone said. "The United States of America wouldn't let them live."

Essex stared over the water at the distant profile of the *Sea Trek*. "I had a random thought about one motive the pirates may have."

"What?"

"Every day for the last month, we've seized at least a ton of cocaine. Its street value's forty million dollars a ton. Think how much tonnage is slipping by us while we're dealing with the *Sea Trek*."

"Could be you're on to something." Stone thought of the Orion P-3 aircraft flying in the general vicinity of the cruise ship. Earlier versions of the Orion had flown out of Moffett Field, California, when it had been a Navy base. The P-3s were equipped to track Soviet and newer Russian Federation submarines. Three P-3s patrolled the oceans for drug smugglers and their fast, homebuilt, fiberglass, cocaine-crammed submarines.

The Coast Guard's recent requests for two new cutters had been denied because of budget cuts. The US coastlines and surrounding ocean waters where the smugglers operated were two times larger than the continental United States. Additional cutters were badly needed. However, other agencies, including US Customs and Border Protection, had received extra money to deal with an onslaught of migrants who crossed the US borders. Illegal aliens continued to stream into the nation, and the US Congress had again deadlocked on taking meaningful steps to stem the tide of desperate migrants.

Stone stopped thinking about his shrinking resources when he spotted a tiny dot in the distant sky. While the flying object neared, he heard the faint sounds of helicopter rotor blades. He shoved his binoculars to his eyes. The aircraft was a civilian chopper. "Tell the pilot to turn his copter around."

FOURTEEN

RYDER STOOD on his cabin's balcony. He was scanning the helipad with his field glasses when he heard a helicopter approaching. He tilted the binoculars up and caught sight of the chopper flying toward the *Sea Trek* from the east. He wondered if the aircraft was bringing a negotiating team to meet with the pirates. A lot could've happened since he'd last talked with Rita roughly two hours ago. When the whirlybird got closer, Ryder thought it was a civilian craft. In short order, he realized it was a television station's chopper, white with red stripes. Its fuselage displayed a large red seven with a circle painted around the number.

Ryder heard yelling coming from the sundeck above him on the aft end of the ship. He caught sight of Tony pushing another man who wore a pistol belt on his waist. Ryder then saw Tony gesturing and speaking. At first he couldn't hear what Tony was saying until he screamed, "Get the friggin' RPG and the range finder."

The second pirate scrambled into a doorway.

* * *

MAY 16, 11:12 AM

A KSIP-TV cameraman was in the front seat next to the pilot while a female reporter sat in the back of the small helicopter, which flew toward the *Sea Trek*.

The cameraman wore a headset with its flexible microphone wand in front of his lips. A minicam propped on his right shoulder, he leaned forward, recording video of the cruise ship. He said, "Standby. We go live in twenty seconds. I'll cue you, Janet."

The pilot said, "The Coast Guard ordered us to turn back."

Janet, the reporter sitting in the back seat, said, "Keep going. This is too big. We'll ask for forgiveness later." She pulled her handheld microphone closer to her mouth and took a deep breath.

The cameraman counted, "Three, two, one." He pointed his left thumb backward toward the reporter.

She began to speak.

* * *

MAY 16, 11:13 AM

Tony stood on the sundeck near the railing. His pulse raced. He watched the white and red helicopter fly toward the *Sea Trek*. He guessed it was a mile away, and he noted it flew low over the water, approaching from the east. All of a sudden, it slowed, turned south, and hovered. Tony yelled behind him through the doorway, "Get your ass moving, Charlie. I need the RPG." He wished he had the Stinger antiaircraft, shoulder-fired weapon, but it was stowed on the Huey, which was tied down on the helipad four decks below him.

Tony stared at the chopper when it again began to fly toward the *Sea Trek* from the south. Behind him someone stumbled and fell. Tony turned and saw Charlie sprawled on the deck holding a Soviet-era, nineteen-pound, rocket-propelled grenade—RPG—launcher loaded with an 85mm projectile. Tony grabbed the weapon, and noticed the blue plastic safety cap was not on the tip of the warhead. If it had struck the deck nose down, the weapon would've detonated and killed him and everyone nearby.

"Get up, Charlie. How far away is the chopper?"

Charlie pulled a small military-grade range finder from his hip pocket. He shook while he peered through the device. He sucked air into his lungs and exhaled half of it. "It's hovering one thousand two hundred meters away."

"Keep your eye on it. Tell me when it's a thousand meters away."

"Yes, Cap."

Tony's brain was working fast. He knew the RPG was an anti-tank weapon, not designed to shoot down aircraft. *Damn*, he thought. But the RPG-7 anti-tank rocket would self-destruct after it had flown nine hundred thirty meters.

Tony flipped up the RPG's front and back iron sights, which were similar to antiaircraft gun sights. They could be set from two hundred to five hundred meters. But he needed to aim for nine hundred thirty meters so the projectile would self-destruct near the helicopter. He'd have to guess where to aim and account for the moderate wind, too.

While these thoughts raced through his head, he glanced at the RPG's simple trigger and hammer, which were similar to those on a revolver. He pulled back the hammer with his thumb, cocking the weapon. He supported the firing tube on his right shoulder and aimed at the chopper.

"He's flying this way again, Cap," Charlie said. "Eleven hundred meters." Charlie was silent for what seemed like ages to Tony. "One thousand meters."

Tony aimed left of the chopper to compensate for the wind. He squeezed the trigger. In a fraction of a second, the firing pin struck the primer on the rocket. The initial propellant charge blew the rocket from the weapon's launch tube. After a few meters of flight, the rocket ignited, spewing exhaust behind it. The heat of it was far enough away, so it didn't scorch Tony.

Gray smoke trailing behind the projectile, the rocket rushed toward the chopper.

Tony had begun to count when the rocket ignited, "One thousand, two thousand, three thou—"

The weapon exploded near the whirlybird in an orange ball of fire with colors ranging from dark, blackish orange to a light tangerine hue. The helicopter burst into flames a short moment later and fell into the sea.

Less than three seconds after Tony had seen the two explosions, he heard a double report of the blasts when their sounds reached his position. He felt like Zeus must've felt when the sound of thunder reached the Greek god shortly after he'd thrown lightning bolts at an enemy.

Tony scanned the cabin balconies along the east side of the ship. Passengers were standing, pointing at the cloud of black smoke rising into the sky. He gulped. He'd just saved his life, if the chopper had been carrying a sharpshooter to ice him. In any case, the helicopter was in flaming bits, and its destruction would surely terrorize the passengers and crew. The ship's owners and Mr. Falcon would take him seriously.

Charlie held the range finder and blankly stared at Tony.

Tony yelled, "Come here."

Tony slapped the thin man across his face. Charlie fell. "You stupid idiot. You shouldn't have unscrewed the safety cap. If you'd hit the nose of the warhead on the deck, you and I'd be dead. Get the hell out of my sight."

Charlie stood and wiped the blood from his mouth and nose. "Yes, Cap. I'm sorry."

Tony sighed and decompressed. "Your apology is accepted." He stared at Charlie. "Label the RPG launcher with simple directions, like, 'Slide projectile in tube; unscrew blue cap; cock hammer; aim and fire.'"

"I'll do it right away, Cap."

* * *

MAY 16, 11:14 AM

A fixed-wing Coast Guard ScanEagle drone had relayed live video of the cruise ship to the bridge of the cutter, *San Diego*. The officers on the bridge had watched their video monitor as a pirate on the *Sea Trek* had aimed a shoulder-fired missile at a civilian helicopter. The drone's video had clearly shown the buccaneer's face. He had a medium-length, sharp-pointed, black beard.

Captain Chuck Stone had observed the pirate fire at the TV station's chopper and destroy it. He'd felt his face turn red. Then he said, "These guys are scum."

Lieutenant Commander Essex pointed at the TV monitor. "The pirate captain, Tony Franco, launched the missile."

The drone continued to send video of the bits and pieces of the helicopter floating on the choppy water. The weather was about to take a turn for the worse, according to recent weather reports.

Stone said, "I doubt if there are survivors, but launch a boat to recover the bodies."

Essex said, "The pirates' M-60 machine guns have a range of eight hundred to eleven hundred meters, depending on if they're on tripods or not, so we should keep the boat twelve hundred meters away from the *Sea Trek*."

"That's true," Stone said. "But let's recover the bodies, even if the wreckage appears to be a thousand meters from the cruise ship and within range of the machine guns. I don't think they'll shoot at a rescue boat."

"Yes, sir."

An ensign on the bridge pointed to a second video monitor. "Captain, men carried a Stinger antiaircraft missile launcher out of the chopper on the helipad."

Captain Stone stared at the screen. "It's definitely a Stinger." The American Stinger, a surface-to-air, shoulder-fired weapon, was far more dangerous to aircraft than the Soviet-era RPG-7 Tony had used to shoot down the news helicopter. The Stinger's targeting range was four thousand eight hundred meters, and the weapon had an infrared system to lock onto aircraft.

Stone took two deep breaths and felt himself calm down. He realized he had to carefully weigh his options before taking further action.

Essex said, "I suggest we take it slow."

Stone nodded. "You're right." He rubbed his chin. "I had been thinking of sending out the MH-65D Dolphin to make observations and intimidate the pirates, but we'll hold back." The MH-65D helicopter carried a machine gun, stun grenades, and men with M-16 rifles. "These pirates are well-armed, and plenty of passengers and crew could die if there was a lot of shooting."

Essex surveyed the *Sea Trek* in the distance. "Let's hope the pirates don't force passengers to be human shields."

Stone sighed. "I bet it'll be the pirates' next move. We've got our hands tied. We may need to wait them out until the SEAL Team arrives."

* * *

MAY 16, 11:40 AM

Ryder stepped off the bed after retrieving his satellite phone from its hiding place in his cabin's vent work.

Layla asked, "What did they shoot down?"

"A TV news chopper cuz it had a big red seven with a circle painted around it. I gotta call Rita ASAP to find out what the FBI plans to do next."

Ryder thought Layla was more scared than when her former pimp had shot at her through a café window a half year ago. It had happened so fast she hadn't had time to be terrified.

Ryder selected Rita's number.

"Hi, Luke." Rita inhaled. "I suppose you know the pirates launched a missile at a news helicopter and downed it." She choked up. "A TV audience of millions saw the live shot from the chopper while the projectile approached and exploded."

"I was lookin' through Layla's whale-watchin' binoculars from my balcony and saw the whole thing. I heard the chopper comin'. Then there was a commotion on the sundeck. Franco was yellin' and ordered a guy to bring him a shoulder-fired rocket."

Rita sighed. "The Coast Guard cutter monitoring the situation told us the same thing. They have two drones flying circles above the *Sea Trek*. But now the fog's a problem. It's too thick for them to take pictures."

"I didn't see the drones."

"They're hard to spot."

Ryder shifted on the bed. "Is the FBI gonna try to take out the pirates soon?"

"No. The pirates have too much firepower. The drones saw a Stinger missile launcher being unloaded from the Huey after the shoot-down. The Stinger poses a much greater threat to aircraft than the Russian RPG Franco used to hit the chopper. Many passengers and crew could die if we were to assault the ship at this moment. Our analysts say Franco's unstable, and he'll sink the ship if we attack."

"How do the pirates plan to get away?" Ryder asked.

"They haven't asked for a plane or safe passage. It's a puzzle. Franco and his bunch could be terrorists ready to die. But the shrinks say a number of the pirates could be ready to give up after having seen Franco kill four people. We can't figure out how he convinced so many men to join him."

"Big money clouds minds." Ryder glanced at his watch. It would be lunchtime in minutes. "I better find Colonel Casa. We gotta do somethin' to disrupt the pirates."

"No. We need you to learn what's going on. You can't do it if you're dead."

"Okay, but I'll hunt for Casa. He could help me monitor the bad guys."

Rita bumped her phone, creating a brushing noise. "I've gotta go. So long."

Ryder wanted to disrupt the pirates' plans, but he feared doing so could endanger Layla. He turned to her. "Layla, we gotta talk about keepin' you safe."

Pounding echoed from their cabin door. "Open up."

Ryder slid his sat phone underneath the mattress.

FIFTEEN

"GOD DAMN IT, OPEN UP," the man outside of Ryder's cabin door yelled again. He pounded harder on the door.

Ryder stood up from the bed and walked to the door while Layla watched. "Hold yer horses. I'm comin'." He unlocked the door and pulled it open. A muscular man, roughly six foot three, with a dark chocolate complexion, stood there. He wore a blue Hawaiian shirt, and a Glock pistol hung at his side in a black holster. "Y'all gotta climb up to Deck Fifteen, go outside along the railing, and stand there. The captain wants the Coast Guard to see how many of you passengers is on this ship."

Ryder turned to Layla. "Let's go." Ryder realized the passengers were soon to become human shields.

The pirate said, "Deck Fifteen's where all the bars and coffee shops is. Step outside so y'all can see the big Coast Guard cutter. After a while, Cap's gonna have the bars break out the booze fer everybody." He took a long look at Layla.

Ryder thought her low-cut blouse had caught the pirate's attention. Ryder had intended to ask her to change before the man had hammered on their cabin door. She needed to keep a low profile and not reveal her shapely body. If she'd put on loose, baggy sweats and skipped her makeup, she'd be better off, Ryder thought.

The tall pirate held up a hand. "Hold it. On second thought, sir, you can proceed up the steps. The lady will come with me. The captain wants four women to make fake people by stuffin' clothes with newspapers. We gonna fool them Coast Guard guys with bogus buccaneers. Lady, let's go." He grabbed Layla's arm and began to lead her along the passageway toward the bow of the ship.

Another pirate went by. "Hi, Horatio," the pirate said to the tall, dark-complected buccaneer.

Horatio nodded and continued on with Layla. The other pirate watched them, smiled, shook his head, and kept walking toward the aft end of the ship.

Ryder saw Layla was worried when she glanced back over her shoulder at him. He winked to calm her and began to climb the steps. When he noticed the pirate wasn't checking behind him, Ryder stepped down the steps into the crowd of people who headed for Deck Fifteen along the passageway.

Layla caught a glimpse of Ryder when he began to walk, furtively following her and the pirate who was guiding her toward the ship's bow.

Ryder wondered where the tall pirate was taking her.

* * *

MAY 16, 12:01 PM

Self-proclaimed Captain Tony Franco sat on a chair on the bridge in front of a microphone on a stand. He closed his eyes, took a brief breath, and opened them again. He stared through the bridge's bank of windows. To the southwest, in the distance on the rough waves, he saw the cutter, *San Diego*. Its four hundred-foot-long profile was a menacing reminder the US government would never quit chasing him. But he had an escape plan. He'd win. He'd change his identity and live like a king.

He depressed the mike's transmit button, and a red light glowed on the switcher box. "Passengers, crew, and fellow buccaneers. This is Tony." His voice echoed across the entire ship. "We're asking our guests to assemble on the open-air decks along the rails, in full view of the US Coast Guard, to remind them there are many of you aboard." He hesitated.

"To help those who can't remain standing for long, feel free to place chairs along the railing. Leave space for people to walk along the decks. I've ordered the bars and coffee shops to provide free drinks for all. You see, we pirates are not the devils you may think we are. Follow directions, and all will be fine."

He covered the microphone with one hand and coughed. "You may have seen the regrettable incident during which a helicopter was lost at sea in a ball of flame. The Coast Guard is wholly at fault for this loss of the aircraft. I've spoken with them and warned them to stay out of an exclusion zone which extends from the *Sea Trek* out to twelve hundred meters. The helicopter crossed into this zone. Ergo, we thought we were under attack and had to respond. We wish shooting down the helicopter wouldn't have been necessary." He uttered a sigh, and its sound traveled through the ship's audio system.

"We don't want any senseless loss of life. Your presence on deck in full view of the Coast Guard will cause them to think twice before assaulting our ship."

He smiled and admired his reflection in the window in front of him. "In a half hour, we'll ask most of you to disperse for lunch. However, at random, we'll choose able-bodied people to take turns standing on the decks in the open. People in plain view will remind our Coast Guard friends they should not put all our lives in jeopardy. We are doing this for your own protection and ours. This will keep you safe."

He exhaled. "We have taken this ship to relieve its insanely rich owners of part of their ill-gotten gold. I've often pledged to my men, like Robin Hood, I will redistribute much of this money to the poor people of the Americas." He smiled, thinking how he'd deposit most of the ransom money into his hidden bank account. "Until next time, this is your humble Captain Tony Franco." He switched off his microphone.

He turned to his third-in-command, Arlo, the first mate. "Please have the two Stingers set up on the top deck, forward and aft. Make sure they're manned at all times. We can't be caught off guard again." He peered down at the water. "Also, put the two RPGs on Deck Two by the two shell doors."

Arlo stepped back toward an exit leading off the bridge. "I'll see to it the rocket launchers are moved right away, Cap."

Tony smiled and nodded.

* * *

MEANWHILE, on Deck Nine, Ryder saw the tall, dark pirate lead Layla toward an elevator on the forward end of the ship.

SIXTEEN

A LONE PIRATE dozed on a folding wooden chair on the sundeck. He sat outside of a room in which one of the two Soviet-era rocket-propelled grenade launchers on the *Sea Trek* was stored. This RPG-7 was the very weapon that had destroyed the news helicopter an hour before.

Arlo frowned when he and two other pirates neared the slumbering guard. Arlo shook the man's shoulder. The pirate awoke. "Huh?"

"You should be guarding the RPG, not nodding off," Arlo said. "Get up, and help us. Tony ordered us to relocate the RPGs, the Stingers, and their rockets."

The pirate stood. "Where we gonna take this one?"

"Near the port shell door." He gestured at a pile of three-pound, rocket-propelled projectiles. "It'll take several trips to carry all these warheads down to Deck Two." Each of the twenty-five projectiles consisted of three parts—the explosive warhead, the attached rocket motor, and a booster charge at the tail.

Arlo thought for a moment. "We also gotta deal with the two Stingers. We'll move them to the upper deck, fore and aft. They're heavier than the RPGs. The rockets are heftier, too."

While Arlo picked up the RPG launcher, the other three men each grabbed three of the twenty-five projectiles. Arlo recalled similar Soviet-designed RPGs and their cousins had a history of destroying US helicopters. Taliban soldiers had shot down a huge Chinook in Afghanistan. In Somalia, two Black Hawk choppers also had been downed.

Arlo thought placing the RPGs near the ship's shell doorways was a first-rate idea. The doors were at midship, a few feet above water level on both sides of the *Sea Trek*, so the RPG-7s could destroy Coast Guard speedboats racing toward the vessel. The two heavier American Stinger antiaircraft, shoulder-fired weapons could shoot down aircraft most effectively if placed on the top of the ship.

When he began to carry three of the three-pound RPG-7's projectiles, the pirate who'd been asleep said, "What do y'all think of Cap shooting down the civilian chopper?"

Arlo said, "It'll haunt us all. The feds will throw us into prison for hundreds of years if they catch us." He hoisted the nineteen-pound rocket-propelled grenade launcher, which had been loaded with one of the 85mm projectiles, into a comfortable position. "I hope Cap's plan for us to leave the ship unnoticed works."

The other two pirates—one tall and thin, and the other short and fat—who also carried RPG ammunition, glanced at each other and shook their heads.

Arlo asked, "You two nervous about how this hijack is going?"

The lanky buccaneer said, "When I signed up for this, it sounded great—a half-million bucks and a foolproof escape plan. But Cap's gone nuts. Odds are the feds will shoot us dead. If not, they'll lock us up, and we'll never get out. I was stupid to take this gig."

The fat, little pirate said, "Ditto. We got ourselves into quicksand, and it's like we're bein' sucked into muck."

The men got into the elevator leading down from the sundeck. After entering a code on the lift's touchscreen, Arlo pushed a button for Deck Two, an area open just to the crew. He heard the elevator descending but nothing else. The men were silent. He realized his question about how they were feeling in regard to their acts of piracy had exposed their deep concerns. Could he trust them to hear a proposal he had for them? Would they keep it quiet? If any of them told other buccaneers about his plan, it could lead to his instant death at the hands of Tony.

Arlo was third-in-command after Tony. Tony would be certain to make an example of Arlo if he wasn't totally loyal. But Arlo knew that the lanky buccaneer was right. There was a significant chance the feds would kill him or throw him in the clink to rot forever if he didn't escape from the *Sea Trek* without delay.

In a few minutes, the four pirates found the rooms near the port shell door.

Arlo surveyed the area. He guessed the heavy, hydraulically-powered shell door was ten feet square. A sturdy rope ladder was next to it along the hull. When a harbor pilot was approaching to board the ship from a large motorboat, the door would be opened, and the flexible ladder would be hung down to the water. The speedboat would match the pace of the *Sea Trek*, and the harbor pilot would climb up and into the ship on his way to the bridge.

The other three pirates also examined the space inside the hull near the door. There were three rooms, the middle area where the shell door was and two adjacent rooms on either side of the central room.

The fat, short buccaneer switched on the light in the room aft of the shell door. "Hey, look," he said. He pointed to scuba suits, air tanks, flippers, and diver propulsion vehicles, or DPVs. The twenty-one-pound DPVs were two feet long and a foot wide. All the gear was neatly arranged, hanging from hooks along the walls and stacked on the floor.

Arlo walked into the room and counted ten sets of diving equipment, enough for more than a third of the twenty-eight buccaneers, including Pilot, who had flown the Huey helicopter onto the *Sea Trek*. Because Arlo was third-in-command of the pirates, he knew the diving equipment would be there since he'd helped write the escape plan. He hoped no one would be rotten enough to open the thin, watertight, pod-shaped cases to steal the cash in them. The containers held money, a set of clothes, a fake ID, a burner phone, and gift cards. A tab with each pirate's name or nickname was wired onto each case. Additional scuba gear would arrive later via a narco submarine.

The black tarp the Huey helicopter had brought would be hung in front of the door and the ladder. Thus there was little chance the Coast Guard would spot the men leaving the ship.

Tony's plan called for the majority of the pirates, all of them handpicked divers, to don their gear near a shell door a few feet above the surface of the ocean. The divers' gear included wet suits, air cylinders, two-stage diving regulators, inflator hoses, pressure gauges, buoyancy control devices, scuba masks, and fins. The divers would strap the thin pod-shaped cases containing their clothes and money to their stomachs. The men would then enter the water sometime past midnight, in the fog and darkness, invisible to onlookers, cameras, and infrared sensors.

Underwater, each diver would position himself on top of his bullet-shaped, battery-powered diver propulsion vehicle —DPV—and grasp its handlebars. The diver's case of clothes and money was thin enough to fit between his stomach and his DPV. The diver would then turn his DPV on to start moving. A propeller in an enclosure similar to those used for portable house fans would pull a diver forward at roughly four miles per hour.

Each DPV's batteries could power the vehicle for ninety minutes. The air in the diver's scuba tanks would last from forty-five minutes to an hour. But since the *Sea Trek* was traveling three miles from shore most of the time, there was a scant chance the divers would have to surface before reaching a beach.

Because the *Sea Trek* was sailing south, the port side was

facing the coast. The ship would slow down for the men to enter the water. Once on dry land, they would hide their gear, dress, and search for one of three semi-trucks. Each truck's trailer could hold all of the men. The other semis had been added for safety's sake. After the truck drivers had been sent a coded message from Tony, each would turn on a string of Christmas lights along the top edges of his long trailer. After picking up the pirates, the big rigs would ferry them to light planes. The small aircraft would fly low and enter Mexico. If any of the buccaneers missed the trucks or the flights, they would walk until they could hitchhike or hire a ride with the money they carried.

Arlo summoned the other three pirates into the room where the diving equipment was stowed. He felt his throat tighten. Then he gulped and cleared his throat. "Men, from what you all said, I think you feel the same way I do. It was foolish of us to sign up to join Tony's crazy plot."

The men nodded. The skinny pirate blinked. "Amen," he said.

Arlo studied the men's faces, one by one. "I question Tony's plan to rely on the Stockholm syndrome to get the passengers on our side by letting them roam the ship and gamble. Some passengers may plot against us." Arlo frowned. "The passengers and nonessential crew should be confined to their cabins."

The skinny pirate nodded. "Damn straight."

Arlo continued, "I propose tonight, at 1:00 AM, we meet here and swim for shore. We can disappear, and there's an excellent chance we won't be connected with this sorry-ass debacle. Anybody who doesn't want to go doesn't have to. I ask you to keep our plan secret. Don't blab to anyone, including those you think are interested in joining us. Agreed?"

Each man smiled, and they all shook hands.

"Tonight we go. If you're late, go. You still can leave." Arlo turned to the tall, skinny man. "You stay here to guard the area until 1:00 AM. I told Tony you'd be here to protect the RPG launcher. I'll bring you food and coffee. The head's right there." He pointed to a restroom door next to the other storage room.

"You got it," the skinny man said.

Arlo and the other two men left to deliver the rest of the shoulder-fired rocket weapons to their new locations. In a flashback, Arlo saw a vivid image of Tex's Ka-Bar combat knife flying by him and then sticking into the security chief's chest. Arlo knew he could never erase the memory of the man's blood soaking the rug in the security chief's cabin. It was especially gruesome because knifing was personal.

SEVENTEEN

RYDER KEPT his distance while he tailed Layla and the tall pirate who gripped her by her upper arm. They followed the passageway toward the bow. Ryder wondered how far the pirate was going. He had started at midship and walked toward the forward elevators, which led down to the ship's two theaters.

The pirate glanced back at the same time a heavyset man crossed in front of Ryder. "Lucky," Ryder thought.

Ryder melted into the crowd in front of a restaurant-grill and watched the pirate usher Layla into an elevator.

Ryder power walked to the lift. He checked the deck-level lights above the elevator. It was descending toward Deck Seven and the theater.

Ryder rushed to a staircase and rapidly trotted down it. He peeked into the elevator lobby. The lift Layla was on had stopped on Deck Eight for a small group of passengers. After the people had entered and the door had closed, Ryder followed the steps to Deck Seven. He leaned against the bulkhead near the entrance of the elevator lobby. A lift's door slid open, and a dozen people exited, followed by the pirate pulling Layla by her upper arm. When the pirate glanced to his right, Ryder stepped into Layla's line of sight. She saw him and nodded. He went into an alcove a moment before the pirate stared Ryder's way.

The buccaneer pushed Layla in front of him and then opened an unmarked rear door to the theater. After the door had swung shut, Ryder jogged to the entrance and opened it slightly, peering inside. He saw the pirate guiding Layla through a doorway marked "Dressing Rooms."

Nobody else was in the foyer in front of the dressing room passageway. Ryder trotted inside, into the open area, and moved toward the dressing rooms.

EIGHTEEN

THE TALL, black pirate shoved Layla into the dressing room. She spied a couch along the far wall. The room was bare and had a blond, maple wood floor.

She thought she'd be raped if Ryder couldn't get into the room soon. She glanced at the door and noticed the pirate hadn't thrown the bolt to lock it.

The man smiled at her, unbuckled his gun belt, and dropped it behind the couch. He had an evil, licentious grin on his face.

She tried not to show fear, but she felt her fingers tremble.

"Strip, lady, strip."

"No." Layla heard a scream and realized it came from her own lips.

The pirate shoved her toward the couch.

She fell backward onto its cushions.

He lunged at her, grabbed her blouse, and ripped it away, its buttons flying everywhere. He yanked her brassiere downward.

Layla braced herself. She'd been raped before when she'd

been an escort. Her mind was on fire, recalling how humiliated she'd been. When she'd told her pimp about the assault, he'd laughed—said it came with the territory—was part of the "life."

She'd find a way to survive, she told herself. Living is better than dying.

Her assailant was pulling her slacks down. Then he reached behind the couch and grabbed his Ka-Bar knife from his holster.

* * *

MAY 16, 12:28 PM

Ryder quietly opened the dressing room door.

The tall, dark-complected buccaneer was on top of Layla, who was face up on the couch and topless. The pirate held his combat knife across her throat and was eyeing her ample breasts.

Ryder felt anger explode inside his brain while he bounded toward the couch and then stopped near the man. Ryder hesitated, fearing the buccaneer would slit Layla's throat.

The man turned, still holding the knife against Layla's throat. "Go away, schoolteacher. I won't kill her."

Ryder remembered this guy was the first pirate he'd encountered on the ship when jogging on the upper deck. This man had stopped him, questioned him, and patted him down.

Ryder said nothing but took a step forward, assessing his options.

The muscular man let go of Layla.

She scrambled aside.

The tall man pointed his Ka-Bar combat knife at Ryder and lunged at him.

When Ryder dodged the knife thrust, he kept his balance. He lifted his right knee, turned his hip, and then snapped his leg outward. The ball of Ryder's foot struck the man's knife hand.

The razor-sharp weapon clattered away across the wooden floor.

The pirate grabbed a heavy glass ashtray from an end table. He swung the hefty chunk of glass.

The ashtray struck Ryder's left shin bone and stunned him like he'd been jabbed by a giant needle. As Ryder fell to the smooth, wooden floor, agonizing pain vibrated throughout his leg. He instinctively rolled, and he pushed himself up on his right, uninjured leg. When he leaned on his left foot, a jolt of pain hit him like a hammer blow. He staggered aside in agony.

The pirate adjusted his grip on the heavy ashtray.

Ryder pushed down on his uninjured right leg and then leaped to the pirate's left side. Ryder's left leg collapsed, and he fell against the left side of the pirate's body.

With his right hand, the tall, muscular pirate swung the ashtray sideways and behind him toward Ryder's head. But the blow glanced off Ryder's left shoulder.

Ryder pivoted behind his foe and wrapped his right arm around the pirate's neck. Then Ryder grabbed his own right wrist with his left hand, putting the buccaneer into a choke-hold. Ryder threw both of his legs backward, parallel to the floor. He pulled the man down and back. In midair, halfway down, Ryder heard the pirate's neck snap with a sickening crack. The two men hit the hard floor. Ryder's left leg pained him so much he thought he'd black out.

Ryder felt the pirate's body tremble. Then it became still and limp. The man had stopped breathing. Ryder tried hard, but he couldn't release his choke hold from the pirate's neck. It was as if Ryder's left hand had a death grip on his right wrist. Had his primal self decided to make doubly sure his enemy was no longer a threat?

After twenty seconds, Ryder felt his left hand begin to relax. With difficulty, he pulled his cramped fingers off his right wrist.

He saw Layla holding the pirate's Glock with two hands,

aiming the firearm at the buccaneer's limp body. She was topless, her bra pulled down to her waist. She'd chambered a round during the struggle.

Ryder said, "It's okay. Point it at the floor."

Another sharp pain hit Ryder. He felt his forehead flush. He noticed his face was sweaty. He touched the pirate's throat. There was no pulse. "He's dead. You can put the pistol down." Ryder felt a wave of regret. He'd had the same feeling after he'd grappled with, and killed, the murderer he'd caught at NASA a few days prior.

Layla set the firearm on the couch. "What are we going to do?"

Ryder glanced at the door. "First, lock the door."

She nodded, walked to the door, and engaged the deadbolt.

Despite trying not to, Ryder groaned when he pushed himself up on his right leg while he kneeled on his left knee. He struggled to stand, swivel, and sit on the couch. "I think my leg's broken."

Layla rushed to him. She tried to move his trouser leg up, but touching his leg made him wince. "I'll use the bastard's knife to cut your trouser leg."

Ryder nodded.

She grabbed the Ka-Bar from the floor and sliced the trouser cloth upward. "It's nasty." Ryder's shin was badly bruised and swollen.

He peered at his injury. "No bone's stickin' out. If it's broke, it's minor."

Layla let her breath out. "I'll get ice."

"Not yet. For one thing, you need a shirt. Plus, I can't stand for long." He caught sight of the end table. "Could you drag the table over here? I'm gonna make a splint."

Layla pulled the table to Ryder. He picked it up and struck one of its legs on the deck at an angle. This loosened the leg enough so he could twist it off.

Layla lifted her bra back into position and then walked to a desk in another corner of the room. "There must be tape around here." She opened a drawer. "I found packing tape. It'll pull the hairs out when we remove it, though."

"It won't hurt like my shin's hurtin' now."

Layla also found a pair of scissors in the top desk drawer. She brought the tape and scissors to Ryder, who'd already placed the short wooden table leg against his shin.

Layla unwound the tape and snipped a piece off. She leaned forward, intending to wrap the tape around the wood and Ryder's leg. But she stopped and stuck the tape on the edge of the broken end table. "We need to pad the wood against the shinbone." She glanced around. "I'll cut cloth from the dead SOB's slacks." She closed her eyes and then opened them again to steel herself. "I need a shirt, too. His could be unisex."

"I'll crawl over and help," Ryder said.

"No way. I got this." Layla stood and walked to the body, which lay face up. The pirate's dark brown eyes stared at the ceiling. Ryder thought they seemed to hypnotize her, like she was staring at a dangerous cobra about to strike. Then she shifted her gaze to the dead man's slacks.

She hastily snipped cloth squares from them, big enough so she could fold them into pads. She started unbuttoning his shirt but stopped and stared away from the body.

Ryder said, "I'll git the shirt off him after the splint's on. I can stand then."

"Don't count on it." Layla finished taking off the dead pirate's fancy, dark blue Hawaiian shirt. It reeked of body odor. She wrinkled her nose and put the garment on.

"It's too big fer you," Ryder said. "But lots of women wear baggy shirts these days."

Layla shrugged. "You need to do what you need to do." She walked to Ryder. "What about the body?"

* * *

MAY 16, 12:37 PM

Tony sat on the bridge of the *Sea Trek*. He enjoyed the smell of cigar smoke, much to the detriment of most women and many men who might come into his close vicinity.

He blew a circle of smoke above him, watched it rise lazily, and then flicked ashes into an empty coffee cup. He swiveled his chair to face Waylen, his second-in-command. "I've been thinking. We need to get the passengers to like us even if they're scared shitless of us at the same time. I want them to bond with us. I'd like to create a mass Stockholm syndrome."

Waylen shifted on his feet. "What's the Stockholm syndrome?"

"In 1973, a man robbed a bank in Stockholm, Sweden. Four bank employees were hostages for a week. They developed a close relationship with the robber and began to mistrust the police."

Waylen cocked his head. "Why? Didn't the robber threaten to kill or beat the crap out of them?"

Tony studied Waylen for a moment. "Books are food for the brain." Tony puffed on his Cuban cigar and sucked the smoke into his mouth to enjoy its flavor. He blew the smoke from his lips. "A book I got out of the library said psychologists think if a hostage's life is at risk, and the captor decides not to kill the hostage, he's grateful. The hostage connects his well-being with his jailers, in this case, us pirates."

Waylen nodded. "What do we gotta do to get on their good side?"

Tony caught sight of a small bunch of passengers on the forward observation deck below him. "It doesn't take great acts of kindness for our captives to start to like us. Small actions we take will work."

"What should I tell the men to do when they interact with passengers?"

"For one thing, they should stop stealing jewels, watches, and money." He rubbed his chin. "I've learned they're robbing folks right and left. Why? They're going to walk away with at least a half-million bucks. And they can't carry a lot of loot when they swim for shore."

Waylen said, "When you declared free drinks for all, it was a great idea. I heard passengers say they liked it and the free gambling chips, too."

"It did do a world of good, especially after the death of the DEA agent. But we did have to scare the bejeebers out of them before the Stockholm syndrome would kick in."

"Yer a genius."

Tony felt satisfied with himself and his new plan to treat the passengers and crew better. He said, "Get passengers to help us make more fake buccaneers. It'll encourage the artistic ones to bond with us."

"Yes, Cap."

Tony smiled. He pushed the button on the microphone box, and its light glowed red. "Passengers and crew. This is your captain. I hereby instruct the casino to issue every passenger and crew member another five thousand dollars from my account to enjoy themselves wagering. Have a great day." He clicked the mike off.

* * *

MAY 16, 12:42 PM

Ryder felt a constant, throbbing pain in his front left shin. He didn't think he could drag the tall pirate's body. Ryder had trouble standing even with the splint Layla had taped to his leg. He peered into her eyes. "I can't pull the pirate very far. Either we leave him put, or we try to hide him nearby."

"I could search for a closet or storeroom down the hall," Layla said.

"Scout around, but be careful." Ryder winced. "I doubt you could drag this guy very far, and somebody could see you."

Layla shrugged. "If someone sees me pulling a pirate's body, odds are he or she would be a passenger or a crew member. I'd tell the truth. The pirate tried to rape me and kill you. They wouldn't say a damn thing to the bad guys."

"You got a point. But pray a pirate doesn't show up."

"I'll be careful."

Ryder noticed a single-pole, wooden coat rack near the door. A light jacket hung on one of its hooks. "Could you bring the coatrack here? I'll use it for a crutch."

Layla threw the jacket aside and carried the rack to Ryder. "We'll need to find something better than this."

Ryder gripped the rack and pulled himself up. He made his way to the door. "I'll lock it after you go. When you come back, knock once, then wait two seconds, and knock fast twice."

"Okay, hon." Layla cracked open the door and peered out. "Nobody's there. I see a door labeled 'Prop Room.'"

"Sounds promising."

Layla smiled briefly and went into the passageway.

Ryder locked the door. He hoped his leg wasn't broken. Was it merely bruised? If it was fractured, he reckoned he wouldn't be able to physically confront the pirates. He might even have trouble observing their movements. If he couldn't gather information, what use would he be to the FBI?

* * *

MAY 16, 12:45 PM

Layla felt a cool draft when she entered the passageway outside of the dressing room. She surveyed the area. It was still deserted, so she turned toward the prop room thirty feet away, marked by a sign above its wide, double doorway.

As she approached the room, footsteps sounded behind her. She felt her heart thumping like the hooves of a race-horse running at a derby. She took a breath and turned.

A buccaneer, armed with the same type of pistol and knife the dead pirate had carried, leered at her. "Honey, you work in the theater?" He spoke in a strong Southern drawl.

She forced herself to smile. "Yes, sir. I'm a dancer." She waited for a moment. "Anything you need back here?"

"I was lookin' for a buddy. He's a black man and tall." The pirate lifted his arm to show the height. "You ain't seen him, have you, dear?"

"Sorry. No." Layla fought to control her breathing, to make herself inhale normally. She realized the worst thing to do would be to broadcast her fear.

"If he shows up, tell him Tex is lookin' for him, okay?"

"I will."

"What's yer name, Miss?"

"Layla."

Tex Curtis, the pirate who'd killed the ship's chief of security when the *Sea Trek* had first been taken, smiled and turned to leave. He took half a dozen steps, then stopped and faced Layla again. "If you'd like to meet me later, Layla, I'd be obliged."

Layla felt a chill run through her body. This guy appeared to be dangerous. "I'm not allowed to fraternize with the patrons. You wouldn't want to get me fired, would you?"

Tex grinned, showing his coffee-stained teeth. "No, ma'am. But if I happen to catch yer show, I can ask special permission from your boss when it's over."

"You could, I guess." Layla smiled. "But they've changed the performance schedule because of the situation."

"Understood. I'll check it out later." Tex ogled her, turned, and left.

Layla let out a breath and continued toward the prop room's double doors. She twisted one of the doorknobs and pulled. The sturdy, blond maple door opened smoothly.

Light from the hallway lit the prop room's light switch, so Layla flipped it on.

Stage backgrounds called flats leaned against one wall. She counted a dozen of the wide, eight-foot-tall, cloth-covered wooden frames. There were also chairs, platforms, fake trees—a wide assortment of objects crowding the room.

The floor was tiled, likely to make it easier for stagehands to move the props.

Layla noticed an alcove labeled "Costumes." She walked to it. Outfits hung on a long clothing rod, as did a half-dozen clothing bags, which were zippered shut.

One gray, heavy-duty plastic bag caught her attention. It was large, taller than the average man, and its bottom edges draped onto the floor. Could this hold the pirate's body? Yes. Layla unzipped the bag and yanked her shaking hand back from the scary dragon costume inside it as if a jolt of electricity had shocked her.

She stood frozen in fear, and then a flashback sent her back in time. She saw a series of rapid mental images of how she and Ryder had first met when she had been trying to escape her pimp's house in Louisville, Kentucky. She recalled how Ryder had permitted her and her young daughter Angela to stay in his apartment. How the pimp had died in a car crash and a ball of flames after Ryder had pursued him. The panderer had proved to be a serial killer. Yes, Luke Ryder had saved her. By then, she'd quit the "life" forever.

Layla snapped out of her reverie. Her hand was shaking when she grabbed the dragon costume and tossed it on the floor, out of sight in the back of the alcove.

She took hold of the large garment bag. She and Ryder could stuff the dead pirate into it. There was a chance they could shove the body into the small closet in the dressing room, but making the corpse fit inside was iffy.

As Layla stepped back from the costume rack, she saw two chrome poles sticking up from behind a pile of pots, beds, mirrors, and artificial bushes. She walked to the objects and peeked around them. The shiny vertical rods were the top parts of a luggage dolly. Perfect.

Layla pulled the dolly clear of its surrounding pile of items and tossed the garment bag on top of the luggage cart. While she worked her way toward the room's exit, she bumped props along her path. Something struck the hard floor with a dry, wooden clatter. She checked behind her. A walking cane had fallen. She was on a lucky streak after almost having been raped and killed.

She felt calmer but excited when she opened the prop room's door. The passageway was deserted. She pulled the dolly toward the dressing room.

* * *

MAY 16, 1:05 PM

Ryder was leaning against the dressing room wall next to the door. He'd heard voices in the hallway, a man and a woman, but he hadn't been able to understand what they were saying. He worried Layla had been gone too long, certainly longer than ten minutes.

Earlier, he'd picked up the dead buccaneer's pistol belt. Its holster had held a Glock 17 pistol as well as two extra seventeen-round magazines. He had shoved the magazines into his pocket and placed the pistol belt on the floor next to the door, minus the firearm. He held the Glock next to his chest with the safety off, ready to shoot. He'd slid the Ka-Bar combat knife into his belt.

A soft knock sounded on the door, followed by two seconds of silence and then two rapid knocks. He unlatched the door and swung it open.

Layla stood outside, grinning, her hands on the dolly's chrome vertical poles. A walking stick lay on the bed of the baggage cart along with the gray plastic garment bag she'd found. "I got lucky." She pulled the dolly into the room.

"You did." Ryder smiled despite the constant pain in his left shinbone.

Layla closed and locked the door. "It was about time I was dealt a winning hand." She glanced at the body, and her demeanor changed.

Ryder thought she might get sick to her stomach.

She pointed to the gray garment bag. "The body will fit inside this, and we can put it on the dolly. There's a place to hide the bag in the prop room."

"Excellent. When you were outside, I heard voices out there."

Layla concentrated on his eyes. "A pirate asked me for a date. I said I was a dancer, and I wasn't allowed to fraternize with the guests. Said he'd find my boss and ask for an exception."

Ryder felt his anger build. "We need to keep you hidden." He stared at the corpse. "We better get movin'." Ryder set the pistol on the floor next to the pistol belt, then grabbed the cane and hobbled toward the body.

Layla unzipped the bag and set it lengthwise next to the deceased buccaneer. "Let's roll him inside."

"Okay."

After the corpse was in the bag, Layla zipped it closed. "I feel better now because I can't see the bastard's staring eyes."

"Let's get him up onto the dolly," Ryder said. "We can pull him heels first onto the cart."

After Layla moved the handcart next to the corpse, they each grabbed a heel and pulled. In two minutes, the body bag was on the pushcart.

Layla stood. "I'll check outside before we move him." She unlocked the door and peeked outside. "It's clear."

"Wait 'til I go down the hall to keep an eye peeled for pirates." Supported by the cane, Ryder shuffled along the passageway and peered around the corner into the open area beyond it. He gave Layla a thumbs-up sign.

Layla tugged the cart to the prop room's double doors. After pulling one door open, she yanked the luggage cart into the room.

Ryder walked toward Layla. He felt the onset of a headache which added to his leg pain, increasing his discomfort. Even so, he pushed himself to move faster. He entered the prop room with her. "Well done, Layla." He leaned on his cane. "After we hide the body, I'm thinkin' I'll get an X-ray. The med center is at midship on Deck Four. I bet I can get a splint or a cast."

"I agree."

Ryder furrowed his brow. "It's a long way to the med center, and I'll take a while to walk there. Me stumbling along would arouse suspicion, but I got an idea. You'll need to get me a shot of brandy."

Layla frowned. "What?"

A recovering alcoholic and on the wagon, Ryder hadn't had a drop of liquor in months.

Ryder laughed. "It ain't what you think." He smiled. "I'm gonna pretend I'm drunk. I sure as hell know how a drunk acts cuz I once was one."

NINETEEN

IN THE SHIP'S craft center, a swarthy pirate sat at a worktable, his head bent down while he remained focused on his artwork. He used a felt-tip marker to trace the fifteenth of thirty outlines of his AK-47 rifle on a thick piece of cardboard. Next to him, a female passenger, who appeared to be at least sixty years old, was cutting out one of the buccaneer's automatic weapon tracings with a razor blade. When the gray-haired lady finished, she handed it to the pirate.

The man smiled. "Thank you, it's beautiful."

Tony had spread the word throughout the ship that all of his men were to be polite to the passengers and crew. He wanted them on his side if the US authorities assaulted the ship.

The old woman smiled. "You guys aren't too bad. I'm enjoying this cruise better than the others I've taken." She glanced around the room and then back at the pirate, who sported a ponytail tied with a rubber band. "It's a cruise to remember."

"Yes, ma'am. That's true for all of us."

At another table, a young woman, a gifted artist, sat with

a filbert paintbrush in hand and a palette of fast-drying acrylic paints at her side. She smiled while she coated the stock of a sturdy cardboard AK-47 with brown paint. She finished by adding streaks of lighter paint to depict grain on the fake weapon's wooden buttstock.

After the pirate left, carrying a dozen of the completed cardboard rifles, the gray-haired woman turned to the perky young brunette who was in charge of the craft center. "They're not so bad. They're cordial."

The brunette sighed. "Yeah, but you can be convicted of piracy for aiding them."

"What?"

"I heard it from two of the older crew members." The brunette scanned the room where three other women were painting the fake firearms. She whispered, "It's against US law to willingly help a pirate. You can be prosecuted for piracy." She squinted. "If I were you, I'd claim they forced you to assist."

The old lady gulped. "It's hard to believe doing artwork would constitute piracy." She shook her head.

The brunette craft center manager nodded. "I'll tell everybody else here what I told you. But please don't say I asked you to lie to the authorities."

The older lady let out a breath. "I won't tell anybody what you said. You have my word."

The young brunette patted the older woman's shoulder. "I better speak with the others."

TWENTY

RYDER SAT on a desk chair inside the dressing room, waiting for Layla to return from a bar with a bottle of liquor. He knew he had to hide the pain he was in. If she thought his pain wasn't too bad, she wouldn't take chances and get hurt or killed. He'd scrounged around and found a bottle of aspirin and a half-full bottle of water in the dressing room's desk. He'd washed down four tablets and wished he'd had something to eat with them because now his stomach burned. The aspirin didn't seem to help, and he also had hunger pangs. He should have asked Layla to bring sandwiches, too.

Ryder heard Layla's soft tapping on the door. He unlocked it.

Layla stepped into the room and locked the door. She had a mini-bottle of Kentucky bourbon, which held one-and-a-half ounces of liquor. "I figured I'd get the brand of booze you like. I can find out if you've really kicked the habit." She grinned.

Ryder hadn't sipped whiskey or beer for months. He accepted the bottle. "I'm gonna rub this stuff on me like rubbin' alcohol." He shook his head. "But it'll be hard not to lick it off my skin."

Layla's body shook slightly. "I need to swallow what's left."

Ryder figured her nerves were frayed. He twisted off the cap of the airline-sized bottle of bourbon. He held it to his nose and took a whiff. Layla was sure as hell testing him. It was his favorite brand, all right, and his leg pain was worsening. He sure could use a drink to dull the discomfort. Damn it all, he thought. He put his palm over the bottle's mouth and tipped it. When he smeared the booze on his face, he smelled the strong odor of bourbon. He felt like he'd go crazy, but he resisted his urge to lick his black mustache.

Layla watched. "Save some for me."

Ryder nodded. He tipped the mini-bottle over his palm again and tapped his shirt and throat with it. "Should do the trick." He handed the half-full bottle to Layla.

Layla put her lips around the mouth of the little bottle and swallowed the remaining bourbon in three big sips. She winced, blinked, and exhaled. "Makes me feel woozy, and the room's unsteady, like it's wavering."

"You're not a drinker," Ryder said. "But this should help you."

"I haven't had undiluted booze in a year," Layla said. "I feel better."

Ryder glimpsed at the floor next to the chair and spied the dead pirate's pistol belt and the Glock 17. "I need to keep the piece and the magazines, but I don't know how I can conceal 'em." Ryder studied the baggy, smelly shirt Layla had gotten from the tall, black pirate. "The Hawaiian shirt's got plenty of room. You can wear the pistol belt with the holster over your belly, and nobody'll notice it."

Layla, who was well-endowed, gazed down. "Okay."

"Keep the magazines, too. Think they'll fit in your fanny pack?"

"Yes." She unbuttoned the pirate's shirt she wore. After taking the pistol belt from Ryder, she fastened it around her stomach. She swiveled the holster sideways so it was parallel to the belt and then buttoned the shirt. "Can't tell it's there unless I lie on my back." She stuffed the two mags of 9mm ammo into her fanny pack.

"I'm worried they'll catch you with the pistol," Ryder said. "When we get back to the room, we gotta hide it."

Layla shrugged. "If they catch me, I doubt they'll kill me. They'll want their way with me." She took a breath. "If they find it with you, you'd be shot."

Ryder sighed. "Let's ride the elevator down to Deck Four. Then we gotta walk a ways to get to the med center at midship."

Layla unlocked the door and peeked out. "It's deserted. Let's go."

* * *

MAY 16, 1:34 PM

Ryder leaned on the wooden walking stick and took a step out of the lift. Layla was on his left, aiding him while they moved away from the elevator lobby. Ryder smelled the bourbon on his clothes, and the addicted part of his brain yearned for alcohol the same way a jilted lover dreams of a final tryst with his lost loved one.

The passageway on Deck Four was busy. When Ryder and Layla passed close to a straight-laced woman, she shot a critical glance at Ryder, who faked drunkenness.

"You cain't beat free licker," he slurred in a loud voice when he saw a pirate walk by. Ryder felt like crap even though he wasn't having a hangover.

The pirate smirked and walked on.

"My acting's getting better," Ryder whispered to Layla.

"How's your leg?" Layla asked.

"Fine," Ryder said. But he felt sweaty and faint. His pain was increasing with each of his shuffling steps. He added to his lie. "Seems better." He wondered if he'd make it to the med center without falling. He knew he had to grin and endure the pain.

A cabin steward dressed in a white uniform neared them, pushing a dolly that held linen, cleaning tools, and supplies. Ryder guessed the middle-aged man was Filipino.

The man halted near Ryder and Layla. "Sir, you seem to be hurting," he said in an accent. "Where are you going?"

Ryder slurred, "To the med center. I slipped on steps and fell. Lucky, a guy loaned me this cane."

The man pointed. "If you wait on the bench, I'll get a wheelchair."

"I'm obliged," Ryder said. He noticed the steward's nostrils flared when he took a quick whiff of the bourbon on Ryder's face and clothes.

The steward said, "You've been drinking. I wish I could get a shot of whiskey. These scary pirates can drive a man to drink. Trouble is my boss said no." The steward smiled. "We gotta be ready to lower the lifeboats. If we're tipsy, it would cause problems." He motioned again at the bench. "Please have a seat." The man walked away.

Ryder sat down. "Lucky he came by."

Layla leaned against his left side. "I can't wait 'til this is over." She shed tears.

"We're gonna be fine." Ryder hoped at least Layla would survive the cruise physically and mentally unharmed. It was no vacation.

The cabin steward came back, rolling a wheelchair. "Let me help," the man said. He steadied Ryder when he stood and then helped him sit in the chair.

"Thanks," Ryder said. "We can take it from here."

"No, I insist on getting you there," the man said. He began to roll the chair forward while Layla walked beside it.

Ryder spoke with less of a slur. "Are you Filipino?"

"Born and raised in Manila."

Ryder smiled. "The Filipinos I've met are like you, real good people."

"What cabin are you staying in, sir?"

"F497 on Deck Nine."

"You're fortunate. I'm assigned to your room. I'll put two buckets of ice in there."

Ryder reached into his wallet and removed a twenty-dollar bill. "Please take this."

"Thank you, sir. But please keep your money. Helping others makes me happy."

Less than five minutes later, the Filipino man was pushing the wheelchair into the med center. "Doc, I got you a patient. He slipped and hurt his leg real bad."

A man in a blue lab coat came from an examining room into the reception area. "Thanks."

The doctor turned to Ryder. "What happened?"

Ryder slurred, "I slipped on steps and fell." He stopped speaking for two seconds. "Somebody must have spilled a drink on them."

"Let's see what we can do."

Ryder wondered if his leg was broken or not.

TWENTY-ONE

TONY STOOD on the bridge of the *Sea Trek* and peered through a pair of binoculars. He studied the Coast Guard cutter, *San Diego,* bathed in a soupy fog bank a mile away. He wondered what the ship's captain was doing. What was he planning? What surveillance tools did he have to keep an eye on the *Sea Trek*?

Tony's best friend, Colombian drug smuggler Gino Gonzales, would arrive with his narco submarine at night. Could he safely slip past the Coast Guard's watchful eyes and deliver a vital cargo of C-4 explosives, rockets, arms, and scuba diving equipment?

Tony needed additional scuba gear so his entire crew could get away when the time came—likely the early hours of Saturday, May 18. The deadline he'd set for the transmission of the half-billion dollars in cryptocurrency was 11:59 PM Friday night.

If he didn't receive the money, he'd decided he would act. He'd set off the C-4 bombs via a special portable transmitter, which explosives expert Tokyo Joe had hand-built. The transmitter would automatically find an open frequency, even if the feds jammed all satellite and cell phone bands. In the chaos, while the cruise ship burned—or sank— Tony would leave unnoticed in the drug sub while the Coast Guard prioritized rescuing five thousand passengers and crew.

Tony would depart in comfort with Gino and Heather, his hostage, instead of having to swim underwater for shore wearing scuba gear. Nor would he have to take a helicopter ride with Pilot in the old man's ancient, Vietnam War-era chopper. Heather would be an excellent human shield, too. Even if he didn't receive ransom money for her, he could keep her. She'd be his personal human pet. Could she become his companion? He admitted to himself she'd affected him like no other woman had since his true love had left him years ago.

Tony's brain then shifted gears. He began to think about Gino's sub. It had cost millions to build it in the jungle between Ecuador and Colombia. Drug lords had found this area to be relatively safe, where narco submarines could be constructed unseen by the authorities. Rivers and bodies of water in the jungle served as conduits carrying heavy parts and materials, which workers assembled into submersible watercraft. The laborers tested and then dismantled the subs for transport to warehouses near seaports for secret reassembly.

Over the years, the drug smugglers' men had learned to build better and better subs. They were painted blue to blend into the ocean water. They produced a very small wake, so they were hard to detect by patrolling aircraft. For the most part, the subs traveled just below the sea's surface, and their diesel exhaust vented through a long pipe running the length of the hull. The water alongside the pipe cooled the exhaust and decreased its infrared heat signature. Hence, it was hard for infrared cameras and sensors to spot these vessels. And since the subs were made of fiberglass, they were almost invisible to sonar and radar.

Gino's fiberglass submersible was a hundred feet long. Its key parts were made from a special plastic, which was ten times stronger than steel. The vessel even had air conditioning, a ten-foot conning tower, and a periscope. The sub could carry ten tons of cargo and a half-dozen people. Its diesel engines charged German-built, lithium-ion submarine batteries so it could run underwater for days at depths of almost a hundred feet.

After aiming his eyes at the sky, Tony then turned to Waylen, who was second-in-command. "I wonder how much Coast Guard drone sensors can see through fog."

Waylen scratched his head. "They don't work well in foggy conditions. They use thermal imaging cameras sensitive to infrared. The cameras detect heat coming out of objects to take pictures of them. The thicker the fog, the more it blocks infrared heat signals."

Tony smiled. "I spoke with Gino, who's on his narco sub, and he said his ETA is eleven o'clock tonight. Too bad there'll be a full moon. I'm worried the Coast Guard could spot the sub even with the fog. Any ideas?"

"First, let's have the *Sea Trek* do an all-engines-stop. We'll be at the mercy of the current. But Gino can surface the sub next to the port shell door. If the Coast Guard cutter stays on our starboard side, where it has been lately, the *Sea Trek* will block the *San Diego*'s line of sight. But if the *San Diego* gets between us and shore on the port side, then Gino can surface by the starboard shell door instead."

Tony nodded. "The cutter's been on our starboard side since they've been keeping pace with us. I'll call Gino back to tell him to surface on the port side unless he sees the *San Diego* has moved to our port side."

Waylen rubbed his chin. "Even if the Coast Guard's infrared cameras and sensors can't see through thick fog, who knows what new surveillance they have? We should hang the black tarps from the shell doors and drape the canvas over the sub's conning tower if the sea's calm."

"Fine idea. What's the weather forecast for 11:00 PM?"

"Calm with the usual heavy fog." Waylen smiled.

Tony gloated. "I knew there'd be soupy fog in mid-May." He had read about the typical foggy weather patterns off

California's central and southern coast. "Mother Nature's on our side tonight."

Waylen nodded. "If the sub is half submerged, our guys can hustle to unload the explosives and scuba gear unseen."

Tony stared upward while he thought out loud. "The more bombs, the better. Tokyo Joe can wire up C-4 in other places on the ship, too." He grinned. "After the cargo's unloaded, Gino can dive, match speed with the *Sea Trek*, and travel next to us. He could take you and me with him when we skedaddle." He took a moment to think as he was visualizing the future. "The rest of the guys can follow the scuba escape plan. A few could ride with Pilot on the Huey helicopter, if they want. He'll fly low under the radar, and with his extra big fuel tanks, he can fly a long way."

Waylen said, "The plan should work if we leave tonight or tomorrow night. The fog will be one big smoke screen."

Tony nodded. "I talked to the moneymen in Bogotá. Everything's set for the money transfer."

Waylen took a deep breath. "Truth be told, I'll be glad when this is all over and we get our money."

Tony stared at Waylen. "Have faith, and you will be blessed." He paused. "We can increase our chance of success by making sure the men don't harass the women passengers." His eyes bored into Waylen's. "I've seen at least half of our guys ogling females. Pass the word to leave the ladies alone. There'll be plenty of time for women after our mission is done."

"You got it."

Tony pictured Heather and her long, blond hair. He should visit her to be sure she was okay. He believed she'd taken a liking to him. Was the Stockholm syndrome affecting her? "I'm gonna check on the rich bitch, Heather."

Waylen smiled. "See you later, Cap."

TWENTY-TWO

US COAST GUARD Captain Chuck Stone stood on the bridge of his cutter, *San Diego*. "Have we intercepted the pirates' satellite phone conversations?"

"No, Captain," replied Lieutenant Commander Ralph Essex. "I received an update from Rita Reynolds at the FBI. She told me the NSA says the pirates' phones are encrypted. NSA folks are working on it."

"If we're lucky, they'll crack the code soon," Stone said. "Heavy fog's predicted for late tonight until dawn. Our infrared cameras and weapons won't be able to see through it. But we could monitor the top decks of the *Sea Trek*. Let's hope the pirates don't try anything tonight."

Essex sipped his coffee. "It's not likely they'll act until after their deadline tomorrow night."

Stone scratched his nose. "The FBI analysts say the pirates could detonate their bombs with a satellite phone. Could we jam the phone frequencies?"

"Yes, but the FBI's man on the *Sea Trek* is using a SAT phone to relay intelligence to the task force. Jamming would cut him off."

Stone bit his lip, thought, and then said, "We could jam the signal if we knew an explosion was about to happen."

Essex nodded. "True, but we'd have to move very close to the *Sea Trek* for our onboard jammers to be effective. It would take time when seconds matter." He sighed. "During a class I took six months ago, I learned bomb makers have been building radio triggers able to search for a clear radio channel and then send a detonation signal. The triggers also scan frequencies not used by SAT phones or cell phones. At the same time, a radio receiver at the bomb is constantly scanning and locks instantly on to the bomber's encoded transmitter signal when it's sent." Essex took a deep breath. "If we jam all radio channels, we'll block our own communications, too."

Stone knotted his brow. "The bottom line is we won't jam all the radio channels."

"Correct." Essex waited for a second and then said, "Also, from a boat at a safe distance, the pirates could reel out a long, insulated wire and set off the bomb. Or one of them could be suicidal or dying of cancer and willing to do the deed right in the engine room."

"What about a timer?"

Essex said, "A timer would work, but it would be simple to disconnect."

Stone said, "This is one big chess match."

Essex nodded. "They could kill a lot of people. But we'll chase 'em to the ends of the earth."

TWENTY-THREE

THE MED CENTER doctor rolled Ryder in his wheelchair to a gurney under what appeared to be a dental X-ray unit. He and Layla helped Ryder get onto the wheeled stretcher. Then Layla helped Ryder remove his trousers.

The physician caught Layla's attention. "Nice job applying the splint."

Layla smiled.

The doctor cut off the tape.

Ryder felt hairs on his leg pull out when the physician yanked the tape off and removed the table leg splint. He leaned closer to Ryder's left shin. "There's bruising but little swelling. Let's take an X-ray."

Ryder nodded.

The physician glanced at the breadbox-sized X-ray unit suspended on a long steel arm. He said, "This machine was developed for the Army for battlefield use." He moved the long, gray arm with the X-ray instrument on the end of it over Ryder's lower leg. He stood back by a computer monitor and pushed a button. There was a beep.

Layla moved to where she could see the monitor, which displayed a picture of Ryder's shinbone.

The doctor studied the X-ray for three minutes. "It's broken. You don't require surgery, and I don't need to set it. The splint helped to keep the bone from cracking further." He applied ice to the injury.

Ryder sat up on the gurney, keeping his legs flat. "Am I gonna need a cast?"

"Yes. I'll put a fiberglass cast on you because it's light-weight and more comfortable than a plaster one. I'd say you'll heal in about six weeks."

"What physical activity can I do?"

"Take it easy. Avoid putting weight on your left leg. Your cane is adequate, and you can keep the wheelchair until you get off the ship. I don't recommend shore excursions." He scoffed, "But with the pirates in control, you don't have to worry about activities on land."

"If I'm careful, can I get around the ship and enjoy the shows?"

"Yes." He peered at Ryder's eyes. "I'll give you a heavy, plastic, bag-like cover. It seals so you can shower. Let's get started."

The physician iced Ryder's leg for twenty minutes and then slipped a stockinette and cotton padding over the shin area. Next, he wrapped fiberglass strips around the lower leg.

The doctor gazed at Ryder and Layla and said, "This fiberglass cast will dry in a few minutes, but it'll take several hours to harden. Come back to see us if you experience tight-ness or swelling under the cast, or numbness, burning, or tingling below it."

"Okay, Doc. Thanks," Ryder said.

"I'd lay off the booze if I were you. No point falling and cracking the bone, so I have to set it, or worse, so you'll need an operation. Too bad the pirates are in control. Otherwise, we would've flown you to a hospital."

Ryder sighed.

Layla and the doctor helped Ryder get into the wheel-chair. She placed a blanket over Ryder's bare legs, grabbed Ryder's walking stick, and handed it to him. "Thank you,

Doctor. I'll keep him in line." She smiled and pushed Ryder into the passageway toward the elevator lobby.

"You're gonna have to fish the sat phone outta the vent," Ryder whispered. "I need to touch base with Rita."

"Okay, hon."

TWENTY-FOUR

BRUSHING HER LONG, blond hair, Heather stared into the mirror in her cabin next to Tony's suite. She thought she must make herself appear like a fashion magazine cover girl to please Tony. She reckoned she had to play the odds to survive. She decided every little thing she did to increase her chance of living through her ordeal could make a big difference.

She applied makeup though she often wore little of it. Next, she put on the best dress she had, made of burgundy linen. It emphasized her youthful, sleek look.

After she walked out of the bedroom, she heard a soft knock at her cabin door. A baritone voice followed. "Heather, this is Tony Franco. May I come in?"

Heather went to the door and leaned toward the peephole.

Tony was smiling and handsome. It was hard to believe he'd cut a man's throat earlier at breakfast time. She trembled when she briefly remembered the bloody incident, which had appeared on the ship's TV system. "I'll be a minute," she said. She had to calm herself. After taking two deep breaths, she smoothed her hair and then opened the door. "Please come in, Captain." She tried to dismiss repeated flashbacks of the retired DEA agent's killing. She willed a smile to form.

"You look extraordinary, Heather." When Tony entered the suite, he held his left hand behind him. "I have something for you." He handed her a single red rose he'd taken from the small onboard floral and knickknack boutique shop.

"Thank you, Captain." Heather's heart was beating fast despite her effort to appear calm.

"Please, call me Tony." He scanned the suite. "Let's take a seat on the couch. We can chat."

Heather gulped. "Of course. Would you like a drink? The bar's well stocked."

"Yes. I'd like a glass of wine if you have it. Why not have one, too?"

Heather walked to the bar and set the rose on it. "I'll try a small glass of cabernet sauvignon."

"It will calm you." He seemed to be studying her face and the shape of her body in her linen dress. "I've come here to check on you. Don't worry. You'll survive this episode in your life. I will see to it you're protected at all times."

Heather handed Tony his wineglass. After she sat on the far end of the couch, she tasted her wine. "It's the drink of the gods."

Tony lifted his glass and motioned a toast.

Heather could hear his lips smack after he sipped the costly California wine.

"Excellent," he said. He eased into the middle of the couch.

"It was a fine year for Napa wines in 2026," she said.

Tony drank half of the wine in his glass and then said, "Yes, ma'am." He slid next to her.

Heather could smell his bad breath mixed with the odor of the top-notch wine. She hoped the alcohol would dilute some of his mouth odor. When he leaned closer, she felt her pulse rate soar. She cleared her throat and took another sip. "Tony, did you ever go wine tasting?"

Tony grinned. "No, but I should one day."

She thought his coffee-stained teeth resembled yellowed ivory.

He took a moment to think and then touched the shoulder of her burgundy dress. "The color of this dress is like the color of the wine."

Heather felt chills and fear. "The colors are similar." Though she tried to slow her respiration, she breathed faster. She forced herself to smile and felt her face warm. She knew it was bright red.

Tony's dark eyes seemed to drill into hers. "I think you like me," he said.

She shrugged. "You have a dark, handsome appearance." She knew she wasn't lying about him. Too bad the man had taken the wrong steps in his life.

She again smiled, this time broadly. She decided then and there if he wanted her, she would yield. She was sexually experienced. Should sex happen between them, it wouldn't be for love, but for survival. She set her glass on the coffee table.

Tony drank the rest of his wine and put his glass down. He examined her with sparkling eyes and asked quietly. "Will you permit me to kiss you?" He glanced up as if remembering something. "I once had a girlfriend who's a dead ringer for you. In fact, you're her doppelgänger."

Heather picked up her glass and downed her remaining wine. "A kiss wouldn't hurt," she lied. She set her glass down.

Tony pulled her close to him and kissed her lips.

Heather felt the power of his arms. She kissed him back. He was an experienced kisser. *If he takes me, I have to pretend to like it*, she thought. Her breathing rate increased.

Tony said nothing, but he reached behind her and unzipped her dress.

Heather felt helpless. She compelled her lips to form a smile and leaned backward.

Tony pulled her dress over her head.

Heather cringed inside yet kept smiling. Yes, she was a survivor.

* * *

MAY 16, 2:59 PM

Tony felt warm though he was nude next to Heather in her bed. He wondered if she feigned sleep or if she truly rested. Her bare body was warm like a hot water bottle, but soft and feminine. Her blond hair was long and beautiful, and she'd pleased him immensely. He smiled.

Indeed, she was the spitting image of Helen, his long-lost love. Helen was the one woman he'd ever loved. He'd thought he wasn't capable of love after losing Helen. She'd split with him after her father had begun a background investigation of him. Too bad Tony had decided to peddle drugs when in college. He'd sold them to pay tuition, room, and board. But his decision to become a pusher had changed his life. Today it was all about drugs and money.

He again studied the slumbering Heather under the sheet, her body lit by window light leaking through the linen. Something had touched his soul. Had he fallen in love with this young woman? She was not like the many whores he'd had. She was a lady—classy, loving, and considerate.

He thought of the retired DEA agent whom he'd killed. He'd required Heather's TV to be switched on prior to the execution, a mistake. She had to have seen the man die. He asked himself, why the hell had he killed the old guy? The passengers and crew were already scared shitless. Tony shook his head.

Could Heather dismiss his error in judgment? Did she love him? Did the Stockholm syndrome make her act like she did? She seemed willing to be with him. He liked this woman a lot. No matter what, he wouldn't allow her to die.

Tony wished he could travel back in time. He would certainly right the wrongs he'd committed throughout his life. He would be better today. Would he be living a drastically different life? Would it be a better one?

Then his musings turned to the present. He awaited the arrival of the drug sub and extra explosives and arms. He'd take Heather with him when he departed on the sub. He would hate to release her to her father. Tony could return her father's money if Heather decided to stay with him. A few million would be okay to keep, though. It would have been her inheritance. He felt hope for the future. He resolved to change himself after this half-billion-dollar gig was done.

TWENTY-FIVE

RYDER FELT the most dependent he'd been since childhood. Earlier, Layla had pushed his wheelchair into their cabin and left him near the big window overlooking the ocean below.

Ryder felt depressed. How the hell was he going to protect Layla from the pirates?

The first thing he had to do was call Rita at the FBI *Sea Trek* Task Force. "Layla, if you stand on the bed, could you reach the satellite phone?" Ryder guessed the vent in which he'd hidden the phone was too high for her to get to, even while standing on the bed.

She smiled. "Let's see." She stepped up on the mattress, held onto the window frame, and stood on the bed's headboard. Reaching into the vent, she got a hold of the pencil stub and pulled the sat phone up with the floss Ryder had tied to it.

Layla grinned and hopped down. "Mission accomplished." She handed Ryder the phone.

He let out a breath. "Rita's gonna have a fit after she finds out I broke my shinbone."

Layla shrugged. "There's little you can do about it."

Ryder tapped in Rita's phone number.

"Luke, I've been hoping you'd call. What have you learned?"

"Not to let a pirate smack my shin with a heavy glass ashtray."

"What?"

"I got a broken shinbone. And there's a dead pirate Layla and I had to hide."

"Holy Christ." Rita breathed hard. "Are you two safe?"

Ryder never recalled Rita ever cussing. "We're in our cabin. We've got the pirate's Ka-Bar combat knife and Glock 17 loaded with eighteen rounds. Plus, we have his two extra magazines loaded with thirty-four rounds."

"Are the other pirates on to you?"

"No."

"How do you know your leg's broken?"

"I faked being drunk by splashing bourbon on my face and shirt. Then I went to the med center and said I fell down the stairs. I got an X-ray, and the doctor put a fiberglass cast on my shin. I've got a cane and a wheelchair."

"Have you made contact with Colonel Casa?"

"Nope. I was gonna find him, but then the pirate tried to rape Layla in the theater dressing room. I fought him there. Layla and I zipped him up in a plastic costume bag and hid the body in the theater prop room." Ryder let out a breath. "Next, I plan to take the elevator down to Rick's cabin. If he isn't there, I'll hunt for him."

"What about the Glock?"

"I had Layla strap it over her stomach. She took a big Hawaiian shirt off the dead pirate and put it on. It hides the pistol real well."

"Hide it someplace else."

"Yer right. I don't want Layla caught with it." He took a moment to think. "I could hide it in the wheelchair."

"Sounds risky."

Ryder asked, "Any news for us?"

"The National Security Agency has been trying to break the encryption on the pirates' satellite phones with no success. We think Franco may use a satellite phone to trigger the bombs. Our team thought about jamming the phone signals but decided against it. We'd have to move the Coast Guard ship closer to the *Sea Trek*, which could cause the pirates to take drastic action."

Ryder scratched his head. "Because the ransom deadline is 11:59 PM tomorrow night, odds are the crap will hit the fan then, right?"

"Yes. FBI analysts say chances are the pirates will make a move whether or not they get their money around 1:00 AM on Saturday. The Hostage Rescue Team could hit the ship then."

"What do you want me to do?"

"Stay safe. If our guys assault the ship, use your passwords, Mr. Bear and Miss Bear. You're in no condition to confront twenty-something pirates." She was silent for a second. "Keep your eyes peeled and report back anything you can, but be inconspicuous."

"Anything else?"

Rita was silent for a moment. "The plan is to wait them out."

"It could take a month," Ryder said. "They got plenty of food and supplies."

"We figure they'll eventually agree to safe passage to Colombia for release of the passengers. So far, they haven't bitten." She took a breath. "I need to go. Take care."

"Wait a sec, Rita."

"What?"

"Tomorrow night, me or Layla will keep the phone with us on vibrate."

"No. I'm ordering you to hide the phone someplace and not on either one of you."

"Okay." Ryder disconnected the call.

TWENTY-SIX

LEANING ON HIS CANE, Ryder stood in front of retired US Army Colonel Rick Casa's cabin, H499, on Deck Eight. Ryder had taken two more aspirin tablets, but his leg was again throbbing under his hardening fiberglass cast. He figured it would be sturdier in two hours, by 5:30 PM.

Ryder's mind was racing. He didn't like to leave Layla alone in their cabin. Before he had left, he'd watched her stack two suitcases on the bed. She had climbed up on them and put the satellite phone back in its hiding place in the vent.

Though the sat phone was well hidden, Ryder worried about the dead pirate's Glock-17, the man's two magazines of bullets, and the Ka-Bar combat knife. Ryder had hidden them in his cabin in a return vent at floor level, which he figured was, unfortunately, more likely to be searched than the second vent, which held the SAT phone high up above the bed.

To hide the pirate's weapons, Ryder had sat on the carpet, unscrewed the vent cover, and realized the pistol belt wouldn't fit inside the enclosure. However, the Glock, the two magazines, and the knife barely did. There wasn't any better place he could find in the cabin to hide the firearm and the knife.

Ryder had asked Layla to discard the belt in the bottom of a trash can in a ladies' room. She had again strapped the pistol belt around her stomach under the dead pirate's large Hawaiian shirt, which she still wore. After returning from the restroom, she reported nobody had seen her place the belt in the bottom of a full waste can. He figured if an FBI assault were about to happen, he'd tuck the Glock in his belt on his backside and the knife on his belt's right side. He'd wear a loose sweatshirt to cover them.

Ryder stopped thinking about weapons for the moment and listened at Rick's cabin door but heard nothing. He knocked.

Fifteen seconds later, the door swung open. Ryder recognized the colonel right away from Rita's detailed description, though he appeared to be older than Ryder had anticipated. Ryder was also surprised at how skinny the man was. From Rita's portrayal of him, he should've been stronger and healthier in appearance.

Rick's deep-set, brown eyes probed Ryder from underneath a pair of bushy eyebrows. The man's skin was swarthy, and his mustache was gray. "What can I do for you?"

Ryder leaned on his cane. "I've been told you're a retired military man, a US Army colonel. I'd like to speak with you about how we could work together against the pirates."

"I'm not sure I can help, but come in."

Ryder grimaced when he entered.

"Have a seat. What happened to your leg?"

"My shinbone got broke this mornin'. The ship's med center doc gave me a fiberglass cast."

Rick lit a cigarette, dropped his match in an ashtray, and sat on a chair. "How'd you get my name?"

Ryder cocked his head. "Don't tell Tony, okay?"

"No sweat. He isn't on my friendly guys list."

"My name's Luke Ryder, and I'm a Kentucky deputy sheriff. I was temporarily working on an FBI task force until last week. I went on vacation, and then the pirates hit the ship. I used my satellite phone to call my FBI contact, and she put me back on the payroll. She told me the only able-bodied law enforcement or military types on board were you, me, and the retired DEA agent Tony killed. The rest of the ex-military and lawmen on board are past seventy years of age. The FBI gave me your cabin number."

Rick took a drag on his cigarette and blew smoke away from Ryder. Still, its smell was strong. Rick said, "It appears I'm the one fit person in the police and military categories on this ship. You couldn't handle a drunken pirate in your condition, much less a sober buccaneer."

Ryder's mind flashed back to his fight with the tall black pirate who'd tried to rape Layla. "I have a loaded Glock-17 9mm pistol, two extra magazines of seventeen rounds each, and a Ka-Bar combat knife."

Rick knocked ashes into his ashtray. "I didn't think they'd make an exception for a cop to carry a weapon on board."

"They didn't. I took it from a pirate. He tried to rape my girlfriend. I broke my leg fightin' him. He's dead. We hid the body in the theater's prop room."

"The pirates better not catch you with the weapons, or they'll make you walk the plank."

"I hid 'em in a vent in my cabin." Ryder squinted. "I'm willing to share either the knife or the Glock with you. Your choice."

"I don't like the odds," Rick said. He wheezed. "The pirates outnumber us. They've got automatic weapons, M-60 machine guns, RPGs…"

Ryder squinted. A sudden bolt of pain had traveled up his leg. "I git what yer sayin'. But if the pirates start shootin', and you plugged one, there'd be one less pirate."

Rick smiled. "I like your attitude. If you were in my unit, I'd promote you this instant." Rick took a long drag on his cigarette and then smashed it out in his ashtray. "Tell you what. Why don't we meet later? I need to talk this over with a buddy of mine who's on the crew."

"A guy on the crew?"

"He works in the engine room and watched pirates place C-4 explosives in there. I want to see if he's willing to work with the two of us."

"The FBI says the pirates' ransom deadline is 11:59 PM tomorrow night. Otherwise, they'll blow up the ship." Ryder glanced at Rick's eyes. "So, we'll join forces?"

"Let's see what my pal says."

Ryder felt hope. "Where and when do you want to meet?"

Rick glanced at the ceiling for a moment. "My buddy works the second shift. He can't get out of the engine room until about midnight. I usually meet him in the casino before he eats dinner." Rick rubbed his chin. "Let's meet for breakfast at eight in the Galileo Dining Room on Deck Seven. It's close to the elevators. Bring your girl. She's gotta be part of this, too, even if it's a minor role."

Ryder rose, pushing himself up with his cane. "We'll see you there at eight sharp."

Rick nodded and then opened the door for Ryder.

Though in constant pain, Ryder began to hustle back to his cabin so he could tell Layla the news.

TWENTY-SEVEN

MAY 16, 3:40 PM

THE ICE BUCKET was empty in the cabin, and Layla needed to refill it so she could cool Ryder's broken shinbone. She figured it wouldn't take long to find the cabin steward who'd provided ice before, although Ryder had asked her to wait in their cabin. He'd gone to find the colonel.

She figured she could also ask the steward for three or four plastic bags to make ice packs. After taking off the dead pirate's stinky Hawaiian shirt, she changed into an attractive top. She refreshed her makeup, and a minute later, she opened the door. She scanned the long passageway toward the stern of the ship. No luck. She didn't see the steward or his cleaning cart.

Layla turned toward the elevator lobby. All of a sudden, Tex, the pirate who'd seen her near the theater prop room, exited an elevator. Their eyes met. She felt fear, turned, and began to walk toward the aft end of the ship along the passageway. She thought if she returned to her cabin, the pirate would demand entry and find the Glock and knife.

"Hey, you." Layla heard the pirate shout. "Stop."

The sound of heavy footfalls behind her made her freeze like a deer lit by headlights.

She felt the man's sinewy hand grasp her shoulder and bring her to a halt. Tex turned her around. "Lady, where the hell are you going? I told you to stop, God damn it." He spoke in a strong Southern drawl.

"Sorry. I thought you were calling someone else."

Tex fingered his Ka-Bar knife dangling from his pistol belt. "There ain't nobody else in sight." He focused on Layla's face. "Yer Layla, the so-called dancer I met by the theater. I went to a dance show, and you weren't there."

Layla briefly glanced sideways, trying to find an escape route. "I had a case of the flu and couldn't dance."

"Yeah, sure," Tex said.

"Okay, I had a lot to drink. The captain said there was no charge for drinks, so I took advantage."

Tex cocked his head. "Yer lyin'. All the dancers in the troupe were there. I checked with the dance director."

"So I lied. So what? I was in the theater to rip off what I could. I found nothing—no money, no jewels. So, I was leaving."

Tex laughed. "Yer one fine-lookin' thief. Any reason why you wouldn't date somebody in the same business? You know, sort of like honor among thieves?"

Layla decided to appear strong. She lifted her chin. "I have a boyfriend. He's a thief, too. Do the honorable thing, and leave me alone."

Tex wrinkled his brow. "Where's your boyfriend?"

Layla felt defiant. "He's having a meeting with a friend."

"Another thief?"

"Could be." Layla shrugged. "Luke's checking him out."

Tex studied Layla for a moment. "Take me to Luke."

"I don't know where he's meeting the guy or what his name is."

Tex scoffed. "Tell you what. I'm gonna take you to meet the big man, Tony, himself."

"Why?"

"It's possible he'll find a use for you." Tex grabbed Layla's upper arm and led her to the elevator to take her up to the captain's suite on the top deck.

While they were walking side by side, Layla bumped into Tex.

"You're clumsy for such a fine-lookin' woman, Layla."

* * *

MAY 16, 3:50 PM

Heather awoke nude in her bed. Following her rape, she'd fallen asleep after she'd realized Tony wasn't going to kill her.

She reviewed how this horrible day had begun. She'd arisen especially early, at 3:00 AM, excited by the first day of the cruise. She'd lit a marijuana cigarette, and then everything had gone to hell. The pirates took her. While Tony watched, she'd called her father to tell him she had been kidnapped. She'd been scared—still was—and was mentally exhausted. Though terrified, she'd slept after Tony had finished with her. She couldn't remember her dreams, but they had been nightmares. Thankfully, the memory of them had evaporated like water hitting a sidewalk on a hot summer day.

Tony had slipped away while she had slept.

Rested but still jumpy, Heather showered and put on her green, trendy dress. Nice clothes made her feel better, cleaner, civilized. Was there a chance she could escape and hide? She walked to her suite's door and tried to twist the doorknob. The door was locked. The moment she released her hand from the knob, the lock clicked, and the knob turned. The door opened. She stepped back. Tex, a pirate who'd guarded her before, held the upper arm of an attractive black woman. Both Tex and the black woman stared at Heather.

"Heather, I brought you company." Tex took a breath. "Layla here has an appointment with the captain, but he's not in his cabin. She'll stay with you until he comes back."

Tex gently shoved Layla into the suite and closed and locked the door.

Heather wondered why Layla had been taken by the pirates. She said, "Dear, come in and sit on the couch. There are snacks in the cupboard, alcoholic drinks, and sodas too. Anything you want?"

Layla sat on the couch. A tear rolled down her cheek. She wiped it away. "A bag of chips and a soda, any kind. Thanks."

Heather handed Layla the snack and a drink and then sat next to her. "I'm Heather." She took a moment to study Layla. "Did the pirates take you for ransom, too?"

Layla shook her head. "Nope. One of them, Tex, wants to quote 'date' me, but I know what he wants. I made up bullshit about being a thief, and he believed me." She stopped talking. "Please don't tell any of them what I just said. Okay?"

"Okay." Heather took in a breath of air and then let it out. "I don't want to scare you, but I was raped by Tony. Don't trust them."

Layla nodded. "You okay? You look calm."

"I'm doing what I have to do to survive. I pretended I liked it."

"Girl, it was the right thing to do." Layla hesitated. "I've been raped a couple of times. I was an escort for a while. Do what you need to do. Stay strong."

Layla took a sip of soda. "You wouldn't be Heather Falcon, would you?"

"Yes. How'd you know?"

Layla held her finger to her lips. She whispered, "My boyfriend's a cop. We took this cruise for a vacation, but also to unwind—for him to unwind—because he had been working undercover for the FBI. We hid his sat phone and have been in contact with the FBI. So, we know they've asked for one hundred fifty million dollars for your release."

Heather felt a wave of relief. Somebody was doing something. She whispered, "Is the FBI going to assault the ship?"

"Not yet. They're waiting. The pirates put bombs in the engine room, and they have machine gun nests in three places. If the FBI tried to take the ship, they think the pirates would kill a lot of people." Layla glanced at Heather's eyes. "Did you know Tony slit a man's throat on the helipad and broadcast it on the ship's TV channel?"

"I saw it. When Tony talked to me after the killing, it was like he was another person. If I wouldn't have known he'd killed the old man, I would've thought he wasn't so bad, even if he'd kidnapped me. But the scariest thing is how normal he acted when he last came to see me. Brought me a flower, and talked like an average person, until he made a move on me." Heather recalled Tony had been strangely gentle with her.

Layla sighed. "Did you know he shot down a news helicopter with a shoulder-fired rocket?"

"No. When?" Heather felt instant distress. How could she have thought well of Tony, even for a second?

"He shot it down around eleven fifteen."

Heather realized Tony hadn't merely killed one man but likely several others, too. Odds are, he had killed in his past as well. She felt sick to her stomach. "Excuse me, Layla. I feel queasy. I'm going to get a ginger ale."

Layla stood. "I'll get it."

"Thanks. Please bring the wastebasket near the bar in case I have to barf."

Layla grabbed a can of ginger ale and the garbage can. She opened the can. "Here."

Heather took deep breaths and sipped the ginger ale. "I think I'm okay for now."

While Layla watched Heather, she began to worry about what Ryder would think and do after he learned she wasn't in their cabin.

TWENTY-EIGHT

RYDER RETURNED to his cabin after meeting with the colonel to tell Layla about the prospect of joining forces with him. But Layla was not there. He'd told her not to leave, but she must've gone to pick up sandwiches. He was hungry, and he was sure she was, too. He waited for at least twenty minutes, and still, Layla did not return. He worried while the seconds ticked by.

There was a knock at Ryder's door. He checked through the peephole and saw a pirate standing in the passageway. Alarm bells went off in his head. Should he open the door? Yep. Chances are the buccaneer's visit had something to do with Layla's absence. He leaned on his cane with his left hand and opened the door.

"You Luke Ryder?" The pirate had a distinctive Southern drawl.

Ryder mustered a smile. "Yep. How'd you know?"

"The ship's computer guy has the passenger list and cabin numbers."

"How come yer visitin' me?"

"We took your girlfriend, Layla, to meet the captain. Seems she's a thief, and she says you're one, too."

Ryder shrugged, not sure what to make of what the pirate had said. "I ain't got nothin' to say."

"Come with me. We're not aimin' to take y'all down. Like they say, there's honor among thieves, but we gotta get on the same page."

Ryder figured he'd better claim to be a burglar and play along with Layla's story. It was lucky this pirate had told him about her lies. "Okay, I'm comin', but I'm slow 'cuz of my leg."

"So, you and Layla are rip-off artists?"

"Yep, but it's slim pickin's since you guys got here. The passengers have already been relieved of their best jewels."

The pirate laughed. "We beat yous to the punch." He held the door open for Ryder. "My name's Tex."

Tex led Ryder along the ship's rail. The air felt cold with the wind coming from the west. The fog floating over the water hadn't thinned all day.

Tex stopped, removed a two-way citizens band radio, and pushed the transmit button. "Tex to Cap."

The sound of static coming from the radio stopped, and a clear voice replied, "Go ahead, Tex."

"I got the boyfriend with me. Be there shortly."

* * *

MAY 16, 4:23 PM

A knock sounded on Heather's cabin door. Layla felt jumpy, but she fought to appear calm. She took a smooth breath and let it out between her parted lips.

Heather glimpsed sideways at the door. "They must be coming to get you for your appointment with Tony." She got up and whispered. "Be careful."

Layla nodded.

Heather opened the door. A fat, short buccaneer entered. His large eyes studied the two women. "Who's Layla?"

"Me."

"Come with me. The boss wants to see you."

Layla stood and followed the pirate. His body odor was strong, and Layla wrinkled her nose.

The obese pirate opened the door to the captain's suite and pointed inward. "Tony's waiting. Go in."

When Layla walked in, she recognized Tony at once by his pointed, black beard and the short ponytail he wore. He sat in a classy leather chair. She scanned the sumptuous cabin.

She noted the suite was two decks high, lit by overhead lights. There was a huge picture window looking out at the sea. The ocean view was foggy, but it was still a beautiful sight.

In front of the big window, there was a modern, Nordic-design dinner table big enough to seat eight. To the left of the dining area, a stairway covered in a thick blue carpet led up to the second level, enclosed in glass.

Layla could see several bedrooms up there. Below the upper level was an entertainment area, which included a baby grand piano; a floor-to-ceiling, theater-sized television; and a wet bar. The floor shone like polished glass.

Again her eyes fell on Tony, who grinned, showing his yellowed teeth.

"So, you're a supposed burglar, according to my man, Tex."

Layla shrugged. "I'm a crook, except I don't kill people. I rip them off."

Tony laughed. "You have a chip on your shoulder, Layla. It's your name, right?"

"Yes, but I don't have a chip on my shoulder. I've got a gripe, though. Why bother with me and my boyfriend—simple burglars—when we don't threaten you? We're in business to steal, but not on the same scale you guys operate on. You must be asking for millions to release the ship and Heather."

"Indeed, we buccaneers stand to come out of this flush with cash, cryptocurrency. But we want the passengers and crew to be our friends until this is over. Therefore, we don't want to take their valuables, because robbery would irritate the very people we want on our side. We'll get all the money we need from the rich owners of this floating hotel and that billionaire, Heather's father."

"So what?"

"We want you and your boyfriend to stop your pilfering until we pirates depart." Tony lit a cigar and puffed on it to get it going.

Layla's stomach felt queasy.

* * *

MAY 16, 4:28 PM

Ryder stood aside while Tex knocked on Tony's cabin door. It opened. Tony stood there, and Ryder recognized him at once.

Tony smiled. "Who do we have here? Mr. Luke Ryder, according to your girlfriend, Layla." Tony pointed to Layla, who sat on a brown leather chair near a large leather couch.

Ryder forced himself to smile.

"Come in, Mr. Ryder."

Tex followed Ryder and sat in a chair near a wall.

When neither Tex nor Tony was facing in her direction, Layla winked at Ryder.

Ryder walked farther into the suite, halted, and leaned on his cane.

Tony viewed Ryder. "You've had a mishap."

"I got into it with a passenger when he caught me in his cabin."

"You're a burglar?"

Layla nodded yes, still out of Tony's and Tex's lines of sight.

"Yeah, but like I told yer partner, Tex, it's been slim pickin's since you guys bin on board."

"Burglary is a noble profession," Tony said. "You don't hurt people, but you do relieve them of possessions they don't need, in particular, if they're wealthy."

Ryder displayed a fake smile. "Everybody's gotta do

somethin' to git by in this world. If yer dealt a bad hand, you gotta do what you gotta do."

Tony slapped Ryder's back. "True, my friend." He pointed to the couch. "Have a seat."

Ryder sat down and set his cane against a cushion.

Layla appeared nervous to Ryder. But he was thankful she was street-smart.

Tony said, "I have no proof you two are what you say you are. Tex told me how Layla's been lying to him about being a dancer, a sick dancer, and then a drunken dancer." He waited and then aimed his brown, dark eyes at Layla. "Tell me, dear, about your burglary techniques."

Layla shifted in her chair and reached for her left side.

Tex drew his Glock-17 and aimed it at her. "What are you up to, Layla?"

"Take it easy, Tex." Layla pulled a brass-colored money clip jammed with cash from underneath her extra-wide belt. She tossed it on the carpet toward Tony.

Tex stood. "It's mine."

Layla grinned. "You didn't feel anything else when I was 'clumsy' and bumped you, huh?"

Tony laughed. "You're a pickpocket."

"Yes, Captain." She stared at Tony. "My ma taught me to pick pockets when I was eight. We'd visit the Grand Louis-ville Mall when it was crowded. I started by picking wallets out of purses. Little by little, I learned to pick men's pockets, too. Later, she taught me the basics of burglary."

Tony smiled broadly. "I'm convinced." He smiled. "An attractive lady like you must distract a man if you bump into him." Tony turned to Tex. "How about it, Tex?"

Tex meekly grinned. "Yeah, she's distractin'."

Tony scanned Layla's and Ryder's faces. "I've been thinking about the situation we pirates have put you two thieves in. You've not been able to rake in jewels and other costly items because my men have already made a sweep, hitting the richest folks on board." He stared at Tex. "I told my men not to pester the passengers, but true to their bucca-neering nature, they did it anyway. Heaven knows, their split of the ransom money will be a hundred times what they'd get from a handful of hot baubles."

Layla nodded, glanced at Tex, and scoffed, "They're gonna wear them?"

Tony laughed. "Let me tell you what I want. Do not rip off the passengers and crew. Lay low. Agreed?"

Ryder nodded. "Sure."

"Please enjoy the rest of the voyage."

"Thanks," Ryder said.

Tony raised his index finger. "Oh, and if we find you've hidden a stash in your cabin, there'll be hell to pay."

Ryder said, "We won't be stealin' anything." He felt nervous. He had to get rid of the pistol and knife, and fast. He figured the pirates wouldn't care if he had the satellite phone, but he'd have to erase the contact list and the recently called numbers. He hoped other pirates weren't already searching the cabin. The buccaneers would be sure to open the vents.

"You two can go. Behave."

Walking with the aid of his cane, Ryder escorted Layla from the captain's suite.

When they were out of earshot, Layla said, "I was kept in a cabin with Heather before Tony saw me. When we get a chance, I'll tell you what I learned. She was raped, for one thing."

"Doesn't surprise me." Ryder felt pain. "We need to move fast to get to the cabin before the pirates search it, if they haven't already."

* * *

MAY 16, 4:45 PM

Ryder opened the door of their modest cabin. He glanced along the passageway toward the ship's stern. He saw a crowd of bustling travelers coming his way toward the elevator lobby behind him. Hunger pangs irritated him, along with the persistent pain in his lower left leg. Dinner-time was near, and passengers were heading to dining rooms and cafés. He could hear the hubbub of their voices while they moved along.

Layla entered their cabin, and he followed. "We gotta move fast to hide the Glock and the knife someplace, but not in here."

Layla moved toward the floor-level vent cover and sat on the carpet near it. She unscrewed the loose vent screws with her fingers, pulled off its cover, and peered inside the vent. "The gun's still here."

Ryder said, "I talked to the colonel about taking this weapon off our hands and hidin' it in his cabin." He thought for a moment. "We need to find him and convince him to do it."

"Okay." She hesitated. "I can hide the pistol in another bra I'll strap around my stomach, but I need to put the pirate's large Hawaiian shirt back on. What about the knife and the two magazines?"

Ryder moved toward her. "Hand 'em over, please."

Ryder slid the Ka-Bar combat knife underneath his belt at his right side and pulled his shirttails out of his trousers. He put the magazines in his right front pocket. "Could you hand me my turtleneck sweater from my suitcase?"

After Layla put on the Hawaiian shirt and Ryder slipped on his sweater, Layla snapped the vent cover back in place and hand-tightened its screws.

Layla stood. "I'm ready to eat."

"First, I gotta wipe out the contacts and history from my phone." Though Ryder's device was password protected, he figured the buccaneers would ask him to unlock the phone, if they found it.

Layla stared up at the vent which held the SAT phone. "I'll get it down."

After erasing the phone's call history and contacts, Ryder moved to a chair near the cabin's picture window so he could get a satellite signal. Then he tapped in Rita's number.

"What's up, Luke?" Rita sounded like she was in a cheerful mood, despite the circumstances.

"Lots happened since we last spoke." He told Rita about his meetings with Rick and Tony.

Rita took a deep breath. "What a story. Y'all managed to get close to the number one pirate, by hook if not by crook. You could keep a closer eye on Franco and the pirates, if you're careful."

"Yep. Layla can tell you about Heather's rape. I don't know the details." Ryder handed the phone to Layla.

"Hi, Rita."

"You had an adventure."

"Yes. Before I met with Tony, the pirates put me in a suite next to his to wait for him to return. Heather was locked in there. She said Tony raped her, but she pretended to like it so he wouldn't harm her."

"What was Heather's mental state?"

"Surprisingly calm. She impressed me. She's a strong woman."

"I'm glad Heather is holding up. If we launch a rescue operation, I bet she won't panic." Rita hesitated. "How'd you manage to take the money clip from Tex?"

"I didn't lie to Tony when I said my mom taught me to pickpocket when I was a small girl. We used to work a big shopping mall in Louisville. Anyway, I figured if I picked Tex's pocket, I could prove I was a crook. It worked."

"Nice thinking, Layla." Rita ceased talking for a second. "But it was fortunate Luke was able to catch on to what you were doing."

"I didn't think they'd grab him, too."

"Thanks, Layla." Rita took two seconds to think. "Please give the phone back to Luke."

Ryder took the phone. "Rita, we gotta eat somethin' and tag up with Colonel Casa. I want to hide the pistols and knife in his cabin cuz the pirates don't suspect him."

"Call me soon if you can."

"Yes, ma'am." Ryder disconnected and erased the phone's call history again.

After Layla replaced the device in the vent, Ryder said,

"I'm hungry like a skinny bear after it's been hibernatin' all winter."

"My stomach's growling, too." Layla stared down at the large Hawaiian shirt she wore. "This isn't fashionable, but it hides the gun."

"Be glad the shirt makes you less temptin' to a pirate." Ryder opened the door. "Let's go."

TWENTY-NINE

LAYLA AND RYDER rode the elevator near their cabin down two decks. The lift stopped on Deck Seven at the Galileo Dining Room's front doors. After entering the eatery, they rubbed their hands with disinfectant, which was required due to a recent surge in flu-like illnesses. Ryder hoped a respiratory bug wouldn't hit him next.

Ryder surveyed the large restaurant. People were lined up at seven all-you-can-eat buffet food islands, where diners chose from a wide variety of dishes. Fellow passengers were filling their plates with food. Ryder figured the vacationers were consuming more than they typically would, even on a cruise ship. He guessed comfort eating was relieving their tension.

Layla tapped Ryder's shoulder. "I'll get your food if you want."

Ryder's leg was throbbing after the short walk to the restaurant, but he thought he'd soldier on so Layla wouldn't worry about him. "I can do it. But thanks fer offerin'." The smell of food diminished his pain. His mouth was watering. He reckoned food was a great motivator, especially when a man's stomach was empty.

"Is your leg better?"

"Yep." Ryder knew he was lying to himself more than to Layla. Sliding his tray along a serving table's rails, he chose his food.

Ryder led Layla to a vacant table next to a window with an ocean view. Fog lingered over the water. In the distance to the southwest, he could see the top half of the Coast Guard cutter, *San Diego*. He slid onto his chair and grinned to hide his discomfort. A surge of pain made his eyes water. "I thought it would be to our advantage to eat in this restaurant cuz Rick asked us to meet him here tomorrow for breakfast." Ryder scanned the crowded space. "He could be here tonight, too."

Layla nodded. "What else did the colonel tell you?"

"I proposed we work together, and he sounded like he was going to agree, but said he'd talk with his engine room friend first. I think Rick'll try to git the guy to join us."

"I want to help, too."

"You can, but I don't want you takin' chances. Angela needs her mother."

Layla sighed. "I'll be careful. But if a bad guy tries to kill me, I need to stop him for Angela's sake."

Ryder nodded. He grabbed a knife and fork and began to cut into his filleted trout. A movement at his side caught his attention.

The colonel stood next to Ryder's table. He held a tray of food. "Mind if I join you?"

Ryder smiled. "Be my guest, Rick. I was gonna go lookin' for you after we ate." The man appeared even skinnier in the daylight streaming through the window than he had in his cabin's artificial light.

Layla slid over to let Rick sit. "I'm Layla. Luke told me about your meeting."

"Ma'am, you could be a movie star."

Layla smiled modestly.

Ryder said, "I've spoken with Layla. She's gonna help us if we band together. But she has a daughter, so I'm requestin' if Layla helps, she do so outta harm's way."

Rick nodded. "Makes sense."

Ryder whispered, "Layla has the dead pirate's Glock strapped to her stomach under her baggy shirt. And I've got his Ka-Bar knife on my belt and two extra mags in my hip pocket."

Rick studied Layla. "They're well concealed, but why not keep them in your vent?"

Ryder leaned forward across the table and spoke softly. "Cuz of Layla, the pirates think the two of us are burglars who've been stealing jewelry and money from passengers. The pirates don't want us to steal from passengers. To make sure we aren't thieving, Tony talked about searching our cabin."

Rick raised his palm slightly. "You want me to hide the weapons in my cabin?"

Ryder shrugged. "Yep."

"I'll do it." He sighed. "After we eat, let's go there, and you can leave the weapons with me."

"I appreciate it," Ryder said.

Rick took a bite of spaghetti and then set his fork on his plate. "I'll give you the code for my door's lock in case you need the weapons when I'm not around." He picked up a napkin and wrote his cabin door's combination down.

Ryder caught Rick's eyes. "I git the feelin' we're close to bein' a team even if your friend from the engine room decides not to get involved."

* * *

MAY 16, 5:45 PM

The colonel had opted to leave first from the Galileo Dining Room so Ryder and Layla could meet him minutes later at his cabin on Deck Eight. He thought walking separately wouldn't draw attention to the three of them.

He reasoned eating dinner with strangers on a cruise ship was common, but meeting in your cabin with those you'd dined with might well raise suspicions. If an alert pirate had seen them eating together and then noticed the three of them later entering Rick's cabin, alarm bells would have gone off. After all, Ryder and Layla had told him how they'd met the top pirate, Tony. The pirates must be keeping an eye on the pair.

After Rick entered his cabin, he rapidly reviewed the last eight months of his life. He'd always been healthy, had run a mile daily, had lifted weights, and had done the same calisthenics he'd always done throughout his military career and as a civilian.

But three weeks after his fifty-first birthday, he had begun to have back and stomach pains, and he had felt bloated. This hadn't worried him at first.

Then he'd often become nauseous and have trouble digesting food. He had a great deal of diarrhea, too. All of a sudden, he lost weight, twenty pounds within a month, without dieting. Sure, he'd lost his appetite. Who wouldn't, with all the stomach aches and bloated feelings plaguing him daily?

He recalled the first day he'd visited his doctor, complaining about his digestive issues. The doc had noticed Rick's skin and eyes were yellowish. The physician had taken a blood sample from Rick, indicating he had type 2 diabetes, which he hadn't had before.

The doctor conducted follow-up tests. A week later, the physician told Rick to return to review his test results. The doc asked him to sit down. He peered into Rick's eyes and gently explained to him he had an aggressive form of pancreatic cancer. He had six months, max, to live.

Rick remembered thinking of all the tasks he had to complete to make final arrangements. He still hadn't told his ex-wife or his children.

Now Rick daydreamed he'd go out in a blaze of glory like a movie star charging the enemy, firing his weapon— exactly what he'd ordered new recruits not to do. He'd be sure to send plenty of pirates to hell.

Should he tell Luke Ryder there was a stash of World War

II-era M1 Garand rifles hidden in the engine room, which he'd planned to smuggle into Canada? No.

The hidden M1 rifles used center-fire cartridges. Weapons that use them were banned in Canada. The M1s would've brought in a pretty penny for Jeff and him. Too bad. He sighed.

If he told Ryder about the rifles, Rick would claim the pirates had brought them aboard and that his friend, Jeff Brooks, had found them stashed in the engine room.

The pirates were heading for Mexico. Whether or not they'd succeed in walking away with a big ransom, the FBI and Coast Guard were sure to find the M1s hidden under the heavy boxes of spare parts in the engine room.

He and his pal, Jeff, would have to shift the blame for the two dozen smuggled M1s and ammo to the pirates. But how? Could Jeff sneak two or three M1s out of the engine room and plant them somewhere near the pirates? And give both himself and Ryder M1s and ammo, too? The pirates had a man in the engine room at all times to guard the C-4 bombs they'd set up. He'd have to be distracted.

A knock at Rick's door ended his train of thought. He peered through the peephole. Ryder and Layla stood outside his cabin.

* * *

MAY 16, 5:53 PM

After Ryder had tapped on Rick's cabin door, Layla noticed he'd kept his eyes focused along the passageway, scanning for pirates. There weren't passengers in sight. Most were likely still at dinner, eating like starved dogs to alleviate their fear of the buccaneers. Layla heard the door's hinges creak.

Rick opened the door. "Come in."

Layla and Ryder hustled into the cabin. Ryder said, "I see you got a return vent on the deck like we do. If it's the same size, the Glock, knife, and magazines should fit in."

Rick pulled out his pocket knife and pried out its screwdriver attachment. He knelt and began to unscrew the vent cover.

Layla asked, "Okay if I use your bathroom? I've got to take off my top to get the gun."

Rick smiled. His jaundiced skin was yellowish. "Don't mind the mess."

Layla went into the bathroom, unbuttoned the dead pirate's Hawaiian shirt, and removed the Glock-17 from the two cups of her second bra. She set the weapon on the countertop near the sink. She figured the easiest thing to do with her second brassiere was to wear it over her first one. After donning the second bra, she realized she seemed bigger in the bust. Luckily, the huge Hawaiian shirt cloaked her size.

She left the bathroom and handed the pistol to Ryder. She saw him check to be sure the weapon's safety was engaged.

Rick had set the vent cover aside on the rug. Layla noticed the two magazines and the combat knife were already inside the vent.

Rick stood, and Ryder handed him the pistol. "There's a round in the chamber," Ryder said.

"I always like insurance, too, an extra shot," Rick said. He sat on the rug, placed the firearm into the vent, and replaced its cover.

Ryder said, "Thanks fer everything. Let's hope we won't need to invade yer privacy to get the pistol."

"No worries. I'll see you both for breakfast at eight in the Galileo Dining Room. I'll have answers then." Rick opened the door.

"Bye," Layla said. She wondered how such a sickly guy could help Ryder fight pirates. Then again, Ryder was in bad shape, too. Any help he could get would be welcome.

While they walked toward the elevator lobby, she said, "Rick seems like death warmed over. How's he gonna help?"

Ryder shrugged. "I'm not sure, but at least his buddy can tell us about the C-4 bombs if he shows up at breakfast."

THIRTY

ARLO, the first mate, approached Tony on the bridge. "Cap, there's a report one of our guys is missing."

"Who?"

"The tall, black guy. I don't recall his name. Last time anybody saw him was during the lunch hour when we were herding passengers to the railing to impress our Coast Guard friends."

Tony scratched his jet-black pointed beard. "Any idea where he is?"

Arlo shook his head slightly and said, "No. But I just got word that our man guarding the RPG and scuba equipment inside the port shell door noticed one diving kit had disappeared. The plastic box with the clothes and money was gone too. It's possible our missing man swam for shore."

"Did you guys scan the water?"

"Yeah, but we didn't see anything."

Tony faced the window toward Southern California's shore. "Maybe a guy hid one set to be sure he'd have scuba gear when the time to abandon ship comes. Do a headcount. If a guy's missing, I bet he's in a bar having a shot."

"Could be, but the shell door was shut, and the ladder

was dry. How would he have gotten into the water?" Arlo cocked his head. "Somebody could've taken the box for the money in it."

Tony shrugged. "You may be right, but if that's the case, why wouldn't they have taken just the box?"

Arlo wondered if Tony would send a guard of his choosing to ensure no further diving kits were taken. If Tony did that, it would screw up Arlo's plan to swim to shore with three others. "You're right, Cap. I'll personally go to the port shell door area and help our man guard the equipment until I can free up another guy. Having three men on duty with the M-60 machine guns eats into our reserve." He squinted. "Until the sub arrives with more air tanks and diving suits, we'll be short if we need to escape early."

"Guarding the equipment's important." Tony took a moment to think. "Could be the guard took the kit for himself, hid it, and plans to crap out."

Arlo nodded and then laughed inside. Tony was being prophetic. Four of them, including the guard, would indeed take to the water at 1:00 AM if all went according to plan. Arlo left for the port shell door on Deck Two. When he departed, he wondered what the hell had happened to the black guy. Had he gotten a rope, tied it somewhere, and lowered himself into the water? Even if a passenger or two would've seen him, why would they have reported this to Tony or any other pirate?

* * *

MAY 16, 7:15 PM

"Man overboard!" the obese, short pirate yelled. He peered through a pair of binoculars focused on a figure floating on the water far behind the ship. Misty fog swirled around him, making it hard to see the floundering man.

A passenger on the sundeck on top of the ship smiled. He'd seen the drunken pirate hold a whiskey bottle in one hand, stumble, and then reach for the railing just above the turbulent water beneath him. The buccaneer had tumbled forward head over heels and across the barrier at the stern of the ship. The doomed man had then vanished into the foamy wake of the *Sea Trek*. The tourist thought it served the pirate right. Good riddance. These bastards had cut a man's throat and shot down a news helicopter to boot. Sunset would be at 7:49 PM. Soon it would be impossible to find the man's body. The passenger felt justified in not alerting the pirates after one of their comrades had plummeted into the sea.

* * *

MAY 16, 7:16 PM

The fat, stocky pirate grabbed his two-way citizens' band radio. "Chester to Cap." The cool wind penetrated the buccaneer's jacket. He shivered when he thought of the man overboard, who'd soon lose a lot of his body heat, suffer hypothermia, and die within the hour. The ocean temperature was in the lower fifties. It would suck the heat from his body like a giant ice cube.

"Go ahead, Chester. This is Tony."

"One of our guys was drunk like a skunk, and he tumbled over the back railing. I caught sight of him a minute ago. He's way the hell behind us. Could you turn the ship around?"

"Hell no. It serves him right. I told you all we need to stay sober and avoid the ladies. We'll have time enough for whiskey and women after our payoff."

"But Cap…"

"The sun's setting, and the fog's building up. Turning this ship around will take a while. You can't take a sharp turn like you're driving a speedboat. We'd never find him." Tony shrugged. "Your share will increase. This is the second guy we've lost in a day."

The obese man sighed. "Okay, Cap. Over and out."

The rotund pirate glimpsed at the sun, close to the horizon above the fog bank. The mist was rising and would engulf the ship and hide it like a giant smoke screen from the Coast Guard cutter *San Diego*. Thank God. They'd need every advantage they could get. Tony was nuts. Signing onto this hijacking was stupid. Too bad the fellows couldn't vote Tony out, which pirates had done hundreds of years ago to men they disliked.

THIRTY-ONE

MAY 16, 7:40 PM

THE SUN HAD DIPPED to the top edge of the fog layer on the horizon. Ryder sat on a white, plastic desk chair and studied the eastern vista through his cabin's wide picture window. Darkness began to blot out the distant gloom of low-lying clouds. Sunset would be in minutes.

Ryder felt his leg pain increase. Its throbbing had become intense. He was faint and warm, but he had to stay strong and not succumb to his discomfort. Layla had to believe he could and would fight off their enemies.

There wasn't an immediate emergency to deal with. He figured it was an opportune time to call Rita again to update her, and he wished to learn what plans the feds had. Would they assault the ship? If so, he had to know how they'd do it and when.

The shower was running. It stopped, and Layla came out of the bathroom in a white terrycloth robe. It contrasted with her dark ebony skin. Ryder could smell the steamy air streaming from the bathroom and the scented oil she'd applied. He relaxed to enjoy a minute of calm and a brief feeling of normalcy, though his leg wrestled enjoyment from him when a wave of agony hit him. "Layla, could you get the phone down?"

Layla placed two pieces of luggage on the bed. She took off her robe. Ryder figured she didn't want to trip on its strap. She wore a pink bra and panties. Ryder felt desire for her while he watched her step up on the cases, balance on the bed's backboard, and take the phone from the vent. She tossed it onto the mattress next to where Ryder sat on his chair.

He tapped in Rita's number.

"Luke, any news?"

"Layla and I had dinner with Colonel Casa. He seemed drained and sickly." Ryder then told Rita how the colonel had hinted he and his engine room friend could join forces with Ryder and Layla. Ryder explained he'd report back to her after he and Layla had breakfast tomorrow with Rick.

"Rick's ill?" Rita asked.

"His eyes and skin are yellowish, and he's real skinny. I doubt he'd be able to fight, unless it's in a gunfight."

"Speaking of guns, what did you do with the Glock and Ka-Bar knife?"

"At dinner, Rick agreed to hide them in a vent in his room."

"Excellent." She waited a moment and then said, "What do you think about carrying your sat phone with you tomorrow after lunch?"

Ryder wondered why Rita had reversed her order that he shouldn't carry the satellite phone. "I could carry it. Are y'all gonna assault the ship?"

"It may happen tomorrow at around midnight. The NSA thinks before then, its information technology people will be able to block the transfer of cryptocurrency to the pirates. If the NSA does it, the pirates are going to be annoyed."

Ryder coughed. "Like a hive of angry bees." He hesitated. "I wager Franco's so crazy he'll set off the bombs if he don't get his money."

"Hold on, Luke." Rita was silent for twenty seconds. "The bomb squad guys are listening." She was quiet for fifteen seconds and then reported, "Because your leg's broken, they want you to convince Rick or his buddy to try to disable the bombs."

Ryder exhaled. "I'll ask 'em. According to Rick, his friend saw the pirates place the bombs. I bet he could tell y'all about the setup."

"Get Rick's buddy on the phone ASAP to describe the bombs," Rita said. "The bomb squad could tell y'all how to disable them."

"There's a problem. To defuse them, we gotta get past the man guarding the bombs."

"Somebody needs to distract him," Rita said.

"We'll try, but first we need the engine room guy's help." Ryder took a breath. "Me or Layla could keep an eye out to see if we can spot Rick and his friend meetin' tonight around midnight to get answers sooner than breakfast tomorrow."

"It might work," Rita said. "The Hostage Rescue Team's making final preparations. We have four Black Hawk helicopters on shore on standby. While the *Sea Trek* continues going south, it's been sailing within four miles of shore or less. Our choppers have been moving southward little by little along the coast to keep pace with the ship. The team's speedboats are ready, too. Also, the Coast Guard's *San Diego* has its powerboat assault teams on high alert."

"Call before they storm the ship."

"We will," Rita said. "Hope you get lucky with Rick and his pal."

"Thanks," Ryder said. Then he ended the call.

* * *

MAY 16, 7:50 PM

Rita set down her phone. She worried defusing the C-4 bombs would be an impossible task for Rick and Ryder, especially if the pirates had set up multiple radio-activated detonators. Because C-4 has a consistency like putty, it is easy to stick in various inaccessible places. Ryder's leg would prevent him from climbing around the engine room to ferret out where the C-4 had been placed.

From Ryder's description of Rick, the retired colonel, he could be too weak to do anything. And the pirates were guarding the bombs twenty-four hours a day. How were two disabled men and a woman going to overpower or fool a pirate armed with an automatic firearm?

Rita recalled the tour she'd had of the FBI's Hostage Rescue Team—HRT—years ago after she'd been in the Bureau for a year and a half. Her bosses were counting on this team to end the *Sea Trek* hostage crisis.

The HRT was the FBI's most elite unit, designed to handle terrorist attacks anywhere in the United States, and elsewhere, too. They'd been deployed overseas in Afghanistan and Iraq in years past. The HRT had been formed in 1982 with roughly fifty men. On this day, the HRT had two hundred men and women in its ranks.

The FBI had modeled the HRT on the US Army's Delta Force and the US Navy's SEALs. The Hostage Rescue Team's responsibilities had grown to deal not only with terrorist incidents but also with biological and/or nuclear weapon threats.

The FBI was highly selective in recruiting HRT members. Some were explosives experts. Others were top-notch snipers, divers, and combat-tested soldiers. They periodically reviewed new weapon developments and terrorist techniques and trends. They stayed in shape and trained routinely, often with foreign military and intelligence services like the British Special Air Service and the German Border Guard Group Nine.

The HRT was more elite than the FBI's sixty SWAT teams. HRT agents would likely rappel onto the *Sea Trek* on ropes dangling from Black Hawk choppers and fire their Heckler & Koch MP5 submachine guns. Hopefully, the passengers and crew would take cover when they heard the firing. Rita hoped a few agents would carry 12-gauge shotguns to limit collateral damage to the innocents.

Rita figured the HRT guys would carry stun grenades,

too. She hoped some of the first to board the ship would be special agent bomb technicians. It was vital to defuse the C-4 bombs.

The HRT's divers, trained in combat swimming with scuba gear which didn't produce telltale bubbles, knew how to board ships, break through locked doors, and sail large vessels.

Rita knew the HRT leadership was weary of waiting and wanted to kick ass by assaulting the *Sea Trek* right away. But cooler heads had prevailed. Too many lives were at risk if the ship were to catch fire or sink. It would be chaos trying to rescue five thousand people.

She wished upon a star Ryder and Layla would survive if there was fighting.

THIRTY-TWO

RYDER HAD ENDED his latest phone call with Rita less than an hour ago. He'd lain back on his cabin's bed and elevated his left leg on top of two pillows. The pain in his broken leg bothered him.

Layla sat next to him. "You should revisit the med center and get pain pills instead of taking aspirin."

Ryder turned to her. "I don't want to get hooked on pills."

"There are new, nonnarcotic ones."

"I don't trust 'em. I don't want to get addicted to them, plus alcohol."

Layla brushed her lips across his cheek and lightly kissed his lips. "Honey, I know a way to make you feel better. I'll be careful not to disturb your leg." She smiled. "Making love releases natural painkillers called endorphins."

Ryder viewed her eyes. "Endorphins?"

"The name's not important, just its effect—super pain relief. In twenty minutes, you won't feel any pain." She stripped off her undergarments. Then she began to unfasten Ryder's shirt.

His body heated like a rock in the noonday August sun.

* * *

MAY 16, 10:55 PM

Sex with Layla had indeed reduced Ryder's pain and had relaxed him. Exhausted, he had fallen into a deep sleep. Layla reclined next to him, also in slumber. At first, Ryder dreamed of watching a doe with its fawn in a Kentucky forest. After they frolicked, they rested in a warm, sunny glade. But all of a sudden, a dark cloud approached, the air turned chilly, lightning flashed, and thunder roared. Ryder smelled ozone and felt fat drops of rain spatter him.

Like a phantom, at once recognizable because of his sharp-pointed, black beard, Tony floated silently from behind the trunk of a large tree, his eyes glowing deep green. He held a small black box, which had a luminous red button. Tony focused on Ryder's eyes and smiled with a devilish grin.

Ryder watched while the forest scene dissolved, and he found himself sitting in a rowboat on the ocean at night. Waves were slapping the small skiff's sides, almost cresting them. He worried the pitiful boat would take on water and sink. He squinted at the moonlit blanket of fog on the horizon. Through a swirling mist, he saw a large passenger ship. It was the *Sea Trek* with its many cabin windows lit. Out of the fog, Tony rose like a ghost, his two pistol belts strapped across his chest like bandoliers. He still held the black box with the flashing red light while he soared through the fog toward the huge cruise ship. He grinned at Ryder, whooping loudly across the water.

Ryder opened his eyes. Fully awake, he saw Layla still sound asleep next to him. He sat up and felt stiff. His leg hurt, but not like it had before. He reached for his cane, propped against the bed's headboard. Quietly, he swung his feet onto the carpet and stood. Leaning on his walking stick, he silently slid open his balcony's door and stepped out into the night air to refresh himself. He heard a splash below him. The *Sea Trek* was sailing at a slow pace. He looked down toward the port shell door. In the inky darkness, he made out the obscure outline of the conning tower of a slender submarine with a man standing on top of the vessel. *What was going on?*

THIRTY-THREE

MAY 16, 11:00 PM

DRUG SMUGGLER GINO GONZALES had matched the speed of his expensive fiberglass narco sub with the slow-moving *Sea Trek*. Both vessels sailed unhurriedly side by side. Gino hoped Tony's pirates could rapidly unload the scuba gear, C-4 explosives, rifle ammunition, rocket-propelled grenade rounds, and Stinger surface-to-air missiles. Then he could again submerge and cruise under-water along the port side of the *Sea Trek*, masked from the US Coast Guard cutter, *San Diego,* by thick fog, darkness, and the massive hull of the cruise ship. Before dawn came, he could go down even farther and sail underwater for up to two days, thanks to the state-of-the-art lithium-ion subma-rine batteries he'd recently installed.

Gino smiled when he recalled how he'd slipped by the Coast Guard's human eyes and advanced sensors with ease. The heavy, misty fog had blocked the *San Diego*'s infrared—IR—sensors and cameras, as well as its IR-guided weapons. And the narco sub's blue fiberglass hull was hard to detect with sonar and radar. He'd turned off his diesel engines, so there would be no noise from them and no warm exhaust which sensitive IR sensors could detect if the fog cleared.

His vessel was tied to the *Sea Trek* with two lines extending from the huge ship's port shell door, which was not far above water level. Tony and his men had moved aside a black tarp hanging from the top of the shell doorway. They'd wanted the large sheet to block stray light from escaping the doorway. But the tarp had gotten in their way when they had begun to unload the boxes of C-4 explosives. Gino stood next to the conning tower near his open hatch. A dozen buccaneers had formed a human chain. They worked fast to hand arms and ammunition up into the cruise ship.

Gino felt someone tap his shoulder. He turned and saw Tony, who said, "Heavy fog is predicted for the next two days. Could you keep your antenna above the water when it's foggy?"

"Sure." Gino thought Tony was like a tiger, able to sneak up on people unnoticed.

Tony smiled. "We can talk by sat phone or CB radio." He thought for a bit. "When I need you to come alongside again, if I use the CB, I'll say, 'Meeting on the bridge, Gino.' I'll repeat it a few times. But if I use the sat phone, I'll talk normally, since it's encrypted."

"You got it, boss," Gino said. "I can drag a wire behind me attached to a mini-buoy antenna."

Tony smiled. "Our payoff should happen no later than 11:59 PM tomorrow night. Be on the alert for my calls."

"I'll route the CB signal and SAT phone to my speaker system." He took a moment to ponder. "But if the Coast Guard moves in, I'd cut the wire to the antenna and crash-dive. Then I'd lose touch with you."

A light bulb inside the shell door switched on. Tony yelled, "Damn it. Kill the light."

* * *

MAY 16, 11:06 PM

In the darkness, Ryder had grabbed Layla's binoculars from the top of his cabin's desk and had gone back outside onto his balcony. He was cloaked by a shadow next to the railing while he peered downward at the submarine's conning tower and a man standing next to it. Although there was moonlight, Ryder could not make out anything in the foggy blackness except for ghostly forms of people and vague outlines of objects. The binoculars were useless. Ryder began to probe the scene below him with the corners of his eyes. His side vision was better at discerning images in the darkness than the centers of his eyes. He heard the shuffling of feet, an occasional grunt, and men mumbling. Then he saw a mist-enshrouded line of pirates handing boxes up and into the ship.

A light went on, blinding him for a moment. He raised the binoculars to his eyes after they had adjusted to the brightness.

A man yelled, "Damn it. Kill the light."

Through the binoculars, Ryder saw the boxes were marked "C-4 EXPLOSIVES." The pirates were passing small rockets, scuba tanks, and flippers up and through the cruise ship's shell doorway.

The light went out after ten seconds. Ryder's eyes began to readjust to the moonlight. After he became accustomed to the dimness, he watched the pirates unload the sub for ten more minutes. Then the buccaneers who were on the sub climbed one by one up the ladder hanging from the shell door and back into the *Sea Trek*. The shell door closed.

One man remained on top of the submarine. He descended through a hatch and closed it. Ryder kept his eyes on the submarine until it submerged below the water.

* * *

RYDER REENTERED his cabin through the balcony's doorway and quietly slid its door closed. He set Layla's whale-watching binoculars back on the desk. When he glanced at the vivid green numerals of the digital clock which sat on a small table next to the bed, he saw the time was 11:31 PM, almost midnight. The colonel and his friend would be meeting in minutes someplace on the ship. Ryder gazed at Layla under the covers, still slumbering. He hated to wake her, but she could help him search the ship for Rick and his buddy.

Ryder's leg throbbed, though making love with Layla had reduced his pain for a couple of hours. He lightly clenched his teeth to help him ignore his discomfort. He felt under pressure, thinking of the effort he'd have to make to coax Rick's friend to help him defeat the pirates. It would be hard to persuade anybody to try to defuse the C-4 explosives.

Still, Ryder figured he wouldn't have to endure stress for long. The FBI's Hostage Rescue Team was bound to attack within twenty-four hours. Would Tony set off his bombs if they couldn't be disabled? Would he try to escape on the covert submarine at the same time five thousand people would be scrambling to abandon a sinking, burning ship?

Ryder decided to wait to call Rita to report his sighting of the submarine until after he and Layla had searched for Rick and his friend.

Ryder leaned on his cane and shook Layla's shoulder. In the dim moonlight coming from the balcony window, he saw her sit up. Her covers fell away, exposing her breasts. "What time is it?"

"It's goin' on midnight in a half hour. We gotta start lookin' for the colonel and his pal."

Layla swung her legs over the edge of the bed, picked up her panties and bra, and put them on. "I bet I'm wondering the same thing you are, Luke. When's this going to end?"

"I'm guessin' it'll be over in twenty-four hours." Ryder blinked. "Sorry for draggin' you into this."

"It's not your fault. It's fate."

Ryder put on his shoes and donned a sweatshirt in case he had to retrieve the Glock pistol from Rick's cabin. The sweatshirt would hide the weapon, he reckoned. "I'm thinkin' we should check the places which are open all night —the bars, casinos, and restaurants."

"I'm ready," Layla said, pulling on a sweater. "Let's go."

THIRTY-FOUR

RETIRED COLONEL RICK CASA walked into the ship's casino at a quarter past midnight. It was Friday, May 17, and he'd heard Ryder say the ransom deadline the pirates had set for the ship was 11:59 PM the coming evening—less than twenty-four hours away.

Rick took in the gaudy sights of the gambling place.

Bright orange strips of lights wound back and forth across the dark blue ceiling. Shiny, brown marble walkways crisscrossed the large space. Islands of slot machines sat in clusters on tan and burgundy checked carpets. Wooden stools with soft leather seats invited patrons to relax in front of the one-armed bandits. A smattering of old people sat at the machines sticking coins and tokens into slots. The old folks and the occasional gambling addicts pulled the machines' handles down, triggering whirring sounds. Once in a while, one of the gambling devices would flash, play a song, beep, or ring a bell.

An old man with white hair whooped when coins cascaded from his machine. He smiled. Rick thought the man didn't give a crap whether or not the pirates had taken the ship. The fellow was enjoying himself nonetheless.

Earlier, Rick had befriended the casino's gaming manager. Rick had told the man he'd like to have a private meeting with a member of the crew, engine room apprentice engineer Jeff Brooks. Rick remembered the manager grinning and saying, "Jeff is one of the best guys on the crew, always smiling and friendly. Sure, you can have card room number two. When Jeff comes in, I'll send him there." The manager had slapped Rick on the back. "Think about what you want to eat. Jeff always eats dinner here because he works the second shift. We know what he wants."

On his way to the card room, Rick passed the roulette wheel around which a half-dozen, happy-looking gamblers stood. After two dozen more steps, Rick noticed a craps table, which reminded him of a pool table, except symbols and words marked its surface. Someday he should try the game and learn its rules. But he didn't have time left. The big "C" would get him before long. He caught sight of his image in a mirror when he neared card room number two. For a fraction of a second, he didn't recognize himself. Damn, he was skinny. Cancer had sucked the vitality out of him along with fat and muscle tissue. A war hero with medals, he wondered what use they were now. The end was near.

His thoughts shifted. He ought to be a hero again and send a bunch of pirates to their maker. It would be noble to die in a blaze of glory.

He pulled open the card room door and set the doorstop so his friend and smuggling partner, Jeff Brooks, would see him.

Within three minutes, Rick caught sight of Jeff, who was wending his way through the maze of slot machines and gambling tables. He wore thin-lens, rimless glasses, and a bright smile. He appeared younger than his twenty-five years. His skin was a pale white, and he was rail thin.

Rick knew the young man was in all respects agreeable. This warm people-pleaser helped folks whenever he could. He enjoyed both human beings and pets of all kinds. He even had a parrot in his quarters.

A frequent cruiser, Rick felt guilty because he'd had no trouble convincing Jeff to help him smuggle dozens of World War II-era M1 Garand rifles and cases of ammunition onto the ship. He'd planned to sell the weapons and ammo in Canada, which was illegal but also lucrative.

Jeff entered the room. His stride and expression showed he was in a cheerful mood despite the fact he had to work with a pirate guard watching his every move in the engine room, where C-4 explosives had been placed. "Hi, Colonel."

Rick stood and grasped the young man's hand. "Hello, Jeff." He grinned. "There's no need to be formal. We're comrades in arms because we have enemies, the pirates. Call me Rick."

Jeff squeezed Rick's hand. "Okay, Rick." He hesitated. "I saw Marsha. She said she'd be here shortly to take your order."

Rick let go of Jeff's hand. "You mean the cute little waitress who always finds a way to be near you?"

Jeff blushed. "Yes." He pulled a chair away from the walnut card table and sat.

An attractive brunette woman entered. "Jeff, would you like the usual?"

"Yes."

She winked. "Later, shall we meet?"

Jeff blushed an even deeper red. "I'll meet you outside the engine room after the third shift's poker game—you know, after the boss comes back from his break."

She nodded and turned to Rick. "Colonel, what would you like?"

"A bag of chips and a draft beer. I'm not hungry, unlike my young friend."

Marsha departed.

Rick rose and closed the door. "I don't want the pirates to see us together." He wondered whether or not he was becoming paranoid.

Jeff asked, "What do we need to do about the M1s?"

Rick cocked his head. "It's complicated. A funny thing happened since we last spoke. I ran into a guy from the FBI."

Jeff's usual smile turned into a frown. "They on to us?"

"Relax, my friend. All's copacetic. The Bureau has no idea about our special cargo."

Jeff's smile reappeared. "So, what's the deal?"

"A Kentucky deputy sheriff, Luke Ryder, knocked on my cabin door earlier today. He had finished serving on an FBI task force a few days ago. He called his FBI contact when he learned pirates were on board. The FBI scanned the passenger list and found my name and cabin number. They know I'm ex-military. They want military and cops on board to help them. I believe the FBI will assault the ship within twenty-four hours."

Rick took a sip of beer and then said, "Here's what I'm thinking…"

* * *

MAY 17, 12:30 AM

Ryder sat in front of a slot machine near the entrance of the casino to watch for Rick. Meanwhile, Layla strolled among the brightly lit gambling machines and tables. Ryder had said Rick was planning to meet his engine room friend at the casino for dinner.

Layla felt her eyes begin to burn and water. Cigarette smoke polluted the place. She rubbed her eyelids and wondered if she could spot Rick.

Strolling among the machines, Layla pretended to search for an appealing one-armed bandit. She reached into her fanny pack and pulled out three quarters and a dozen pennies.

I'll try my luck and blend in, she thought.

She inserted a quarter into a machine. There were enough colored lights on it to decorate a Christmas tree. She pulled the handle. Three pictures of a rose lined up. The machine jingled. A dozen quarters fell out into a metal tray. She scooped them up and walked to a second machine. She continued to scan the big room, trying to spot an emaciated man with swarthy skin. No luck.

She sat on a plush stool in front of another sort of slot

machine. She lost ten quarters, but on her eleventh try, the gambling device dumped out a dozen quarters.

Time flies when you're having fun, she thought. She checked her watch. It read 12:40 AM. She circled back to the front of the casino and edged up close to Ryder, where he sat in front of another slot machine. She tapped his shoulder. "Any luck?"

Ryder sighed. "No. I'm wonderin' if they decided to meet somewhere else, likely a bar." He glanced into her eyes. "You see anything of interest?"

"No, but I got jackpots on two quarter machines." She smiled. "I'm ahead two bucks. Want to try? I have a lot of coins."

Ryder held out his hand. "I'll try one. If it doesn't win, I'm done."

Layla laughed and held out a quarter. "I know you kicked your drinking habit. Doing it must've affected your gambling, too."

Ryder shrugged. "I never gambled, not even penny-ante poker." He slid the quarter into the machine next to him and pulled its lever. The machine ate the coin. "Lately, I'm not lucky," he said. "What time is it?"

Layla glanced at her watch. "12:47."

Ryder stood, supported by his cane. "Let's check the bars and lounges. Rick and his buddy must've changed their minds about the casino."

* * *

MAY 17, 12:47 AM

Rick studied Jeff, who continued to shovel food into his mouth, and then said, "I think we ought to get our ducks in a row before the FBI assaults the ship."

Jeff nodded, continuing to chew.

Watching Jeff voraciously devour his dinner and smile between bites, Rick sipped his beer. The kid had an appetite. Rick lit a cigarette and filled his lungs with smoke while he considered what he'd say next.

After Jeff set his fork down, Rick said, "The cop, Ryder, told me the pirates' ransom deadline is tomorrow night, technically still today, at 11:59 PM, or they'll blow up the ship. We have less than twenty-four hours before the bombs could go off."

Jeff stopped eating. "I'll call in sick tomorrow morning and make a beeline for the lifeboats if the bombs explode." He shook his head. "I'll bring Marsha with me."

"I doubt the pirates will do it." Rick let out a breath. "They'll get their money because this ship's new. It cost billions." He studied Jeff's face. "But we've got our own problems, the M1s."

"I was wondering about them."

"The FBI will assault the ship, or they could wait to board after the pirates leave." Rick tapped his cigarette against the ashtray. "Either way, they'll scour the ship for weapons. They're bound to find our rifles. We have to make it appear like the pirates brought them on board."

Jeff wiped his lips with a napkin. "The pirates brought AKs. Why would they bother to bring semiautomatic, World War II-era rifles which take eight-round clips?"

Rick smiled. "Luckily, I included two cases of armor-piercing .30-06 Springfield rounds. AP rounds would be useful if you're a pirate shooting at steel-hulled FBI speedboats."

"Except don't AKs shoot armor-piercing bullets, too?"

"They're comparable." Rick shrugged. "Let the FBI figure it out."

Jeff laughed. "Yeah." He sighed. "I'd still have to tell the FBI a lie, namely I saw the pirates hide the rifles and ammo under the pile of wooden crates. The feds won't buy it."

"Say you didn't see them do it."

"What if they suspect the pirates didn't do it?"

Rick scratched his head. "Do you have a big canvas bag you could stuff four or five rifles into?"

"I have an old sea bag more than four feet long. Should hold several M1s, even assembled."

"Excellent." Rick rubbed his hands together. "Put three or four rifles in it with ammo, whatever you can carry. Each rifle is nine and a half pounds." He paused. "Three are enough. Then plant the bag where the pirates hang out."

Jeff frowned. "How am I going to open up the M1 boxes with a pirate guard watching, let alone sneak rifles out?"

Rick thought for a moment. "I met Luke Ryder's girlfriend. She's a real looker. She'll be able to convince the guard to abandon his post."

"If she'll do it."

"If you don't ask, you won't know. They say, 'Faint heart ne'er won fair maiden.'"

"Huh?"

"It's an old saying. It means if you don't ask a lovely lady out, you'll never get a date with one."

"Makes sense. It took me a while to ask Marsha out. But she surprised me and said yes."

Rick thought it would be smart to invite Jeff Brooks to breakfast to meet Ryder and Layla. Jeff was a likable sort.

Rick forced himself to smile. "Why don't you meet me, Ryder, and Layla for breakfast at 8:00 AM in the Galileo Dining Room? You can tell Ryder about the C-4 explosives."

"It's early for me, but sure." Jeff smiled. "I thought of a nice place to put the M1s, if I can get them out of the engine room."

"Where?"

"A side room near the port shell door." Jeff leaned closer. "A crewmate said he saw a pirate there guarding small rockets and a shoulder-fired RPG launcher."

Rick sat up straight. "It's what the pirates used to shoot down the TV news helicopter."

"The guy also saw a lot of scuba gear, tanks, and small battery-powered diver propulsion vehicles, DPVs."

"DPVs?"

"Divers hold on to their handlebars, and the DPVs pull swimmers along underwater. Even small ones can go for miles on one charge."

"They must have plans to escape underwater." Rick wrinkled his brow. "How many sets of gear are there?"

"The guy said enough for most of the pirates."

Rick sighed.

Jeff took out a large, dark chocolate candy bar, ripped off its wrapper, and binged on the chocolate. Between bites, he said, "I checked where the pirates stuck the C-4 putty. On the farm, I used to blow tree stumps out."

"You know about explosives?"

"Just dynamite." Jeff set his candy bar on the table. "The guy who set up the C-4 was called Tokyo Joe. He's a short, white guy. He stuck the explosives at different places along the bulkheads. Instead of daisy-chaining them together, he ran separate wires to a bunch of them. So, even if you can figure out how to disarm one, the others would blow up. He also hooked them to our wired telephone system, which means the bombs can be detonated through the telephone wires. There are four different phones in the engine room, each with its own set of wires."

Rick worried Tokyo Joe could have been the guy who'd blown up the Tokyo high-rise a year or two before. The Japanese cops had known about the high-rise bomb, but they still couldn't defuse it. In fact, they didn't. Instead, three bomb squad members were blown to bits. To this day, nobody knew how the bomber had rigged his bombs, according to news reports. Rick cleared his throat. "You think you could disarm the bombs?"

"I'm not suicidal. He booby-trapped them. I saw him set up at least one hand grenade. I try to stay away from a bunch of different places where he put C-4 on the hull and bulkheads."

"How many places did he stick the C-4 to?"

"At least a dozen." He stopped smiling. "The bomb setup is why I'll call in sick after breakfast." He took another bite of chocolate. With a half-full mouth, he said, "I could tell Ryder I saw the pirates bring M1s in from the chopper and put them under the spare parts boxes."

"He'd believe you." Rick inwardly smiled.

THIRTY-FIVE

ARLO ARRIVED at the port shell door, where three other buccaneers met him. He could feel the sea breeze whipping past the black tarp hanging out of the yawning doorway. The men had opened the hydraulically powered shell door, which was ten feet square. They'd also lowered the sturdy rope ladder to the surface of the water, several feet down.

The tall, thin man who'd guarded the rocket-propelled grenade launcher, scuba diving gear, and go-packs containing clothes and money stood in a side room. He wore most of his diving gear, including a 7mm thick wet suit to keep him warm. The waters off California's coast were cold. Because diver propulsion vehicles—DPVs—would pull the buccaneers through the water, they wouldn't use their muscles to swim, which otherwise would've warmed their bodies.

The tall, thin pirate's gear also included two air cylinders, two-stage diving regulators, inflator hoses, and pressure gauges. His mask hung from his neck, and his fins were on the deck next to him. He was strapping a thin, pod-shaped case containing clothes and money to his stomach. Each diver would have a luminous-dial compass to guide him to land since he wouldn't be able to surface to sight the shore. Even if he did surface, heavy fog would certainly have disoriented him.

Air supplies were an important consideration for the divers. Since DPVs would do the swimming work for the divers, they would need less air, and it would last longer. Also, they wouldn't dive deeper than forty feet because the farther down divers go, the more air they'd need to inflate their lungs. Go too deep, and they could run out of air. Therefore, each diver would carry a luminous-dial depth gauge. The buccaneers would have to take care to check their gauges and compasses often to safely reach the shore.

Arlo was jubilant. He couldn't wait to flee the ship. Tony was a total nut job. Arlo believed Tony's plan would fail. He smiled. "You guys ready?"

"Yes, sir," said the tall, thin pirate who had helped unload a dozen diving kits and ammunition for the RPGs and the Stingers from the sub. "Because of all the extra C-4 the sub delivered, this ship's gonna burn to a crisp and sink when Tony pushes his radio trigger."

"I'm glad we're going to miss the fireworks," Arlo said. He stared at the two other buccaneers—the short, fat guy and the third, nondescript pirate. They were slipping into their wet suits. "When we're ready, let's leave together. We'll turn off the lights first."

The fat, chunky man asked, "Won't it be easier to see us if we're together?"

Arlo shook his head. "It would be, except the fog's thick. Our bubbles won't be seen, and the Coast Guard's drones are worthless because their infrared cameras and sensors can't spot us through heavy fog." He nodded. "Sound thinking, though. We'd have to leave separately if the fog were thinner."

The fat pirate said, "I'm so ready for this swim." He grinned.

The nondescript buccaneer asked Arlo, "Will we get paid?"

"Could be, especially if the shit hits the fan, and there's

chaos. We can say we got away in the confusion. The Bogotá cartel will pay off because they reward loyal people. Tell a lie, and you'll live and get paid to boot."

Arlo knew the *Sea Trek* was sailing at two or three knots because Tony had decided to prepare to stop the big vessel as fast as possible. If the big ship were drifting on a calm ocean, Tony could easily board the narco sub and escape.

Ready to flee, the four pirates helped each other put on their air tanks and adjust their equipment. Arlo checked each man to see if he'd properly donned his diving gear. "We're ready, men." He scanned the men. "Line up, and go down the ladder one by one. We'll tag up and swim to shore together. If somebody has an equipment failure, we'll help him."

After Arlo switched the lights off, the men descended the ladder and got in the water. Previously, they had tied four of the twenty-one-pound diver propulsion vehicles to ropes and dropped them below the surface near the ladder. After the band of four was in the water, each diver untied his DPV; mounted his bullet-shaped, battery-powered machine; grabbed its handlebars; and turned his vehicle on. The DPV batteries could power each unit for ninety minutes. The air in the diver's scuba tanks would last forty-five minutes to an hour.

With their backs to the ship, the four escaping buccaneers headed due east for California's shore at four miles per hour. The beaches were two miles away. The men would be walking in the surf in a half hour. Arlo felt euphoric. He'd stay alive and remain free. At least, he believed he'd survive. He felt safe under the thick layer of fog.

THIRTY-SIX

RYDER WAS EXHAUSTED. He sat on the edge of his cabin bed. Dull pain was a constant reminder of his broken shin. Unexpected twinges of discomfort had kept him awake despite his mental fatigue. He had to call Rita.

Layla had already gotten his sat phone from the vent. Now she dozed on top of the bedcovers.

Ryder guessed Rita would sleep next to her FBI satellite phone, if she wasn't still awake. He tapped in her phone number.

The phone rang eight times. Rita cleared her throat. "Luke, what's new?"

"A lot."

"Hold on. I need a pen and paper, even if this is being recorded." Ten seconds later, she said, "Go ahead."

"We searched the ship, but we couldn't find Rick and his pal."

"Do you have additional info about the C-4 explosives setup?"

"No, but I saw a submarine along the port side of the ship. The pirates unloaded boxes of C-4, rockets, ammo, and scuba gear from the sub."

Ryder could hear Rita scratching notes on her paper. Then she said, "I wonder if they plan to place explosives in other places on the ship."

Ryder said, "I'll find out more at the eight o'clock breakfast with Rick."

Rita coughed. "The submarine is big news. I'll wager it's a drug smuggler's narco sub. Franco may have planned to leave on it. They're made of fiberglass and are hard to see on radar and sonar. And the fog's better than a smoke screen because it blocks infrared cameras and sensors."

"How could Franco get a submarine?"

Rita took a breath. "He's big into drug smuggling."

"I saw the sub go back under the water."

"We'll alert the Coast Guard," Rita said. "Odds are they never saw the sub because of the fog."

"Sorry to cut you short, but I'm tired like a plow horse after a full day's work. Plus, my leg's painin' me. I gotta sleep. I'll call after tomorrow's meetin' with Rick."

"Okay." Rita disconnected.

Ryder woke Layla so she could stow the phone in the vent. Then she quickly fell asleep again.

* * *

MAY 17, 2:40 AM

Ryder tossed and turned. He slept on top of the bed covers, still dressed.

Layla awoke and placed a blanket over Ryder. He moaned in his restless sleep. Figuring he was in severe pain, she debated whether or not to wake him and convince him to revisit the med center. She'd heard new nonnarcotic painkillers were miraculous. Certainly, Ryder would need to ignore his pain if the FBI's Hostage Rescue Team were to assault the ship in the next twenty-four hours. What if the bombs went off? She and Ryder would need to move fast to a lifeboat to get away from a sinking ship.

Layla gritted her teeth and then exhaled to relax. She shook Ryder's shoulder. "Luke, wake up."

"What time is it?"

"Early." Layla chose her words with care. "I'm going to take you to the med center to get pain medication. You need to get through the next day or so, if the situation gets dicey."

"I don't wanna be a recoverin' alcoholic and a drug addict, too."

"The new pain pills are nonnarcotic, not addictive. I've read about them." She kissed him. "Come on. Please."

Ryder sat up and felt a surge of pain. "Okay, you win."

"You won't regret it." Layla handed him his cane. "I promise you another round of loving and the natural painkillers which come with it, too."

"You got my attention." Ryder squinted while he pushed himself up with the aid of his cane.

* * *

MAY 17, 2:50 AM

Layla began to move the wheelchair toward Ryder.

Ryder bit his lip, trying not to show his pain. "We should return the chair." A thought hit him. "I'm gonna ask the doc for sleeping pills."

"Sleeping pills?" Layla showed puzzlement. "You need to be on the alert."

"They're not for me. I figured how to get the man guardin' the engine room to take a nap."

Layla helped Ryder into the wheelchair. "How are you going to convince him to take sleeping pills?"

"All I need is a fifth of whiskey. I'd dribble whiskey out so it would appear somebody had taken two or three nips. Then I'd smash the sleeping pills, pour the crushed pills into the bottle, and shake it."

Layla cocked her head. "Liquor and sleeping pills can kill." She rolled the chair toward their cabin door. "How would you plant the bottle in the engine room?"

"Rick's friend could leave it where the guy would find it." Ryder smiled. "Bein' a drunk, I know most of these buccaneers are heavy drinkers. A bottle of whiskey is a temptation they wouldn't pass up."

"What if someone else in the engine room drinks it?"

"Rick's buddy would have to clue in his coworkers."

Layla nodded. "But first, Rick's sidekick would have to agree to help us." Layla opened the door and pushed the wheelchair toward the elevators.

Ryder felt better. This sleeping pill idea could work. Somebody could defuse the C-4 explosives after all. But first, he needed the pills.

* * *

MAY 17, 3:00 AM

Ryder was happy when Layla pushed his wheelchair through the med center doorway because he reckoned he'd be able to convince the doctor on duty he needed sleeping pills. Layla tapped a bell on the counter. The same doctor who'd put on Ryder's cast came out of an examination room.

The physician yawned and combed his disheveled hair with his fingers. Then he smoothed his blue scrubs uniform. "You're back, Mr. Ryder."

"Yep. I bin havin' trouble sleeping due to my leg pain. Could you give me a bottle of sleepin' pills?"

"I'm sorry, no. You reeked of whiskey when you came in for treatment yesterday." He frowned. "Mixing alcohol with prescription sleeping aids can cause death."

"I promise not to drink, Doc." Ryder wondered what to say next. It was vital he acquire sleeping pills. Without them, disabling the engine room guard would be trickier, if not impossible. "Doc, I gotta sleep. I'm gettin' dizzy for lack of it."

The doctor leaned against the counter behind him. He sighed. "I'm not going to give you sleeping pills. We've had enough death on this cruise already."

"But Doc…"

The physician held up his hand. "Let me finish. Stay in bed. Eventually, you'll fall asleep. Also, lay off the sauce." He sighed. "Since you're here, let's take another X-ray. Have you been taking it easy like I instructed yesterday?"

"The most I could, Doc."

The doctor pushed Ryder and his chair to the mobile cot where he'd been X-rayed before. After Ryder climbed onto the gurney with the aid of Layla, the doctor took three X-rays from different angles. "The crack in your shinbone has grown longer, which tells me you've been overdoing it." He shook his head. "If there's stress, the crack could go through the entire bone. Then you'd need surgery. I'm going to remove the cast, set the bone, and put a new cast on."

Ryder figured the only way he could get sleeping pills from the physician was to tell the truth. Would the doctor believe him? "Doctor, I need to be honest with you."

Layla perked up.

The doctor frowned. "What?"

"You've gotta promise not to tell the pirates what I'm about to say. Agreed?"

The doctor squinted and then nodded. "Okay."

"I'm a Kentucky deputy sheriff on vacation, but last week I was on an FBI task force. I called the task force agent in charge after I found out the pirates took the ship. I'm back on the FBI payroll, working to stop the hijack of this ship. I got in a fight with a pirate, and I broke my leg then. I splattered whiskey on myself so you'd believe I'd been dead drunk and fell down steps. Can you help me?"

The doctor sighed. "If I won't get killed."

"I need sleeping pills."

"What for?"

"There's a pirate guarding the C-4 explosives in the engine room. I want to lace a bottle of whiskey with sleeping pills and have a friend plant it near the guard. If he drinks it, he'll take a nap, and my friends can try to defuse the explosives."

The doctor pulled a chair up and sat down. "You know the pirate could die if the dose is excessive, don't you?"

Ryder nodded. "But I figger you'll know how many pills to put in a fifth of whiskey, minus two shots, which would ease him into a deep sleep."

The doctor let out a big breath. "How big is this guy?"

"I'm not sure, and they switch guards every so often."

The doctor walked to a cabinet and unlocked it. "I'll grind up enough pills to mix with whiskey and safely put an average man to sleep with one or two shots. But if he's small or has a disease making him vulnerable, he could die."

Ryder blinked. "Don't feel bad takin' a chance with the dose size. These guys could sink this ship and kill thousands of people."

The physician removed a brown bottle from the cabinet and put pills into a small granite bowl, a mortar. He ground them with a club-shaped tool, a pestle. Then he poured the resulting powder into a small envelope and sealed it with tape to avoid licking the power. "I don't know if I've broken my Hippocratic oath to do no harm or not. Hopefully, this won't kill the man."

"Thanks, Doc." Ryder sighed. "I don't know if I'm doin' the right thing or not either. Let's pray my pals can defuse the bomb. I can't 'cuz of my broken leg. There's no tellin' how many places the pirates put C-4 explosives."

The doctor sat back on his chair. "What happened to the pirate you fought?"

Ryder cleared his throat. "He's dead. His neck broke. He tried to rape Layla and had a knife to her throat."

The physician sighed. "Anything else I could do?"

Layla asked, "Could you give him the new nonnarcotic painkiller I've heard about in the news?" She cocked her head. "It's not habit-forming, is it?"

The doctor glanced at Layla and then at Ryder. "It's safe and nonaddictive. I'll give you a dose. The danger is you won't feel pain if your break is getting worse."

Ryder focused his eyes on the physician. "I need to keep goin'. People are dependin' on me."

The doctor picked up a small, white plastic bottle. "Here's enough painkiller for a week. Take one tablet every eight hours. You don't have to take it with food." The doctor went to a sink and filled a small paper cup with water. He dropped a pill into Ryder's left hand.

Ryder swallowed the pill with the water. "How fast does it work?"

"In thirty minutes, you'll feel better." His stare grabbed Ryder's undivided attention. "Protect your leg. It's fragile in its current state." He sighed. "If it gets worse, get back here right away."

"I appreciate it, Doc." Ryder glanced at the floor for a moment. "Doc, how can I get the elevator to go down to Deck Two?"

"I'll help you, but I've noticed there's always a pirate there guarding scuba gear."

"I'll be careful."

"First, I need to set your shinbone and put on a new cast."

* * *

MAY 17, 3:15 AM

A minute after the stocky, older engineer-in-charge had left for his break, Jeff Brooks entered the engine room to meet with his coworkers for their weekly secret poker game. They played it in a small side room, which had enough sound-suppression insulation to block a great deal of the roar of the ship's engines. Also, the engineer-in-charge couldn't see them playing cards there when they should've been working. Each week one of the men took a turn standing watch to make sure his boss wouldn't catch them.

Often, engine room workers from different shifts would join the games. This evening, as Jeff neared the makeshift cardroom, he noticed the pirate guard was not at his post.

Jeff felt a tap on his shoulder. He turned and saw a fellow card player. The middle-aged man yelled over the roar of the engines, "The guard's got the shits. I had to hand him a roll of toilet paper." The man smiled. "He'll be in the crapper a while."

"That's what he gets for not washing his hands," Jeff said, and he grinned.

The card player laughed and coughed. "That's not all," he yelled. "There's no guard at the port shell door. I bet he swam for shore. The door's wide open." Jeff's coworker waved and took a step toward the cardroom. "You'll be late if you don't get in the room before the first deal."

"Be there later," Jeff yelled. He couldn't believe his luck. He went to his locker and took out his oversized duffel bag. Next, he went to where he'd hidden the M1 rifles and pulled out a case of them. He placed three weapons and two metal ammunition boxes in his large canvas bag.

Within two minutes, he was lugging his stuffed duffel bag along the passageway on his way to the port shell door where the guard was missing.

* * *

MAY 17, 3:20 AM

The physician finished putting the new cast on Ryder's left shin. "Don't put pressure on this cast for three hours to give it time to harden. Ride in the wheelchair when you go down to Deck Two." He rubbed his chin. "I'll give you the elevator code."

"Layla, can you write it down?" Ryder asked.

"There's no need to," the doctor said. "The code's 1492— the year Columbus landed in the Bahamas."

"It's easy to remember," Ryder said.

The physician nodded. "Enter the code. When the screen asks you what deck, type in the number two."

Layla smiled at the physician and then pushed Ryder out of the med center toward the nearby elevator lobby. "When we get out on Deck Two, I'll push your chair out of sight. I'll check to see if anybody's around."

Ryder shifted in the wheelchair when Layla pushed it into the elevator car. "Okay, but take no chances." He glanced at her. "The painkiller kicked in fast. I can ditch this chair."

Layla typed 1492 on the elevator keypad and chose Deck Two. The lift gently went down two decks and halted. When its doors opened, Ryder saw the lobby was devoid of people.

After guiding the wheelchair into an alcove, Layla said, "You can wait here."

"No. I feel fine." Ryder's left leg was pain-free. He reckoned he would be okay if he put most of his weight on his walking stick and his right leg. "I'm goin' with you."

Layla frowned. "Be careful. The cast's not hardened."

Ryder gestured toward a sign pointing to the port shell door. "Let's go."

Layla whispered, "If we're stopped, I'll say I'm a dancer. What about you?"

Ryder tried to imagine a job he could have on a cruise ship. He was hard-pressed to think of anything except security man. Then an idea hit him. He could claim he was a teacher as well as a wildlife expert and guide for onshore Alaska excursions. After all, he'd been a Kentucky game warden for years before becoming a deputy sheriff. "I'll be a wildlife guide."

Layla smiled. "You'd be a great guide."

Ryder stood, supported by his cane.

The two of them set off toward the port shell door. They were vigilant, checking around them, stopping to listen at each passageway intersection. They crossed a long central passage, which Ryder thought must run the length of the ship. When they neared the port shell door, he felt a chilly breeze sweeping along their darkened pathway.

Ryder could barely see a black tarp flapping in the breeze and hanging from the top of the ten-by-ten-foot, open shell doorway. In the gloom, Ryder could see the tarp was hanging down past the bottom edge of the doorway. Because there was a slight slapping coming from the bottom of the tarp, he thought the tarp must've been dipping into the waves.

Ryder held his finger to his lips to caution Layla to be extra quiet.

She nodded. They both crept forward. Nobody was in sight in the dimness of the large space in front of the doorway. Ryder inched closer to a side room on his right. He peered around the corner into the room. He saw wet suits, scuba tanks, flippers, and other diving equipment, including one pod-shaped case near each set of gear. He noticed first names and initials on labels affixed to each case, presumably the names or initials of each pirate. He also saw small, bullet-shaped machines. The label on one of them read, "Diver Propulsion Vehicle." He guessed most of the pirates would swim for shore under the cover of darkness and the persistent fog when they decided to abandon the ship.

Ryder surveyed the room's far corners. He saw no guard. He squinted to check beyond a pile of boxes should someone be dozing there. Nobody was in sight. He quietly crossed the large space in front of the shell doorway. He worried a guard could be in the room Layla had entered on the left. He peeked inside. Layla was examining a pile of blue-tipped projectiles, each two to three feet long. He surmised they were ammunition for the RPG launcher Tony had used to shoot down the news helicopter. Then he saw a launcher in a far corner.

Ryder approached Layla and tapped her shoulder.

She recoiled from his unexpected touch. She whispered, "You see anybody?"

"No." He gestured at the blue-tipped projectiles. "Let's throw these in the water. The door's open." He stared at them. "I think a rocket like these blew the news helicopter outta the sky."

Layla appeared nervous to Ryder. "Could they explode if we touched them wrong?"

"I doubt it. The one Tony used didn't have a blue tip. I reckon somebody took the tip off to activate the warhead." He hesitated. "I'll throw one out and see what happens."

Layla began shaking. "Be careful."

Ryder picked up a projectile. He thought it weighed between three and four pounds. After moving to the black tarp, he pushed it outward and dropped the small missile into the water, causing a large splash. He smiled. "It's one less shot they can take with the RPG." He took a moment to think. "I should toss the launcher in the water, too."

Ryder grabbed another RPG projectile and started to walk to the open shell doorway. "Could you pick up one or two of these and dump them in the water while I get the launcher?"

"Okay," Layla said. All of a sudden, she held up her hand and then put her finger over her lips. She pointed along the passageway that ran to the center of the ship. "Somebody's coming," she whispered.

Ryder set the projectile on the deck. He and Layla went into a janitor's closet near the port shell door area. After he heard a person shuffling past the closet and toward the shell doorway, Ryder cracked open the closet door. He saw the backside of a lanky young man with pale white skin walking toward the shell door. He was lugging a heavy duffel bag. Ryder thought the thin man was a crew member because he wasn't armed. He entered the space near the shell door and turned left into a side room.

Ryder touched Layla's shoulder. "Let's go. Seems he's a regular crewman, but he could be a pirate guard for all I know."

THIRTY-SEVEN

TONY WALKED ONTO THE BRIDGE, exhilarated. He felt sure the ransom payoff would happen in less than twenty-four hours. He and his men would leave the ship rich men under the cover of darkness and fog. But he noticed Waylen, his second-in-command, had a frown pasted across his face. Tony guessed something had gone haywire. "What's up?"

"We got trouble, Cap." Waylen let out a sizable sigh. "When Elko went to relieve the port shell door guard, he was missing. Four diving kits were gone, too. One of them belonged to Arlo. We called him on the CB radio, and he didn't answer. We found his radio on the deck near the diving gear. We can't find two other guys, either. We figure four of them swam for shore after we unloaded the sub."

Tony shook his head. "The bad thing is we could have used those four fighters. The upside is we have fewer men to divide the ransom with." Tony walked to a chair and collapsed onto it. "Friggin' Arlo lost his nerve. I knew it after I found out he got upset after Tex took care of the security chief."

Waylen gulped. "There's more to report."

Tony sat up straight. "What the hell else could go wrong?"

"We found Marco sitting on the crapper with a bad case of diarrhea around 3:15 AM, and he admitted he'd been in the head for at least fifteen minutes instead of guarding the engine room." Waylen sighed. "Anybody could've gotten in there and fiddled with the explosives."

Tony stood. "God damn it." He pounded the console near him with his fist. "I thought we vetted these guys. How the hell'd we get such a bunch of losers?" He shook his head.

Waylen bit his lip and seemed to be carefully choosing his next words. "We did check these guys out. It was hard to find scuba divers who we could trust." He took a quick breath. "And we're both aware most of them drink, smoke weed, or do hard drugs."

"I should've hired mercenaries." Tony stepped toward one of the bridge's doors. "I'm going to make surprise visits. It won't be long before it's 11:59 PM."

Tony left. Waylen began to decompress.

* * *

MAY 17, 7:17 AM

Tony strolled along the passageway on Deck Two toward the port shell door. When he approached, he saw one of his men, a tough-looking fellow who was unshaven and burly, sitting in the wide space near the ten-foot-square door. Tony managed to contrive a smile and said, "Good morning. I'm checking on everyone today. Tonight's the deadline for the ransom payments. I want everybody on their toes."

"Yes, Cap."

"If one of us screws up, it may allow the FBI to take the ship before we can escape." Tony nodded at the scuba equipment in a side room next to the shell door area. "Make sure nobody takes anything else."

The burly buccaneer's face grew red. "Cap, I counted the

RPG rounds. One's missing, and I found another near the shell door."

Tony scowled. "One of the regular crew must've sneaked in here and dumped an RPG projectile overboard. He must've been surprised and dropped the second one on the deck when he heard you coming."

The burly pirate frowned. "I saw a skinny guy turning the corner to the main passageway, but his back was turned."

Tony gazed down at the deck. "Did you know four of our guys swam away last night?"

"Everybody knows."

"Make sure nobody else goes 'til I say so, or Waylen okays it." He squinted. "We may leave the ship at once if the money's wired ahead of schedule."

The burly buccaneer grinned. "I'll see to it that nobody takes scuba gear until you say so."

"Excellent." Tony caught sight of the black tarp, which was rolled up above the hydraulic shell door. "Open the door, and hang the tarp out. We may have to leave in a hurry. It's foggy enough. The Coast Guard won't notice us."

"Yes, Cap."

Tony left.

* * *

MAY 17, 7:55 AM

The big, burly buccaneer who'd been guarding the port shell door and diving equipment got up from his chair when a short, thin pirate came to relieve him.

"How'd it go?" the smaller man asked.

The bigger pirate shrugged. "Cap was here. He's on edge. Wants us to be on the alert in case other guys decide to swim for shore and desert."

"Why go early?"

"If the FBI drops in, it'd be best to be gone before then," the big man answered.

"You thinkin' of gettin' away early?"

"I'd say keep your eyes open and your ears tuned to the scuttlebutt." The big man winked. "I gotta eat somethin'. See ya later."

* * *

MAY 17, 7:58 AM

Drug dealer Bert Holmgren sat in the Challenger's Lounge, waiting for the big, burly buccaneer who'd been guarding the port shell door. The husky pirate had told Bert to meet him there. The pirate wished to buy ecstasy and oxycodone pills from Bert.

Fifty-year-old Bert nervously scratched his salt-and-pepper hair. Most of the time, he smiled, but this morning he frowned. One of the *Sea Trek*'s crewmen had informed Bert he'd been reported to the Drug Enforcement Administration for selling drugs, and DEA agents would meet the ship at its next US port to arrest him.

Bert felt his body shake each time he thought of being detained by DEA agents. If he went to federal prison, it would be for a long time. There was a chance he wouldn't complete his sentence because of his advancing age, and then there was also the danger fellow prisoners would pose.

Still, Bert figured he had the potential to thrive in prison because he was an extrovert. He prided himself on making friends with ease. This would be vital if he were to survive behind bars. But would his fellow inmates be so hard-assed they wouldn't warm up to his friendliness? Would they think he was weak because he talked a lot?

What could he do to evade arrest? His mind was busy calculating, thinking of options. He brainstormed, but the ideas he had were so far-fetched he became depressed. This was not normal for him. He was usually cheerful, full of fun, uninhibited, restless, and able to change direction and adapt at a moment's notice.

Bert shifted in his wrinkled, blue shirt. He'd spent the

night smoking weed. It was his one vice, the one drug he used and also sold. His best sellers were Mollies, oxycodone pills, and M30s. To provide a special service, he always carried an antidote for fentanyl, naloxone, in case one of his pills contained deadly fentanyl. He thought himself a businessman, not a killer—a man who had the well-being of his customers in mind. After all, if a consumer died, his death would cut into Bert's revenue stream. He knew himself well enough to realize money was truly important to him. It supported his unrestrained, fast-moving life. Without it, he would slip, fall, and careen over a cliff.

Bert glanced at the lounge entrance and saw the big, gorilla-like pirate enter. Bert raised his long arm and waved his big hand.

The burly pirate sat in the booth where Bert nursed a cup of coffee. The buccaneer asked, "You got what I need, Bert?"

Bert displayed a broad grin. "You bet." He reached into his pocket and withdrew two small plastic bags. "Here are your Mollies and M30s. I'm throwing in the antidote for fentanyl in case there's an overdose." He pulled out a third plastic bag.

"You think you got bad shit mixed with the good pills?"

"No, but you never know for sure. I want live customers, not dead ones."

"I like the extra effort." The big pirate reached into his pocket and pulled out greenbacks. "Here."

An idea flashed into Bert's brain. He held up his big hand. "This one's on me." His smile morphed into a genuine grin. "In fact, I'll pay you fifty thousand if you can slip me a set of scuba gear."

The burly buccaneer took the three bags. His eyes seemed like lasers probing Bert's head. "Why do you need a diving outfit?"

Bert inhaled, shrugged, and then thought, *what the hell, tell him the truth*. He stared into the pirate's inquiring eyes. "I heard the DEA knows I'm selling drugs. Agents are waiting to arrest me when I get off the ship. I can't use fifty K if they catch me. I figure I can swim and make it to shore because the fog's thick. If I wait any longer, the FBI could board the ship."

The pirate scratched his unshaven face. "You'd be taking diving gear from one of our guys."

"I don't think so." He glanced around the room and whispered. "I heard one of your guys fell overboard, drunk. Another guy went missing. Could've fallen overboard, too."

The pirate laughed. "You know what's going on better than Tony."

"I've been peddling my wares to most of your brothers, and to passengers. Everybody talks."

The muscular pirate held his hand out, grabbed Bert's hand, and shook it. "You got a deal. I'll meet you at the shell door at nine when I'm due back after breakfast. Bring the cash. Be ready to swim then."

"I will. I'm glad I took scuba lessons during my last cruise." Bert held the pirate's hand in a firm grip.

"I'll miss you, Bert." The burly pirate smiled. "I respect your honesty."

Bert felt his true smile project happiness. "See you at nine, brother."

THIRTY-EIGHT

THOUGH HE WASN'T HUNGRY, Rick had selected pastries and coffee with cream and sugar for his breakfast in the Galileo Dining Room. He sat at a table for four in a far corner of the eatery. He kept a close lookout for Jeff Brooks. He was easy to spot because of his youthful appearance, slender body, and rimless glasses. He resembled a college student instead of an engine room crewman.

Rick hoped Ryder and Layla would be late and Jeff would arrive on time. Then Jeff and he would have time to get their stories straight. Rick had chosen this particular table because a partition hid it, and Ryder was less likely to see it. Still, Rick had a clear view from the table of the dining room's entrance through a gap between the partition and the wall.

By happy chance, Rick caught sight of a reflection from Jeff's glasses when he passed under a bright LED ceiling light outside the restaurant. Rick got up and waved to Jeff, who nodded and approached.

Rick again sat down behind the divider to better conceal himself from Ryder and Layla.

Jeff stopped to choose food from a self-serve table.

Rick got up and vigorously waved Jeff to come to the table right away.

"I didn't get anything yet," Jeff said.

"We need to talk fast before Ryder and Layla get here." Rick sighed.

Jeff sat down, and his usual bright smile appeared.

"First, tell Ryder about the bomb placements," Rick said quickly. "Second, tell him you saw pirates carry boxes of rifles into the engine room and take two of the weapons out to inspect them. Then say you saw a pirate shove the boxes of rifles under the crates of parts. Don't say they're M1s. Ryder would wonder how you'd know."

"Okay." Jeff held up his hand and grinned even wider than he normally did. "I have great news." He told Rick the story of how he was able to sneak three M1 rifles from the engine room and plant them near the port shell door in a storeroom.

Rick smiled, his olive skin creasing. "Great news." Though his cancer made him weary, he felt a surge of energy at Jeff's good luck. "The pirates will take the fall for the M1s."

Jeff leaned closer. "Also, the shell door was open, and a black tarp was draped down to cover the open doorway." Jeff whispered, "I saw four ropes hanging down into the water. I bet the missing guard and three other pirates hung DPVs there, put on scuba gear, and swam for shore."

Rick felt elated. "Excellent news. The fewer pirates, the better." He picked up a pastry and held it. "Their leaving tells me there's fear in the ranks of the pirates."

Jeff asked, "Should I tell Ryder four pirates left?"

"Say you heard a rumor the shell guard pirate was missing and swam for shore, but don't say anything about the four ropes. If the FBI learns you were near the shell door, they'll figure out you planted the M1s there."

"Okay."

Rick glanced at the restaurant's entrance, wondering when Ryder and Layla would arrive.

* * *

MAY 17, 8:06 AM

Ryder and Layla walked toward the Galileo Dining Room on Deck Seven to meet Rick for breakfast. Ryder's leg wasn't hurting, but he was careful not to lean on it so the crack in his shinbone wouldn't get worse. His gut told him to keep his eyes peeled.

Tony turned a corner in the passageway ahead. His sharp-pointed black beard made him easy to spot. He walked straight to Ryder and Layla. "If it isn't our two jewel thieves and pickpocket." He smiled. "I hope for your sakes you've decided to take a holiday from your usual vocations."

Ryder shrugged. "We're on vacation."

Layla said, "It's nice to relax and enjoy the cruise."

Tony peered down at Ryder's leg. "You seem to be in less pain."

"The med center doc gave me pain pills."

Tony nodded. He glanced at Layla.

Ryder knew the buccaneer liked her physical appearance.

Tony smiled lustfully at her. Then he said, "Glad to hear you're both keeping out of trouble. We searched your cabin and found no loot." He smiled. "I need to do my management by walking to make sure my men are on the alert. Bye." He departed.

Ryder said, "Lucky he didn't see us with Rick and his engine room pal." Ryder watched while Tony turned a corner and disappeared. "Let's go into the Galileo before he comes back."

Layla nodded. "We can get Rick to change tables if he's someplace in clear view."

They walked into the dining room and began to search for Rick.

* * *

MAY 17, 8:09 AM

Ryder and Layla entered the Galileo Dining Room nine minutes late, thanks to their surprise meeting with Tony in the passageway. Though Ryder scanned the large room, he didn't see Rick. Had he overslept?

A movement in the far corner of the place caught Ryder's eye. Rick was waving his arm. After Ryder lifted his arm to acknowledge Rick, the man slipped behind a divider, which sectioned off five tables in the rear of the eatery.

Ryder tapped Layla's shoulder. He pointed at the partition. "I saw Rick step out from behind that divider."

After Ryder walked behind the partition, he saw Rick and a young man who appeared to be a teenager. The pale fellow had dark brown, neatly cut hair and rimless glasses.

Rick stood. "Luke and Layla, thank you for coming." He gestured at the young man. "This is my friend who works in the engine room, Jeff Brooks."

Jeff smiled and seemed to be in a fine mood.

Rick said, "I've told Jeff about you, and he's promised to keep your identities secret, right Jeff?"

Jeff nodded. "Yep."

Rick's eyes zeroed in on Jeff. "Tell them about the C-4."

Jeff's smile left his lips for a moment and then returned. "The bomb guy is a short, little, white dude they call Tokyo Joe. I saw him wire up at least a dozen bombs and connect them to four of the engine room's telephone lines. He climbed a ladder to get to hard-to-access spots to place the explosives. After he finished the setup, he used electronic instruments to check the wires for signals going to each of four bomb clusters." Jeff blinked.

Rick said, "Tell them what else Tokyo Joe did."

"He wired small plastic boxes of electronics between each of the four telephone lines and the four groups of C-4 explosives."

Rick said, "The plastic boxes could be receivers, and the phone wires could be attached to outside antennae on the top deck. A pirate could set off the bombs from miles away with a satellite phone or a homemade radio transmitter, which uses a frequency the feds don't expect him to use."

Jeff shifted in his chair. "I also saw him carrying a plunger and a long reel of wire, but I'm not sure if he hooked them up."

Rick gazed at Ryder. "I think the plunger and reel of wire are a backup. The pirates could detonate the explosives with them."

Jeff leaned forward. "He set up a grenade booby trap, too. If anybody fiddles with the bombs, it could set off the grenade, but it's not real close to the C-4 putty. He pulled the pin on the grenade and held down the safety lever with a thin wire. I'm not sure how the lever still stays in place and doesn't spring off and set off the grenade. I try to stay away from it."

Ryder said, "What if the ship gets in a storm, and something falls, hits the grenade handle, it flies off, and the grenade explodes?"

Rick said, "If it went off, it wouldn't explode the C-4 unless the grenade is touching it or is fairly close to it. You can shoot bullets into C-4, and it won't explode. It looks and feels like putty. You have to embed a detonator in it and set off the detonator to trigger the main explosion."

Jeff shrugged. "The grenade could be a fake one to scare us."

Ryder nodded. "Yeah, but we can't be sure exactly what Tokyo Joe did."

Rick leaned forward. "I heard about Tokyo Joe before. He's the guy who blew up the high-rise in Tokyo two years ago. Killed three Japanese bomb squad guys and two dozen people in the building he brought down."

Ryder took a deep breath and then said, "I've got a favor to ask you, Jeff."

"What?" Jeff smiled broadly, and his body language showed he was inclined to help.

Ryder studied Jeff's eyes. "The FBI wants somebody to defuse the bombs."

Jeff's smile vanished. He gulped. "Sorry, I think Tokyo Joe set up at least four separate bombs, and I bet he's booby-trapped them all." He stared into the distance. "I used to blow tree trunks out of the ground with dynamite at the farm, but C-4 is way beyond me."

Rick sighed. "Okay, I'll examine the setup if we can get the guard to leave. I worked with C-4 when I was in the Army." He shifted his emaciated body.

Ryder wondered if Rick would be able to climb into hard-to-reach places to defuse a bomb. The man appeared feeble. Yet Ryder forced himself to be positive. "I have a plan to put the guard out of play—sleeping pills."

Rick asked, "How do you get a pirate to take them?"

Ryder smiled. "We put them in a bottle of whiskey. Jeff could plant the bottle where the pirate is bound to see it. These guys are all drunks."

"I got most of a fifth left in my cabin," Jeff said. "I work the second shift, but I can go in the engine room anytime and tell the guys not to drink it."

"Can you trust them?" Ryder asked.

"Yep. They're all scared shitless. If Rick goes in there to check out the bombs and defuses one or two of them, the guys would welcome it. If the guard's asleep, the engine room crew could leave while the colonel does his thing."

Ryder reached into his pocket and took out an envelope. "There's sleeping pill powder in this. The med center doctor ground up the pills. He says it'll put the average man into a deep sleep if he drinks it with whiskey."

Rick nodded. "Whiskey and sleeping pills are usually deadly."

Ryder set down his fork. "If those bombs go off, the ship will burn and sink. There are five thousand people aboard. A lot of 'em would die."

"Will the FBI go after me if the guy dies?" Jeff asked.

Ryder fingered the envelope. "The doc thinks it won't kill the pirate. I don't think the FBI would tell us not to do it. They want us to defuse the bombs, if we can. What other way is there to do it? We'd have to disarm, kill, or wound the guard by using a knife, which would be risky. A gunshot would attract the rest of the buccaneers. The sleeping pill plan is the safest for us and the pirate, too."

"Okay, I'll do it." Jeff held out his hand.

Ryder passed the envelope to Jeff. "Here."

Rick said, "Tell them about the rifles."

Ryder perked up. "Rifles?"

Jeff gulped. "When they carried in boxes of C-4 explosives, the pirates also brought in three long crates. I saw a pirate open a box and take out two rifles."

Ryder asked, "What were they? AKs?"

"No. They were heavier with big, fat wooden stocks. I saw a pirate put a clip of bullets into the top of a rifle at the back end."

Rick said, "From what Jeff observed, putting the clip into the rifle at the top, chances are they're eight-shot, semiautomatic M1 Garands, although other rifles load on the top with clips, too. The M1 has a fatter stock, though."

Ryder asked, "Aren't those World War II rifles?"

Rick said, "They could be." He took a deep breath. "Jeff and I could take a few of them out with us when the guard's asleep." He peered at Jeff. "You told me you saw them bring in boxes of ammo, too?"

"Yes. They opened a box of ammunition. Those were the bullets they put in the gun."

Ryder said, "We need to grab three rifles and enough ammo for the three of us." He turned to Layla. "I think you should lay low if shootin' starts."

"You need to be careful, too." She peered into his eyes. "Don't forget Angela's been calling you Daddy."

Rick hesitated and then addressed Ryder. "What if the bombs are set up so we can't disarm them? Then what?"

Ryder let out a breath. "We could use them M1 rifles. Kill enough pirates, and they could skedaddle." Ryder was silent for a moment. "Let's meet later today to learn if Jeff was able to plant the laced whiskey."

Rick said, "How about Jeff and I meet you at eleven

fifteen this morning in the Columbus Dining Room on Deck Six. It's at the stern above the engine room." He glanced at Jeff. "Okay, Jeff?"

"Yep."

Ryder nodded.

THIRTY-NINE

HAPPY-GO-LUCKY drug dealer Bert Holmgren felt anxious when he pressed the 1492 code on the elevator's keypad and then chose Deck Two, where the burly pirate waited for him near the shell door. The fog was thicker than it had been during the two previous mornings. Bert carried a bundle of cash, fifty grand, in a paper bag. In a separate bag, he'd put his remaining drugs, a bonus Bert hoped the big, unshaven pirate would like enough to dissuade him from changing his mind. If all went as Bert hoped, the pirate would look the other way while Bert put on scuba diving gear, dropped into the salt water with a diver propulsion vehicle, and headed for shore.

Earlier, Bert had noticed the fog layer was roughly twenty feet thick and hid the water's surface. In the distance, he had seen three coastal hilltops three miles away. There was little wind. He hoped the waves wouldn't be too large. But he reminded himself he'd be underwater most of the time while he headed for shore.

Bert scratched his left shoulder through his sweatshirt. He felt scared but giddy, too. He would soon evade the clutches of the DEA. He'd head for Mexico and, perchance, hook up with a cartel there. He'd tell the cartel he knew how to sell drugs to Americans. Many of them vacationed south of the US border.

The lift doors opened on Deck Two with a smooth, mechanical sound. Bert realized his brain had been on autopilot. He drew his fingers through his salt-and-pepper hair when he neared the port shell door. The large, muscular buccaneer whom Bert had planned to bribe sat on a deck chair near the entrance of a small room, where at least a dozen sets of scuba diving gear were neatly stacked. Bert wondered if the man would take his cash and then push him overboard in the fog. Bert would be reluctant to shout. Would he have the stamina to swim three miles to the shore with no wet suit and no diver propulsion vehicle? If he had to swim, it would be doubtful he'd reach shore alive, though he was an excellent swimmer. Hypothermia would set in. The fifty-six-degree ocean water would suck the heat from his body and immobilize him, and he'd drown.

Bert knew death would occur within one to six hours when the water was between fifty and sixty degrees. So, he'd worn a long-sleeved sweatshirt over his blue shirt, an extra pair of socks, and a second set of underwear, in case he was shoved overboard.

The pirate rose from his chair. He caught sight of the two ordinary brown paper bags Bert carried. "You got something for me?"

"Yes, sir." Bert felt jumpy when he handed the pirate the cash-stuffed bag. "Here's fifty thousand." He waited a few seconds and then handed the muscular man the second bag. "There's lots of M30 and Molly pills in here and naloxone nasal spray for fentanyl overdoses. You can use the drugs, sell 'em, or dump the whole lot overboard, if the feds attack."

"Thank you, brother." The pirate gazed at the bags in his hands and nodded. "We crooks gotta stick together. Look me up. My home base is in Mexico City. Ask around at the Bar del Charro for Mr. Matador. It's the name people know me by." Matador held out his hand.

Bert gripped it. "Thanks, I will. I'll be heading south. I got no future in the States."

"I'll fix you up with a job."

"I appreciate it, Mr. Matador."

"It's nothing." The big pirate pointed at the diving kits. "They're all the same. The small case has loose clothes which fit most men, cash, a burner phone, and gift cards. Suit up before somebody sees you."

Bert rushed into the side room and donned the scuba equipment. He grabbed a DPV and carried it to the shell door, which the pirate opened.

The thick fog offered no view of the horizon when Bert moved closer to the opening. The buccaneer guided the rope ladder down to the water and unrolled the black tarp hanging from above the door. The heavy black cloth extended outside the doorway and down to water level to conceal the open doorway.

Bert climbed down the ladder and eased into the water. The burly pirate smiled while he tied a rope to the DPV and lowered it to Bert, who then submerged.

In his wet suit, Bert felt free like a vagabond on a warm spring day. He switched on the battery-powered DPV. With both of his hands firmly grasping the DPV's handlebars, the unit began to pull him faster than four miles per hour toward shore. He relaxed like he was heading for heaven.

* * *

MAY 17, 9:30 AM

After Tony had returned to the bridge, he received a SAT phone call. "Cap, this is Tex. I found Mr. Matador dead near the port shell door."

"Shit. How'd he die?"

"He OD'd. He's blue-lookin', and his skin's clammy. He's got a container of naloxone nasal spray clutched in his hand. He wasn't quick enough to spray it into his nose holes, or he'd still be with us."

"I'll be there in five minutes." Tony disconnected his phone. He began to add up the men he'd lost. One guy was missing and likely overboard. Another had fallen into the water drunk; four had swum for shore, and Mr. Matador was dead, likely killed by a bad pill laced with fentanyl. Seven guys gone. He'd started with twenty-eight men, including himself and Pilot, a respected old man—but not a fighter anymore. Wait, there also was his friend, Gino, who had sailed his narco sub to meet the *Sea Trek*.

Tony began to worry. Did he have enough men to hold the cruise ship for fifteen hours until 11:59 PM?

When Tony neared the port shell door, he saw Tex standing by Mr. Matador's body. It was sprawled on the deck near the dead man's folding chair. There was a brown paper bag next to him, and his hand held a container of naloxone in a death grip. "What's in the bag, Tex?"

"A bunch of pills—ecstasy, oxycodone, and M30s. Plus, there are three or four naloxone nasal sprays."

Tony stared at Mr. Matador's body. "Find any cash?"

Tex appeared nervous to Tony. "No, Cap." Tex shrugged. "I didn't check his pockets."

Tony suspected Mr. Matador had been selling drugs to the passengers, crew, and even to fellow buccaneers. But where was his money? Tex may have snatched it, or else Matador had stashed it. It was chicken feed compared to the ransom they'd split up, though. "I think he was selling drugs, Tex. What do you think?"

"I agree."

Tony scratched his head. "He didn't bring the drugs with him. He had to have gotten them from somebody. I'd say the doc at the med center had the best opportunity to smuggle drugs on board. Matador could've strong-armed him and got the doc's stash. The oxycodone must be counterfeit, contaminated with fentanyl. Matador's sure blue in the face. Poor bastard."

"Yeah, but like you said before, one less guy means the rest of us get a bigger split of the money."

Tony pulled Mr. Matador's chair away from the body

and sat. "Bring the med center doctor here to me. Also, have the guys search the med center to see what drugs are there."

"Yes, Cap."

* * *

MAY 17, 9:45 AM

The med center physician was caught off guard when Tex strolled into the examination room. The doctor was listening to the heart of an elderly man suffering chest pains.

"Doc, yer comin' with me," Tex said. He grabbed the physician's stethoscope from his hands and tossed it in a chair. The doctor felt fear course through his body but kept a stiff upper lip.

The obese patient gasped and began to pant.

The doctor said, "Let me finish the examination."

"No way, Doc." Tex grabbed the physician by the front of his blue scrubs and pushed him toward the door. Tex peered back at two other buccaneers. "Y'all search the place and see if you can find illegal drugs like Mollies and M30s. If you do, bring 'em to Cap and me at the port shell door. Also, write us a list of the legal drugs the doc's got here."

The two pirates began opening cabinets.

The doctor felt disgust and anger when he saw the two ruffians knock down equipment and toss items from the cabinets. Tex then pushed him through the med center doorway.

Within four minutes, Tex was shoving the doctor along a passageway toward a man's body lying on the deck.

Tony sat on a chair near the corpse. "You're quick, Tex." Tony turned his attention to the doctor. "See this man? He died from an overdose, counterfeit oxycodone with fentanyl in it."

"I'll check to make sure he's passed."

Tony shook his head. "The man's as dead as fresh road-kill." Tony turned to Tex. "Did the guys find illegal drugs in the med center?"

"I don't know, Cap. They started checkin' when we left."

Tony turned his gaze toward the doctor. "I believe you've been supplying pills, including ecstasy and M30s, to drug pushers on board this ship. You're the one person who can bring drugs aboard."

The physician shook his head. "I don't have illegal drugs. But we do have a new painkiller we've begun to use. It's not a narcotic and isn't addictive. Those new pills have almost the same shape, markings, and color of M30s, though."

"You're lying, Doc," Tony said. He struck the arm of his deck chair with his fist. "Let's see what my men come across in the med center. I bet they'll find a bunch of illegal shit. I think you work on this boat so you can peddle drugs."

The doctor shook with rage but kept quiet.

A pirate with a beer belly approached. "Cap, we found some funny-looking pills in the med center." The buccaneer held up a bottle of pills and shook them. They look like M30s."

Tony grabbed the bottle, unscrewed its cap, and poured two pills onto his palm. "These appear to be M30s." He stared at the doctor and then at Tex. "Lock him in the brig."

Tony turned to the second pirate. "You, empty Matador's pockets, then open the shell door and dump his body into the water."

FORTY

AN IDEA HIT Ryder like a lightning bolt while he and Layla walked out of the Galileo Dining Room on Deck Seven after their leisurely breakfast. They could arm themselves with blackjacks. Nobody would suspect them of carrying weapons, if he used the right materials to make them.

Ryder turned to Layla. "Let's go to the casino. It's on Deck Six."

"You want to gamble?"

"Nope. I'm gonna make blackjacks for us."

"What?"

"A blackjack's a weapon you kin hit a person with. It can be deadly."

"Why are we heading to the casino?"

"I need four rolls of quarters." He began to walk toward the elevator lobby at midship. "To make a blackjack, you can stuff two rolls of quarters into a stocking or a handkerchief and knot it so it'll keep the quarters in one end."

Passengers had begun to gather near the lift's doors. Ryder leaned closer to Layla and whispered, "If you hit somebody on the back of the head with the blackjack, you can knock 'em out. If you do, and nobody's around, untie the sock's knot and put the quarters back in your fanny pack."

Layla sighed. "I hope I don't have to do it."

"It's better than bein' taken advantage of by another pirate."

Layla stared at Ryder. "We'll have to go back to the cabin to get a sock for me."

Ryder grabbed his cotton handkerchief from his back pocket. "I'll be usin' this right away, if need be."

* * *

RYDER AND LAYLA waited in the elevator lobby closest to the bow of the ship near the casino on Deck Six. They were headed to their cabin on Deck Nine. There Layla could get a cotton sock for her blackjack, and Ryder planned to phone Rita. He wished to update her about his scheme to use sleeping pills and whiskey to put the engine room guard to sleep so Rick could examine the C-4 explosives.

Ryder's left leg throbbed again. He leaned on his cane. Peering at his watch, he noticed the time was 10:10 AM. He was due to take his second pain pill in an hour. If his discomfort were to rapidly increase, he reckoned he'd take a pill early.

The elevator was slow to arrive, and Ryder studied the blue herringbone pattern on the lobby's carpet. He pondered whether or not the FBI would have qualms about drugging a buccaneer.

The elevator doors slid open.

Tony stood next to Tex in the elevator car. Tony stared at Layla and then at Ryder when they boarded the lift. "Mr. Ryder, I assume the doctor at the med center put on your cast. Correct?"

"Yep."

"Are you hurting?"

"Some."

Tony nodded. "Did the doc give you pain pills?"

For three microseconds, Ryder wondered how to answer.

He recalled he'd told Tony earlier about his medication for pain. While Ryder prepared to answer, he fingered the knotted end of his handkerchief, which held two rolls of quarters—his improvised blackjack. Ryder considered whether or not he should clobber Tony. But Tex stood next to him, and he was resting his right hand on the Ka-Bar combat knife in its scabbard. Ryder's shinbone injury shot a wave of pain up his left leg. Despite his effort not to show any weakness, he winced.

Tony's two Glock-17s were within easy reach of the pirate.

Ryder heard himself say, "Yeah, the doc gave me a new kinda nonnarcotic pain pill. Why?"

"Because we locked up the doctor. We think he's been dealing drugs." Tony's stare seemed to pierce Ryder's head. "One of my men died of an overdose. We think he took counterfeit M30s laced with fentanyl. The one person who could bring drugs onto this vessel without being suspected is the ship's physician. We tossed the med center and examined all the meds he had there." Tony held out his hand. "Let me see your pills."

Ryder shrugged. He felt in his hip pocket below the blackjack and pulled out his small bottle of pain pills.

Tony grabbed the container, uncapped it, and shook three pills into his palm. "These are similar to the ones we found on the body of our dead man." Tony returned the pills to the bottle and twisted its cap back on. "I'm going to keep these, Ryder. If you took any, you've been lucky. A contaminated one could have enough fentanyl in it to kill you."

Ryder wrinkled his brow. "I think this batch is okay. I took one, and it worked fine." He squinted. "Since the bad ones are counterfeit, don't they make 'em to appear exactly the same as the genuine ones?"

Tony rested his hand on the grip of one of his pistols. Ryder noticed the weapon hung loose in its holster. "Ryder, I'm doing you a favor. You're in the same business I am, though in another specialty." He smiled. "You can live through pain, but fentanyl can kill you fast. I'm going to throw this bottle overboard."

Ryder nodded. The lift stopped on Deck Nine. "Thanks for lookin' out for me."

Tony winked. "No problem." He leered at Layla as she and Ryder exited the elevator.

* * *

MAY 17, 10:17 AM

Ryder sat at his cabin's desk. After Layla retrieved Ryder's satellite phone from the vent near the ceiling, he tapped out Rita's FBI phone number. He knew the entire upper echelon of the FBI Hostage Rescue Team—HRT—would likely be patched into his call.

"Luke, how are you?" Rita sounded alert.

"I have a lot to report." He gathered his thoughts. "At three this mornin', I visited the doc at the med center to get pain meds, and he gave me a new kind which works great."

"I'm glad it helps," Rita said.

Ryder purposely didn't reveal the break in his shinbone had worsened, and the physician had put a new cast on his left lower leg. Nor did he say Tony had confiscated his pain pills. Ryder also neglected to mention his leg was throbbing again, and his pain was severe.

Ryder dug a thumbnail into his palm to distract himself from the discomfort in his leg and continued. "I got the doc to help us."

"You admitted you're helping the FBI?"

"Yep. He's not gonna blab to the buccaneers."

Rita huffed. "He better not."

"The doc helped me with an idea I got, which would make it possible for us to examine or defuse the bombs." Ryder told Rita how he had obtained crushed sleeping pills, and he outlined his plan to drug the engine room guard to put him to sleep.

Rita said, "You know whiskey and sleeping pills kill a lot

of people every year." Rita hesitated. "I'm not sure we can permit you to proceed with your plan."

"What? Y'all wanted me to figure out a way to defuse the bombs. There are five thousand passengers and crew who could die if those son-of-a-bitchin' pirates blow holes in this ship, burn it, and sink it. Come on."

Rita sighed. "Our FBI teams will debate it, and we'll let you know what we decide."

Ryder wondered if he should admit having given the sleeping pill powder to Jeff. He calmed himself. "Goin' on to another subject, Layla and I found more than twenty small blue-tipped rockets near the port shell door on Deck Two."

Rita told him a blue-tipped projectile had been used to shoot down the news helicopter.

Ryder continued, "During breakfast with Rick Casa, we met Jeff Brooks, his friend who works in the engine room. Jeff said he saw a man the pirates call Tokyo Joe set up four clusters of C-4 bombs. From what Rick and Jeff said, the bomber is an expert, and it'll be hard, if not impossible, for one of us to disarm the explosives." Ryder went on to tell Rita the rest of what Jeff had reported. Ryder explained Jeff didn't want to try to defuse the bombs, but Rick said he'd try if he could get into the engine room unseen by the pirates. "Then I brought up my plan to use sleepin' pills and whiskey to put the guard outta commission."

The sound of Rita's rapid breathing made Ryder think she was exasperated. Even so, he decided, because his plan to drug the engine guard was already underway, to tell her everything. "I gave the envelope of sleepin' pill powder to Jeff. He agreed to pour it into a bottle of booze he has in his cabin. I'm guessin' he's already put the spiked bottle near the guard."

Rita took a deep breath. "I'm giving you a direct order. Stop Jeff."

"There ain't any other chance to get to those bombs."

Rita was breathing hard. "The ship's within US waters. The FBI has jurisdiction. US laws apply. If we give an unwilling person drugs, and we don't have a warrant to do so, it's a constitutional violation. Just a trained medical professional can administer drugs without a warrant."

"The doc can't do it cuz Franco locked him up," Ryder said, and then he told Rita how a pirate had died of a probable fentanyl overdose.

"Jesus Christ," Rita mumbled.

Ryder took a breath. "Jeff told us when he first saw the pirates bring the C-4 into the engine room, they also carried in boxes of rifles. If the guard's asleep, we could grab a few of them and ammo when we're checkin' out the bombs."

Ryder heard static on the line. A deep male voice boomed through the receiver of Ryder's phone. "Mr. Ryder, this is Duke Duncan. I am the agent in charge of the HRT, and I am in command of this operation. I order you to drop everything, contact Mr. Brooks, and retrieve the spiked whiskey at once." Duke sounded irate. "If you fail, and somebody dies because you okayed giving poison to an unsuspecting person, I'll have your head. We'll find a way to charge you. Even if we can't, your law enforcement career will be over. Get moving, sir."

"Like hell I will. I'm not gonna stand by and let thousands of people die because of shit like this."

"You are insubordinate, Mr. Ryder."

"I'd prefer to take action to save this ship instead of covering my ass like the police chief in Parsons, Pennsylvania, did last year. You remember how twenty-five school children died in their classroom cuz a chief of police was listenin' to bureaucrats?"

"Ryder, if it were up to me, we would've rappelled to the deck right after those bastards took the ship. I was overruled."

"So, yer not in charge." Ryder scoffed.

"You have one last chance, Ryder. Stop Jeff Brooks, and get the doctored whiskey back."

"You can't order me to do a damn thing."

"Like hell I can't."

"You can't order me around cuz I quit."

Rita cleared her throat. When she spoke, her voice was an octave higher. "Gentlemen, this is not the time to argue."

Duke said, "Miss Reynolds. I'm your superior. I will not be chided by a subordinate."

Ryder felt his heart pounding. "I'm gonna disconnect. I ain't workin' for you, but I'll pass on info when I get it. Bye."

Layla's face showed concern. "What happened?"

"I quit. I don't want to work for the FBI. I don't want to see five thousand people die." He handed the satellite phone to Layla. "Please put this back in the vent." His leg pain was worse, and his head was pounding.

Layla put two suitcases on the bed, stepped up on them, removed the vent cover, and began to lower the phone downward.

Ryder heard the device tumble down into the vent.

Layla gasped. "It fell. The sharp sheet metal must've cut the floss."

Ryder shook his head. "We gotta find Rick and get the M1 rifles. We're on our own now."

FORTY-ONE

AFTER BREAKFAST, Jeff had gone to his cabin on Deck Two to take a nap because he hadn't slept well. He'd set his alarm clock for 10:30 AM. After he awoke, he found his open fifth of whiskey and poured the sleeping pill powder into it. When he shook the bottle, he hoped the mixture would put the pirate to sleep forever.

Jeff felt jumpy, and his pale body was cold. After taking three deep breaths, he stuffed the bottle into a lunch bag. Then he put on his light jacket so he could conceal the spiked liquor underneath his windbreaker. Finally, he slipped his sound-suppression headset around his neck. Because the ship's engines were so loud, the engine room crewmen had to wear ear protection to avoid permanent damage to their hearing.

Both hope and dread coursed through Jeff's body as he approached the engine room. One moment his mind told him not to drug the buccaneer guard because if the man realized what was happening, he'd execute Jeff on the spot. The next moment, Jeff felt a sense of adventure, though he was still aware of the danger he would be in. But at last, he plucked up his courage because Rick, Ryder, and Layla were all counting on him to disable the guard.

There was a problem. He worked the second shift, and the first shift crew was still at work in the engine room. The guys would question why he'd shown up. Though his coworkers would be surprised to see him there early, especially after he was marked down for sick leave for the next shift, he'd have to tell them about the bottle of spiked whiskey anyway. They had to be warned not to touch it. It could kill them. Would any of them squeal to the pirates? He doubted it. They were all going to die if the bombs exploded. They'd welcome anyone who could defuse the explosives.

While Jeff power walked along the corridor toward the engine room entrance, his brain was still busy. He'd tell the guys that if they saw the guard asleep or passed out, hopefully dead, to pour the remaining whiskey down a drain and leave the bottle near the sleeping buccaneer. If the man died, it would appear excessive drinking had killed him.

How would Jeff get the pirate to find the bottle? The moment Jeff neared the engine room doorway, an answer came to him. Keeping his lips closed, he'd tip the bottle against them while the buccaneer watched. If Jeff kept the bottle in the paper bag while he pretended to drink, he'd appear to be secretly boozing on the job.

After slipping his headset over his ears and entering the engine room, Jeff moved behind storage shelves near the pirate. The brute sat on a chair with his AK-47 rifle across his knees. Jeff readied himself, building up his nerve. He noticed a wrench sitting on a shelf. Perfect. He tipped his head back, pretended to drink, and knocked the wrench down. It fell close enough to the buccaneer, so it grabbed his attention, despite the noise of the ship's engines.

The pirate, a skinny guy with a wart on his chin, rose and moved toward the shelves. He yelled over the engine noise, "What you got there, son?"

Jeff purposely slurred, yelling, "Nothing."

"Hand it over!"

Jeff passed the bottle, wrapped in the brown bag, to the ruffian.

The bully glanced at Jeff, who acted unsteady on his feet.

"Don't tell my boss, please," Jeff shouted, again slurring.

The thug cocked his head and bellowed, "Go sleep it off in a corner someplace, so your foreman don't get wind of your whiskey breath."

Jeff slumped on the floor behind the shelves and feigned nodding off. From his vantage point, he'd have a great view of the pirate through the open shelves.

The buccaneer sat back in his chair, set his rifle against the wall, and sealed his lips around the mouth of the bottle.

Jeff saw the pirate tip the bottle and sip the spiked alcohol. A short time later, his eyelids drooped, and his chin fell against his chest. Within thirty seconds, he began to snore, his arms hanging down at his sides.

Jeff stood, moved promptly to the pirate, and took the bottle from the man's grasp. In moments, Jeff went to a sink and poured the rest of the liquor down the drain. Then he placed the open bottle on the deck next to the slumbering man.

The other three engine room crewmen were nowhere to be seen, so Jeff rolled a large trash barrel toward the spare parts boxes. He pulled out a wooden box containing M1 rifles and removed three weapons and two steel ammunition boxes. He emptied trash from the barrel and placed the forty-four-inch-long weapons and the ammo-filled boxes inside the container. To hide the M1s, he replaced trash on top of the rifles and added dirty rags.

He was pleased. Nobody but the guard had seen him. He grabbed a small toolbox, which he carried in one hand while he pushed the barrel out of the engine room. He planned to roll it to Rick's cabin. If anyone asked, he was going to make repairs in the cabin.

FORTY-TWO

IT WAS 10:55 AM when Ryder saw Rick enter the Columbus Dining Room. He discreetly nodded at Ryder and Layla and then picked a sandwich from one of the food stations. Ryder thought Rick should eat. The man was as skinny as a walking skeleton. Did he have cancer, *anorexia nervosa*, or TB?

Rick sat across from Ryder next to the window.

Ryder studied the man for a second and asked, "You heard from Jeff yet?"

"No." The ship was rocking on the waves. Rick peered out the window. "I can't see the water under this fog, but it must be rough out there."

Ryder wondered if the weather would change for the worse. If a storm were to develop, would the Hostage Rescue Team rappel agents from helicopters to the *Sea Trek's* deck? Ryder supposed it would depend on the severity of the storm, if one came. Would a squall stop the pirates from leaving the vessel even if they'd gotten their ransom payment? Ryder wished to have an M1 rifle and plenty of clips of ammo in case the buccaneers failed to leave and got into a firefight with the authorities.

Ryder said, "I bet Jeff is sitting in the engine room waitin' for the guard to fall asleep."

Rick nodded. "Let's keep our fingers crossed." He smiled. "Most of these pirates drink to excess, take drugs, or both."

The three sat quietly, eating and waiting for Jeff. Ryder checked his watch. It read 11:05 AM.

Rick cocked his head toward the dining room's entryway. "There's Jeff."

Jeff grabbed a hamburger and fries, approached, and sat at Rick's side. "The guard took the whiskey from me. In a few minutes, he was asleep, snoring like an old hound dog."

Ryder leaned forward. "What about the M1s?"

"I put three into a trash barrel with plenty of ammo and wheeled it out. I went into your cabin, Colonel, and hid them under your bed. I put a do not disturb sign on the door. Plus, I told Jennifer, your stewardess, not to go in there because you've got the flu."

"Excellent." Rick set his coffee cup next to his empty plate. "What about your fellow workers?"

"They didn't see me." Jeff bit his lip. "I've been thinking. If Tokyo Joe set up the bombs the same way he did when he blew up the high-rise in Japan, we shouldn't even think about defusing them. The three Japanese bomb squad guys who died trying to disable them were experts, according to a news story I read."

"I should examine them anyway," Rick said. He zeroed in on Jeff's eyes. "Do you have a digital still camera?"

"Yes. The pirates didn't ask for cameras. We can get it from my cabin on the way to the engine room. I need to pick up my noise-suppression headset and get earplugs for y'all, too."

Ryder raised his palm. "I shoulda told you. My SAT phone fell down into the vent. We have no way to contact the FBI." He felt the ship rocking on the waves more than it had before. "Me, you, and Jeff should get to the engine room fast. Colonel, takin' pics could help. If we're lucky, somebody else has a satellite phone. Layla, it's best if you go in the colonel's cabin and wait." He touched her shoulder. "Remember his door code?"

"Yes, darling. Stay strong."

FORTY-THREE

SUPPORTED BY HIS CANE, Ryder followed Rick and Jeff toward the engine room. Noise-suppression headgear hung from Jeff's neck. He'd given Ryder and Rick clear capsules the size of plastic pill containers. Each held two expandable foam earplugs.

When the men came closer to the engine room, Ryder could hear the loud noise of the ship's massive machinery.

Thirty feet from the engine room entrance, Ryder said, "Jeff should go in first. He can check on the guard and tell the engine room crew what's goin' on."

Jeff nodded. "Be out soon." He pulled his headset up and over his ears.

When Jeff entered the engine room, Rick yelled, "Let's get in and out fast. No telling when somebody will come to check on the guard."

"Yep," Ryder said. "They'll come to get the guard if Tony decides to abandon ship early."

Ryder recalled seeing a spot where the passageways leading to the engine room crossed. From there, a lookout could see a long way and run back to warn them if a buccaneer approached. There were many alternate paths they could take to leave the engine room and not be seen.

Jeff stepped out of the engine room and waved Ryder and Rick forward.

Ryder leaned close to Jeff. "Could you stand guard where this passageway crosses the main one?"

"Sure." Jeff reached into his trousers pocket and pulled out a small, cheap digital camera. He gave it to Rick before leaving.

Ryder and Rick put in their earplugs. When Ryder entered the engine room, he saw, but couldn't hear, the snoring pirate guard.

Rick began to examine the C-4 putty stuck on the bulkheads and the overhead. When he went from spot to spot, he snapped photos. Finally, he took pictures of the hand grenade booby trap. He caught Ryder's attention and pointed at the four bomb clusters and shook his head to indicate it was useless to attempt to disarm them.

Within four minutes, Jeff rushed back into the engine room and frantically motioned Ryder and Rick to exit the room.

Ryder hustled even though his leg throbbed. He reckoned if he put most of his weight on his cane when he stepped forward with his left leg, he'd be okay.

Jeff led Ryder and Rick to a lesser-used side passageway. He removed his ear protection. Ryder and Rick did the same.

Jeff spoke quietly. "A pirate's heading for the engine room."

FORTY-FOUR

PIRATE QUARTERMASTER WAYLEN DEVOR walked along Deck Two's main passage toward the engine room at the stern of the ship. He could hear the roar of the engines, and he felt the temperature rise. He reached in his pocket for a pack of cigarettes, withdrew two cigs, and twisted the filters off them. He dropped the rest of the mauled smokes on the deck.

Close to the engine room entrance, Waylen stuck the filters into his ear canals to block the roar of the massive machinery which propelled the *Sea Trek*. He hoped his man with the wart on his chin who was guarding the C-4 bombs was more reliable than the big guy who'd been watching over the diving equipment near the shell door. The burly man had OD'd on a fentanyl-laced counterfeit pill, and now his body was at the bottom of the sea, decomposing.

Waylen entered the engine room. He instantly saw the guard with the wart slumped forward on a chair near the bombs. His chest was moving up and down while the sound of his snoring was overridden by the roar of the engines. Waylen moved closer to the slumbering man and saw an empty whiskey bottle on the deck.

"God damn it," Waylen mumbled. He shook the man's shoulder, but he didn't wake. He merely fell back into his original sleeping position.

His mouth open, the man wheezed.

Waylen could smell whiskey on the man's breath. Cap will go ballistic when he hears about a second man screwing up on guard duty, he thought. The drunkard was useless. Waylen lamented the fact he'd chosen both of the unreliable men. If he ever needed to select men for another gig, he would employ someone else to do the hiring.

Waylen sighed. He stepped out of the engine room and into the passageway. He moved toward the port shell door at midship. He figured he could send the man guarding the scuba equipment to relieve the drunk in the engine room. From there, he could open the shell door to get a signal and phone Tony, who was on the bridge. Waylen would watch the diving gear until a replacement guard could be found for it.

When Waylen neared the shell door, he saw Jacob was alert, sitting near the scuba kits. It was a relief. The men had made fun of Jacob because he didn't smoke, drink, or do drugs. His addiction was gambling. "Jacob, I need you to go to the engine room. The wart-faced shit there is dead drunk and asleep. I can't wake him up."

Jacob stood.

Waylen pulled out his pack of cigarettes and pulled out two butts. "Wait." He ripped the filters off and handed them to Jake. "Stuff these in your ears. It's friggin' noisy in there."

When Waylen pushed the button to power open the hydraulic shell door, cool air rushed across his face. The misty fog was refreshing. He hadn't realized how hot he'd been in the engine room. Waylen knew the brisk breeze would help revitalize him, especially since his next task was to call the mercurial Tony.

FORTY-FIVE

AFTER EVADING the pirate who had headed for the engine room, Ryder, Rick, and Jeff had split up to avoid arousing suspicion on their way to Rick's cabin. Ryder said, "Colonel, why don't you go first? I'm slow 'cuz of my leg. And Jeff's gotta be careful because he normally wouldn't spend time near yer cabin."

Rick said, "Sure." He left.

Ryder turned to Jeff. "I'm wonderin' if you've ever used firearms."

"Yes, sir. I grew up on a farm." He shifted his gaze aside for a second. "I don't think I'd have a problem shooting the M1. The eight-shot clip loads on the top."

Ryder nodded. He thought about his next words. "The colonel's been in combat. I've had to deal with armed men. You're a young man. There's no need to put yourself in harm's way."

"No worries, Officer Ryder. If pirates blow up the ship, we could die. It's best we confront them, if need be."

"Yer right, Jeff. But we'll hold off the best we can 'til the FBI, the SEALs, or the Coast Guard guys arrive. Okay?"

"Yes, sir. I better go." Jeff departed.

Three minutes later, Ryder limped toward the elevator at midship to catch a ride up to Deck Eight, where Rick's cabin was. Since Ryder had no way to communicate with the FBI, he'd get no warning before the authorities assaulted the ship. The four of them—he, Layla, Rick, and Jeff—would have to watch the horizon and the water around the ship for an assault force. They could take turns as lookouts from the top decks.

If there were an FBI attack, somebody needed to take out the engine room guard. He, or another pirate, would be able to use the plunger and wires to set off the explosives if they couldn't be ignited remotely via a radio signal. Jeff knew every nook and cranny of the engine room and was the ideal person to send there. Would he be prepared to die in an explosion?

Ryder tapped on Rick's cabin door. Rick opened it. Ryder limped in. "I got ideas on how we could proceed. Let's compare notes."

Rick smiled. "I've been thinking of options, too," he said.

* * *

MAY 17, 11:50 AM

Waylen was near the open shell door when he chose Tony's number. The satellite phone on the other end of the call rang. Waylen felt sick to his stomach. It was not because of the increasingly rough sea.

Tony asked, "What have you got?"

Waylen bit his lip and then said, "I found the skinny shit who has the big wart on his chin so drunk in the engine room I couldn't wake him. There was an empty bottle on the deck next to him."

Tony's hard breathing sounded like a steam engine to Waylen. "We need to do a better job of vetting potential employees if we ever do another job like this one. They're deserting, overdosing and dying, getting drunk on the job—what's next?"

Waylen was silent for two seconds, his thoughts zipping across his brain while he tried to think of an answer. "Cap, we gotta take it one step at a time 'til we reach our objective, and then evaluate what happened after we're done. We'll improve our procedures in the future."

"If we don't, we could die." Tony hissed when he let his breath out. "What have you done about the engine room?"

"I sent Jacob to guard it," Waylen said. He studied the diving equipment. "I'll stay with the scuba gear until you send another guy down here to the shell door area."

"I'll send the real short guy, Bob." Tony didn't say anything for a second. "Who's Jacob?"

"The gambler who doesn't smoke, drink, or do drugs. At least there are no roulette tables or slot machines down in the engine room."

Tony sighed. "Jacob's a fine choice. Next time, let's hire a bunch of monks or schoolteachers." Tony disconnected.

* * *

MAY 17, 11:55 AM

The four allies sat in Rick's cabin, talking. Ryder and Layla sat on the bed, Jeff on the carpet, and Rick eased back on his desk chair. Ryder had outlined his thoughts of how the four of them could operate until the FBI Hostage Rescue Team or the Navy SEALs assaulted the ship. Ryder predicted an attack could occur anytime from the present until dawn the next day, Saturday. But he reckoned it would happen after dark in the early morning hours when most passengers would be asleep, and the pirates would be sleep-deprived.

Ryder asked, "What do y'all think of us goin' up to the top deck to watch for the FBI assault?"

Rick rested his arm on the top of his desktop. "Fine idea. We can see three hundred sixty degrees around from there."

Lying on the carpet, Jeff stretched. "Speedboats would be hidden by the fog."

"We'll be able to hear 'em," Ryder said.

"If I were attacking by boat," Jeff said, "I'd use a quiet electric motor or old-fashioned oars."

Rick smiled. "I like how you think outside the box, Jeff." Rick glanced at Ryder and Layla. "Jeff was in my unit during the Congo Conflict. He's an expert shot and a hell of a soldier."

Jeff blushed.

Ryder knew it wasn't always physical strength which made a man formidable, but his attitude and endurance. "Thanks for your service, Jeff," Ryder said. Then he gazed at Rick. "Because I can't call the FBI anymore to give them info, I figger my new role is to back up our rescuers. We could pick off pirates, if we get a chance."

Abruptly, Rick stood and studied his colleagues for four long seconds. His voice broke. "I'm dying of pancreatic cancer. I have six months to live at best. God damn it, I'm going to send a bunch of those friggin' pirates to hell. Especially that pig, Tony." Rick sat down on his chair and bowed his head.

"I'm all in," Jeff said. "The pirates don't expect anyone on board to have firearms. We have the element of surprise."

Ryder felt sympathy and admiration for Rick. Ryder rubbed his stubble. "How about we check out the M1s, split up the ammo, and set up a watch schedule?"

"Okay," said Rick.

"I'll stay in the engine room while you two do lookout duty," Jeff said. "I can go to the shell door every so often to see if pirates are putting on scuba gear."

Ryder peered into Jeff's eyes. "If all of them pirates run to the port shell door, yer gonna have your hands full."

Rick said, "I agree. But somebody has to deal with the engine room guard if the FBI assaults."

Layla raised her hand. "What can I do?"

"Stay here and hold down the fort," Ryder said. "If there's an explosion, head for the lifeboats."

Layla huffed. "I could help Jeff by the shell door." She stared at Ryder's eyes. "Remember the closet we hid in along the passageway near the shell door?"

Ryder nodded. "Yep."

Jeff's face colored.

"I'll hide there," Layla said. "If I see pirates putting on diving gear, I could slip away and tell you guys."

Ryder shook his head sideways.

"You're not going to stop me," she said. "The pirates wouldn't pay me any mind." She inhaled. "I'll take the knife we got off the first pirate. I could have the Glock, too. You guys have rifles…"

Ryder sighed. "You'd be better off without weapons if a pirate catches you."

"I have the blackjack you made."

Ryder bit his lip. "Let's think about it. We've got hours before the deadline. You don't have to rush out there."

Layla shrugged and inhaled. "Okay if I take first watch? It's daylight. The pirates won't notice me like they'd notice a man scanning the horizon."

Ryder nodded. "Is it okay with you guys if Layla takes a shift 'til five this afternoon?" He peered at both Rick's and Jeff's faces.

They both indicated yes.

Layla left for the elevator.

"She's a brave lady," Rick said.

Ryder smiled. "Layla's more street-smart than an alley cat."

Jeff pulled the M1s and ammunition boxes from under the bed.

Rick said, "Luke, okay if you take a watch starting at five? I could join you on the top deck after sunset."

"Yep," Ryder said.

Jeff stood. "I'll stay in the engine room unless the FBI attacks, and if they do, I'll take out the guard. I'm just gonna take the Ka-Bar knife because it'd be hard to sneak an M1 back into the room. I'll get another M1 and ammo from the wooden box there if I need it."

Rick took a step toward Ryder and glanced at him. "The pirates have kept the lights off across the ship after dark. When it gets dark, we should meet back here, grab and conceal our M1s, and take them to our positions on the top deck."

Jeff set an M1 on the floor next to him. "I know where the stewards keep uniforms and laundry carts. You two could wear stewards' uniforms. I'll get one for Layla, too. The pirates won't pay attention to stewards pushing carts, even at two in the morning. You can put the rifles and ammo in the carts under dirty sheets."

"That'll work," Ryder said.

"The white stewards' uniforms will keep the FBI from shooting at us, too," Rick said. He took a moment to compose his thoughts.

He caught sight of Ryder's eyes. "Since you're not quick because of your leg, you could take the lift up to the top deck and stay at midship near the pool. You'll have a clear shot toward the bridge and the bow. I'll find a place near the jogging track where I can cover the helipad."

"I agree," Ryder said.

Ryder thought about what Rick had proposed. When it got dark, there would be shadows where Rick and he could hole up, though the brilliant white stewards' clothing could make them visible in the moonlight.

Layla would be safe in the janitor's closet by the shell door. She could claim she was getting cleaning supplies if a pirate found her. Ryder zeroed in on Jeff's eyes. "I can see why the colonel thinks highly of you. It's a great idea to get those uniforms and carts."

Jeff stood. "I'll get three uniforms and a cart to start out with."

All of a sudden, Ryder remembered he and Layla had passwords the FBI had assigned to them. "We still could be mistaken for pirates if we're toting M1s. The FBI gave me and Layla passwords, Miss Bear for Layla and Mr. Bear for me. Shout, 'Mr. Bear,' if a fed's comin' at you."

"Thanks," Rick said.

Jeff departed.

Ryder felt ready even if his leg was throbbing, but he was

concerned about Layla. He wished she would've stayed put in Rick's cabin.

* * *

MAY 17, 3:20 PM

Layla had been sitting in a folding beach chair overlooking the swimming pool on the top deck for roughly three hours. The air smelled fresh, better than the smog she'd endured in Louisville when she was a child and later when she'd been an escort and young mother. There was a slight smell of fish. She decided the sea had a distinct aroma, the smell of something powerful and wild. The ship rocked, and she noted it continued to sail south, but at a snail's pace.

From her vantage point, she could see all the way around her. Though the fog formed a blanket of thick mist at least twenty feet thick, California's hills on the shore, three miles away, were visible through the thin haze above the fog.

There was a chilly breeze, but it wasn't too cold. She wore Rick's gray sweatshirt. She'd removed her blackjack from her fanny pack and put it in the hip pocket of her jeans before she'd left Rick's cabin.

She tried not to be obvious when she turned her head every so often to survey the horizon. But no one noticed her.

Though the temperature was in the mid-fifties, the sun warmed her skin. Like Ryder, she hadn't slept enough in the last two days. Though she fought to keep focused, at times, her eyelids slipped downward. She relaxed in the darkness that her closed eyelids created and fell asleep. She may have dozed for nearly an hour, when something disturbed her slumber.

"Darlin', you lonely?" The gravelly bass voice of a swarthy pirate woke her.

"Huh?"

The full face of the unshaven, stocky buccaneer almost made her pee in her knickers. She sat up. "My husband's waiting for me." She hoped this wouldn't be a repeat of the first encounter she'd had with a pirate. "I have to leave." She stood.

The man grabbed at her with his meaty hand. "Hold on, honey. How about a kiss before you go?"

Layla reached under the sweatshirt and grabbed the end of the knotted stocking, which held eighty quarters.

The man tightened his grip on her left arm.

"Stop it."

"You're coming with me, darling." The pirate began to drag her toward the men's changing room, fifteen feet away.

"Hey, what do you think you're doing?"

"I'm gonna have me a little lovin'." The pirate pushed her into the changing room and began to close the door behind them.

When he glanced at the door, Layla swung her blackjack hard and struck the big man on the back of his head. He fell like a brick, out cold.

Layla stumbled backward. The man didn't move. She saw a hook on the wall where a sign hung. It read, "Out of service." She took it, pushed the door open, and hung the placard on the doorknob. Then she dragged a heavy, steel deck chair toward the changing room and braced the heavy piece of outdoor furniture under the doorknob.

She checked her watch. It read 4:45 PM. She started back for Rick's cabin on Deck Eight.

FORTY-SIX

TONY SAT ON THE BRIDGE, his eyes aimed at California's coastal hills, which were visible above the blanket of fog. He picked up his satellite phone and chose the private number for Heather's billionaire father.

"Howard Falcon here."

"This is Tony. You told me during our last conversation the hundred and fifty mil would be sent via my instructions. My partners say they have yet to receive it."

Howard took three deep breaths. "I did line up the money in cyber cash. My people attempted to transfer it, but the transaction failed. The fault is not on my end. I'm told your digital pathway is blocked."

"I'll check into it, and I'll get back to you shortly with new instructions if need be."

"You better figure this out because the money's there." Howard stopped talking for a moment. "Once the transfer is verified, I want Heather put on a lifeboat at once with two *Sea Trek* crewmen."

"I'm a man of my word, Howard." Tony disconnected.

* * *

MAY 17, 4:50 PM

Although Layla had the keypad code for Rick's cabin door, she softly rapped on it. She feared if she entered unannounced, her three male companions might think she was a pirate.

Jeff opened the door. "You're back early."

She was surprised Ryder and Rick wore white stewards' uniforms with black and gold epaulets on their shoulders.

Layla felt jumpy. "It happened again, Luke. Another pirate tried to take advantage of me. He dragged me into the men's changing room near the pool. I hit him with the blackjack."

Ryder's face showed anger. "You hurt?"

"No." She explained the man had been out cold when she'd left, and she'd blocked the changing room door.

Ryder frowned. "We'll need to finish off the guy, but you gotta stay here 'til the hijack's over unless you need to run for the lifeboats."

Layla thought about how to reply to Ryder's edict. "I see you found a uniform for me. I'll look like a stewardess in it." Layla exhaled. "I need to help. Another person could make the difference as to whether we live or die."

Ryder sighed. "Let's not quarrel."

Layla grabbed a uniform and abruptly headed for the bathroom. "You don't control me. I'll do my part."

When she emerged from the bathroom, all eyes were on her. "Y'all, I'm sorry." She slipped Rick's gray sweatshirt over her uniform. "I need to look more like a cleaning lady. I'll mess up my hair and wash off my makeup. Nobody's going to bother me. I'll carry the Glock under my uniform and the sweatshirt."

Ryder shook his head. "I ain't gonna stop you."

Rick said, "Tell her about our plans for after sunset."

Ryder nodded. "Okay, Layla. Here's what we're all gonna do come sunset. You can go to the janitor's closet, where we hid near the port shell door." Ryder outlined the rest of the plan.

Layla had a serious expression on her face after Ryder finished talking. "I'm ready." She forced herself to appear strong.

Jeff grabbed the Ka-Bar combat knife from the desktop. He slid the knife under his belt. "I'll deal with the pirate she hit." He donned a light jacket and left. In three minutes, Ryder followed Jeff to take a lookout position on the top deck.

* * *

MAY 17, 4:52 PM

Tony chose the number of his cartel moneyman in Bogotá. He touched the call button on his encrypted satellite phone.

"*Hola*, Tony."

"Julio, Mr. Falcon says he tried to send a hundred fifty million, but the transfer was blocked."

"We blocked it. We have a reliable informant in the NSA who warned us the US government is able to follow our cryptocurrency trail. So, we must reconfigure the pathway, or find another way to receive the payments."

"God damn it, Julio. We're talking about a half-billion dollars in total."

"To set up a new, encoded digital pathway will take days, even weeks. It could be impossible."

"What are you doing about it?"

"We have installed new software to detect problems when they occur. Our NSA informant provided it for a fee."

"Did you get the three hundred fifty million from the cruise ship company before you had to block the hundred fifty million?"

"I'm sorry." The man sighed. "These NSA guys know their business. I hope they don't break our phone encryption. Then we'd be totally out of luck."

Tony wondered how Ricardo Cortez, the head of *Los Hermanos* Drug Cartel in Bogotá, would react. Tony thought for a moment and then said, "I can't hold the FBI, the US

Coast Guard, and the Navy SEALs at bay for long." He took a few moments to ponder his situation. "Tell Ricardo I'm aborting the mission. I'll blow up the ship. But I'll keep the billionaire's daughter when I leave on Gino's sub. We'll still get a hundred fifty million for her even if it has to be paid in greenbacks."

"Ricardo won't be happy."

"Tell him if we don't leave soon, we won't get anything."

"I'll tell Ricardo."

"If you set up a new transfer method, call right away." Tony disconnected.

* * *

MAY 17, 4:58 PM

Silicon Valley billionaire Howard Falcon sat in his fancy office in Palo Alto, California. His satellite phone sat on his shiny, walnut desk. Howard's forehead felt overheated, like he needed to sweat. But it was not hot in his office. He was flustered for the first time in many years. What was the problem with the money transfer? He'd given Tony's instructions to his finance department, and the best two men in the office had told him there would be no problem. The ransom money transfer would be easy. They had asked him if he still wanted to do it because the FBI thought the pirates might not release Heather alive.

Of course he would do it. Why would they ask? Did they think he was so in love with amassing a vast fortune he wouldn't save his own flesh and blood? He was going to change people's opinions of him. Yeah, he worked hard, and money gravitated to him. Money attracted other money like magnets attract iron filings. His fortune had grown like a weed. After this he'd start a charity—one to study ways to cure cancer.

He didn't think an FBI wiretap team monitoring his phone was any help. He'd prefer to pay the money and get Heather back. The FBI could screw it up and get her killed.

His phone rang. "Hello, Tony."

"I have bad news. Indeed, your money transfer was blocked. Our people had to stop it so the NSA would not trace it to our remote location."

"What happens next?"

"I will keep your daughter safe until we can set up a new transfer system. I know you are a man of your word because you attempted to send the funds, and your effort was blocked. Therefore, I will be in contact in a few days to let you know how we will proceed. Your daughter will remain safe." Tony disconnected.

* * *

MAY 17, 5:00 PM

Tony was livid. The FBI had promised the two transfers of cryptocurrency would not be interfered with. However, the cartel's money man in Bogotá had blocked the money transfers because the NSA could track them.

Tony's index finger shook when he selected "FBI" on his satellite phone.

"This is Agent Duke Duncan."

Tony felt as if his brain were boiling. "You deceived us. Our people have discovered the NSA can track the money transfer to our remote location. Therefore, we've blocked the transfer."

Duke sighed. "I didn't realize the NSA could do that."

Tony had already decided he would abandon the ship with Heather via the narco submarine and blow up the *Sea Trek* if the ransom wasn't paid by 11:59 PM. He had to delay an FBI assault until after midnight at the earliest. He wanted the fog and the obscurity of night to cover the escapes of his men and of himself. They would leave on the sub, swim in scuba gear, or fly away in Pilot's helicopter. Though tonight there'd be a full moon, some darkness was better than bright sunshine or even the gloom of a cloudy day.

Could Tony convince the FBI he planned to remain on the

ship until tomorrow morning, thus avoiding an assault by them that evening? He gritted his teeth, relaxed his jaw, and then said, "At eight tomorrow morning, I will begin executing passengers one by one if you continue to impede or track our money transfer." He was bluffing.

Duke was silent.

Tony said, "I'm going to line up passengers along the rails all the way around the ship. Don't try anything."

Tony wondered if he'd said the right thing. His forearm shook. Would the feds now wait to strike the *Sea Trek* until tomorrow, after he and his men had escaped? He wished he could read Duke's mind and precisely predict what he'd do next. Had Tony blundered? What if Duke called Tony's bluff?

Negotiating with the feds was like playing chess. Once, he'd liked to play it. But he'd quit because he often lost after he'd try a new sequence of moves for the hell of it. He enjoyed winning.

Duke said, "You're making a big mistake, Mr. Franco. I urge you to continue to negotiate. We can work out a solution. We can provide free passage for you and your men."

Tony disconnected. Let the FBI worry. While they fretted, he'd take decisive action. If they wanted a fight, he'd give them one.

Tony figured the feds were using delaying tactics so they could plan and prepare their forces to attack. But if they attacked, he had surprises for them. He had modern, US Stinger antiaircraft missiles in addition to the old Soviet-era RPG-7 shoulder-fired weapons. Likely, the feds didn't know about the Stingers. They'd just seen the less accurate RPG-7 down the news helicopter. The weapon had a relatively short range.

The narco sub had brought more Stinger and RPG ammunition, a case of hand grenades, and a dozen Claymore mines—battlefield antipersonnel weapons. Each flat, five-inch by nine-inch, arc-shaped Claymore had one side labeled "FRONT TOWARD ENEMY." This weapon contained C-4 explosives which would shoot seven hundred eighth-inch-diameter steel balls at the enemy. Because the back of the flat weapon was a metal plate covered with a layer of C-4, the explosion sent the steel balls in one direction in a fan-shaped spray seven feet high by fifty-five yards wide. This weapon was most effective up to fifty-five yards. It could be set off remotely. Each mine came with a hundred feet of electric firing wire, and the Claymore could be fired using a clacker. The weapon could also be detonated by anything which could set off its blasting cap.

Tony decided he'd have his men set up Claymores along the whole of the starboard side of the ship, aiming down-ward at the water. His men could hook a string of the mines together, and the daisy-chained weapons could be detonated all at once. On the port side, he'd have his fighters aim the mines so they wouldn't shoot steel balls near the port shell door, where many of his men planned to swim away using scuba gear. Thus, if SEALs or anybody else planned to send teams in small boats to board the big ship using grappling hooks, they'd face ball bearings streaking at them at four thousand feet per second.

Of course, the three M-60 machine guns could also do a number on the FBI. Plus, his men had plenty of rocket-propelled grenade ammunition to launch at small boats and helicopters venturing too close to the *Sea Trek*.

Tony had divided a dozen hand grenades among his men, which they could toss down at small boats alongside the cruise ship. The FBI, the SEALs, or whoever would certainly get a bloody nose and retreat.

But there was one problem worrying Tony more than anything else—his men. At last count, there were twenty able-bodied guys left, including himself. Pilot didn't count. He was too old to fight. Gino didn't count, either. He had to pilot the fiberglass submarine to keep pace with the *Sea Trek*. The sub was Tony's preferred avenue of escape. He needed to take Heather with him so he could still collect at least a hundred fifty million from her megarich father.

* * *

MAY 17, 5:05 PM

FBI Hostage Rescue Team Agent in Charge Duke Duncan frowned after Tony cut short his phone call with him. Duke slapped the table in the conference room in his San Diego hotel. It was the ad hoc FBI command post because the *Sea Trek* was offshore close to the city of San Diego.

Coast Guard and Navy officers, DEA agents, NSA representatives, San Diego policemen, and twenty-five FBI agents, including Rita Reynolds, could feel the tension in the air. They had heard the last conversation between Duke and Tony.

Psychologist Dr. Emma Frosthill spoke. "Franco is impulsive. He could begin killing passengers sooner than he has threatened." Emma peered around the group through thick, black-framed glasses. "Mr. Franco likes to challenge authority. His psychological type needs to control everything—his surroundings and people. His fear of being controlled by others may drive him to a suicidal decision to blow up the ship."

Duke breathed faster. "Emma, do you think he'll detonate his bombs soon?"

"Hard to say, but there's another important point." She doodled on a yellow legal pad while she spoke. "He is a resourceful type of person who's charismatic, but he has a severe anger control problem. He may have alienated his men, which may reduce their willingness to fight. However, he's unlikely to give up, even if his men do. The worst thing about his type is he refuses to surrender and feels everything is a test of wills. He's become combative. He believes he's invincible. He's a human bomb ready to explode."

Duke shook his head. "Okay, people. I'm ready to announce my decision. All of you have expressed your opinions. Having taken everything into consideration, I have decided we will assault the ship at 1:00 AM unless Franco starts killing people before then." Duke hoped to act before Tony roused passengers and used them for human shields in the wee morning hours.

While he spoke, Duke felt the pressure of leadership and the agony of having to make hard decisions. But his team had advantages. First, the four FBI HRT helicopters were the quietest whirlybirds available. Second, HRT agents had practiced rappelling to ships' decks numerous times, even at night. In addition, two of the four FBI choppers each carried two of the best bomb squad guys the Bureau had. They'd conferred with the Tokyo bomb squad and learned how Tokyo Joe had assembled bombs in the past.

One downside was the light from the full moon, which would make the helicopters easy to spot. He wished the blanket of fog would rise enough by one in the morning so the choppers could fly through it cloaked, like they were flying through a smokescreen. *Damn*, he thought. *Too bad we don't have the resources to make a smokescreen.* However, he knew the choppers were equipped with lasers designed to blind enemies.

Other advantages were the HRT team knew the locations of the three M-60 machine guns, and many of the pirates had to be sleep-deprived. The HRT's men were fresh. Though the pirates had one Soviet-era rocket-propelled grenade launcher and lots of ammunition for it, the weapon had no heat-seeking capability. The man wielding it had to aim it, and the RPG-7 was only fifty percent effective at a range of two hundred meters in hitting a slow-moving target. Beyond five hundred meters, it was almost useless.

Since he'd made the decision to assault the *Sea Trek*, the best resources and people the HRT could muster were on a timeline to attack.

FORTY-SEVEN

TONY WALKED ONTO THE BRIDGE. He noticed large seagulls flying above the blanket of fog, which had grown six feet higher over the water in the last hour. The *Sea Trek* was two miles from the California beaches. Scanning the bridge, he caught sight of his second-in-command, Waylen, who appeared composed.

Waylen sat on a chair near one of the bridge's consoles. His pale blue eyes were icy cool. Those eyes, his blond hair, and his six-foot-one height made Tony think of him as a modern-day Viking marauder. He'd been elected quarter-master by the other pirates, and he carried himself confidently. He also had the appearance of a boxer, but in reality, he was a blacksmith by trade. He loved to fashion knives and swords from raw steel. Instead of a Ka-Bar combat knife, he carried a homemade knife in a scabbard on his belt.

Tony started to feel better as he watched Waylen, who was unruffled. Tony leaned back against the bridge's main console. "Let's implement the evacuation plan."

Waylen smiled. "Okay."

"Have the guys set up the Claymore mines along the rails. Everybody should be ready for an assault by the FBI or

Coast Guard by air, sea, or both. Little fat Oscar should take the stern Stinger position, and Tex should take the forward Stinger post. They should not hesitate to fire if they see a chopper approach. Three men should stand ready to set off the Claymores, one man on the starboard and two on the port."

"Yes, Cap."

"Pass the word. We'll evacuate the ship at 12:20 AM. Remind everyone they will be paid in full in cryptocurrency. Those swimming in scuba gear should suit up at the port shell door starting at 12:01 AM unless they're manning the Stingers or the Claymores. Those already in wet suits should help the men who arrive later to put on their gear."

"Anything else?"

"Tell Pilot to take off at 12:30 AM and take stragglers with him. Gino will take me, you, Tex, Tokyo Joe, and Heather. Also, have Tex move Heather to Deck Two to the deputy security chief's cabin. From there, I can move her to the sub faster."

"What if the FBI attacks before the deadline?"

"We'll teach them a lesson. Then we'll evacuate, using the same plan, but sooner." Tony let his mind rest for a moment. "Gino has his antenna sticking out of the water, so I'll phone him to tell him what the plan updates are. He'll come alongside the port shell door when we do an all-engines-stop."

Waylen stood. "I'll be glad to get off this floating hotel." He began walking. "I look forward to drinking tequila in old Mexico."

Tony raised his hand. "Make sure you get the second radio bomb trigger from Tokyo Joe. I want a backup."

"Aye, aye."

* * *

MAY 17, 5:13 PM

Heather sat in the luxury suite next to the captain's cabin. She smoothed her long, thin, blond hair and sat straighter on the tan leather couch. Her back was sore. Did tension cause her discomfort? A young, athletic woman, she hadn't felt back pain since she'd overdone pre-meet calisthenics when she was on her high school's swim team. But once she'd entered the water back then, the pain had disappeared. She had earned her letter in swimming. In college, she'd decided to do without sports and focus on academics.

She felt lonely and hungry. She'd taken a bath, applied makeup including red lipstick, and dressed in warm slacks and a long-sleeved, silk blouse. Dressing and putting on makeup had made her feel better for a while. But it wasn't long before worry again plagued her. Tony had said her father had come through with the ransom money, and it would be a matter of hours before she'd be released. Tony had also told her he would describe how she'd be set free. But he hadn't spoken to her in hours.

She gazed across the sumptuous cabin at a six-foot-tall oil painting of a female Spanish dancer. She wore a fancy red dress and held castanets. Heather smiled.

There was a rapid knock at her cabin door. Before she could go to the peephole, the pushy buccaneer, Tex, entered the suite. He threw a laundry bag toward her. It landed on the couch. "Git enough clothes fer three days, and stuff 'em in the bag. Yer goin' on a trip real soon."

"I'm being released?"

"After yer daddy wires the coin." Tex glared at her. "Don't sit there. Git yer ass in gear, honey."

Heather rose and grabbed the bag. She felt relief mixed with dread. "When am I leaving and how?" She walked toward her bedroom.

"Ever bin in a submarine?"

"No."

"You'll git a chance soon." He grinned. "It's big for a

narco sub. Holds up to eight people and a dozen tons of drugs."

Heather stopped abruptly. "Where are we going?"

"First, we got to evade the Coast Guard, and then I'm thinkin' we'll end up in Mexico. The money exchange would occur there."

"Won't the Coast Guard drop depth charges or chase us?"

Tex laughed. "No. They don't want to blow you up." He took a second to admire her. Then he said, "The sub's made of fiberglass, and sonar and radar can't pick it up. With the fog hoverin' over the water, the feds won't know the sub's swimmin' alongside the *Sea Trek*."

Heather entered her bedroom, snatched underwear, socks, a blouse, an extra pair of jeans, a nightgown, dental supplies, a hairbrush, and a light jacket. She exited her room and walked to Tex. "When are we going to leave?"

Tex opened the suite's door. "Tonight. But first, yer gonna go to a cabin on Deck Two, near the shell door where the submarine will be." He took the laundry bag from her and smiled. "I'll be on the little sub with you along with Cap."

"What if the Coast Guard sees us?"

"Cap's got an orange-colored plastic box. It's a radio trigger which can set off the bombs in the engine room." He grabbed Heather's upper arm. "If the FBI, the Coast Guard, or the SEALs is stupid enough to attack us, Cap's gonna blow up the ship. The feds will be too busy savin' passengers and crew to bother with us."

Heather shuddered. She wished the FBI would let them leave. She merely wanted peace and to get back to her normal life. Then again, she felt adventurous because she was dealing with pirates. To survive her ordeal, she figured she'd do whatever was necessary.

FORTY-EIGHT

RYDER WAS at his post on the top deck at midship near the railing, with a view of the port shell door and the foggy sea. The ship's swimming pool was behind him, but no one had ventured into it except for an old couple who appeared to enjoy its warm water. The air temperature had fallen. Ryder estimated it had dropped to the upper fifties. He was glad he'd worn a windbreaker.

Every so often, Ryder raised Layla's whale-watching binoculars to his eyes and scanned the California coastal hills poking up above the foggy mist. He reckoned if the FBI launched an aerial raid, it would come from the coast. Helicopters would be the best transport for the Hostage Rescue Team. His side of the ship, facing east, was shadowed from direct sunbeams. The sun was sinking lower in the western sky. Flying choppers toward the setting sun would be stupid. Sunset would be a bad time to assault the ship from the east. Of course, the helicopters could also fly west, out of sight of the *Sea Trek*, and then circle back east toward the ship. The sun would then be at the back of the choppers. Horizontal sun rays could blind the pirates.

An attack by boats was also possible under the blanket of

fog. Jeff could be right. The raiders could row the boats instead of use powerboats, which would make a great deal of noise.

Ryder believed the most likely time for the FBI to act would be in the wee hours after midnight. The pirates would be weary by then. Ryder, too, was exhausted. His leg hurt. Sharp jolts of pain were frequently irritating him. He wished he could take a pain pill.

To force himself to quit thinking about the pain, he stood to get a better view of the decks below him. He leaned on the railing and peered downward. He noticed a pirate lowering a small, bullet-shaped, black machine into the water. The device was attached to a rope, which was tied off inside the shell door. Ryder had seen the bullet-shaped units before, when he and Layla had gone down to Deck Two. The small machines had been lined up next to the scuba diving gear in the room near the shell door. He recalled the product label on one of them had read, "Diver Propulsion Vehicle." Ryder thought the pirates could abandon ship soon and swim to shore.

Then Ryder saw motion on the helipad. An older man was putting items in the ancient Huey helicopter. Three or four buccaneers could get away on the chopper, if it were to fly ten feet above the waves, concealed in the fog bank. In the time Ryder had been at his post, he'd watched the blanket of fog thicken and rise until it was forty feet high.

Ryder heard a noise like metal hitting metal below him. He peered toward the bow of the ship. A pirate was using tie wraps to attach olive-colored squares to the rails along Deck Four. What were they? The answer hit him. Claymore mines.

He checked his wristwatch. The time was 6:15 PM, roughly two hours to go before sunset. Before then, he would return to Rick's cabin to get his M1 Garand rifle. Ryder noticed the ship was going slower than it had before. The vessel was quieter. The air was calm, like the atmosphere before a storm.

FORTY-NINE

IT WAS ALMOST SUNSET. Ryder rested on a plastic chair. From his position on the top deck near the swimming pool, Ryder estimated the cold, west wind was gusting to at least twenty miles per hour. Underneath his light jacket, he pulled the collar of his bright white steward's uniform tightly around his neck. Not just fashionable, the crew's clothing had a military appearance because there were black and gold epaulets on the shoulders. The downside was the crew's garb was so brilliant pirates could target him in the light of the full moon. He hoped Tony or Tex wouldn't spot him. It was almost dark, and even if the uniform's trousers were visible in the darkness, the features of his face would be hard to make out.

The ship was rocking with the waves. Ryder viewed the western horizon and saw charcoal-black clouds above the fog while the orange disk of the sun popped in and out of view through the mist. Was a storm coming at them from the west?

In the rapidly darkening east, he could hardly see the hills along the coast. For the last two hours, he had also watched the Coast Guard cutter, which had stayed two miles southwest of the *Sea Trek*. He hadn't spotted any drones or aircraft.

When the sun finally dipped beneath the blanket of fog in the west, Ryder stood in the gathering darkness and prepared to find his way to the elevator at midship, which would carry him down to Deck Eight and Rick's cabin. There he'd pick up an M1 rifle and ammo, return to the top deck with the weapon hidden in a laundry cart, and conceal himself in the gloom of the rising fog. Layla, Rick, and Jeff would also hide in strategic places and await a potential assault by the FBI's Hostage Rescue Team. Ryder's gut told him the shit was about to hit the fan.

* * *

MAY 17, 8:12 PM

Ryder tapped on Rick's cabin door on Deck Eight, not far from the elevator lobby. He heard the door's hinges creak. Rick opened the door, and Ryder saw the weapons and ammo were laid out on the floor.

Rick asked, "Did you see anything of interest?"

Ryder explained he'd watched a pirate tie-wrap Claymore mines onto the railings of the ship while another buccaneer had lowered diver propulsion vehicles into the water from the port shell door. "Pirates could be swimmin' for shore soon. The fog's thicker, and it'll hide them gettin' in the water."

Rick scratched his curly, graying hair. "We won't be able to watch the port shell door effectively from above."

Ryder squinted. "Yep. I think the narco sub will pull up to the port shell door hidden by fog. Two or three pirates could escape on it."

Jeff nodded. "Makes sense." He directed his attention to Rick. "If I were a pirate, I'd want to take the sub instead of swim. The FBI must have the beaches staked out."

Ryder said, "We'd all better git to our positions. An assault could happen fast."

"True," Rick said. He picked up an M1 and clips of ammo and placed them in a laundry basket. He pulled a sheet off his bed and laid it above the weapon. "I'll go first. I'll be covering the aft end of the top deck. We should leave separately." He grabbed a cardboard cup of steaming coffee from the desktop. Earlier, Layla had gone to a café and carried back four coffees on a tray.

"Before you go, do you agree if shootin' starts, we'll shoot too?" Ryder asked. "We got the element of surprise."

"Yes," Rick said. He left.

Ryder turned to Layla. "Please stay in the shell door closet and peek out just once in a while."

"Okay." She wrapped the Glock 17 pistol into an extra bra and strapped it against her belly. Then she put on Rick's big sweatshirt and snatched a cup of coffee.

Ryder sighed. "I thought you were gonna leave the pistol here. And what advantage does your uniform give you if all you can see is white trousers?"

Layla's dark brown eyes appeared steady to Ryder. She said, "The white collar still shows. I'm not going to carry just a blackjack."

"Be careful, hon."

Layla kissed him, smiled, and left.

Ryder picked up an M1 and ammo and placed them in a laundry bin. As he stuffed a blanket over them, he glanced at Jeff. "I better go first, Jeff. I'm slower than you are."

"Makes sense." Jeff looked down at his belt. "I still have the Ka-Bar knife. I'll get an M1 from the box in the engine room if shooting starts. I'll leave the other one here. Don't worry. I'll check on Layla every so often."

"Thanks, Jeff." Ryder took a coffee and left. He needed to stay awake and alert.

* * *

A SHOCK of pain traveling up his left leg woke Ryder. He was sitting on a chair in the dark shadows along a bulkhead near the ship's swimming pool. He focused on the luminous dial of his wristwatch. It was 11:35 PM. Tony's deadline would come in twenty-four minutes.

"Holy shit," he said softly.

Hot blood rushed to his forehead, though the air temperature was in the fifties, and the wind was gusting up to twenty-five miles per hour. He knew he'd been lucky. There had been no FBI assault during the last fifty minutes he'd dozed.

He was glad the colonel hadn't seen him. Falling asleep on watch or guard duty was among the worst sins you could commit in the military. Rick would think he wasn't worth a damn. In this case, his offense could have been fatal to him and a great number of the five thousand passengers and crew. He scolded himself. He knew he'd never forget falling asleep when all hell was likely to break loose.

The sounds of feet shuffling across the deck near the railing put him on high alert. Lit by the full moon, two pirates emerged from the misty fog. They carried AK-47s and appeared to be on watch, scanning the horizon. The moonlight was so bright the two men's features were easy to distinguish. Ryder sat still in the dark shadows. He tried to breathe quietly. By happy chance, the stock of his M1 rifle was butt down on the deck and behind his chair, where the shadows were darkest. He held the weapon with his left hand. The rifle was locked and loaded, but he'd set the safety.

The two buccaneers stopped at the railing eight feet away. A misty haze swirled around them. They appeared like ghosts in one of Ryder's dreams. But they were as real as a kick in the ass.

The taller pirate said, "Tony's orderin' us to start swimmin' at 12:20 AM. It don't make no sense to me. Them feds is gonna attack sooner. I feel it in my bones."

The shorter one said, "I'm going down to Deck Two. If nobody's there, I'm gonna get my butt off this ship and scuba to the beach before the shootin' starts."

"I'm with you, Zeke." The tall man shifted his grasp on his AK. "Let's swim northeast 'til the batteries in the DPVs give out, or we run outta air. We can drop the tanks and swim the rest of the way. We'll end up a lot farther north than them feds would think we'd land."

"I like your logic," the short man said.

Ryder's throat was tickling with postnasal drip. He fought not to cough, but he was forced to clear his throat as quietly as he could to avoid hacking.

The tall man turned toward Ryder. "Hey, you, what the hell you doin' out here?"

Ryder's pulse kicked into high gear. He thought fast. He'd fake being drunk, like he'd done before. Who better to play a drunk than a recovering alcoholic like himself? He slurred, "I'm coolin' off. Had a few too many." He kept a firm grip on his M1 rifle in the shadows.

"You got any with ya?" the tall man asked.

"I drunk it all. Sorry, fellas."

"If I was you, steward, I'd dry out in my cabin. Otherwise, somebody will get nervous and pop you by mistake."

"I'll be goin' soon," Ryder said, speaking indistinctly.

The pirates moved on.

Ryder could see them go down the steps. Their bodies and their rifles were softly silhouetted by moonlight in the midst of the eerie fog.

FIFTY

TONY AND QUARTERMASTER Devon stood on the *Sea Trek*'s bridge. Tony held his satellite phone. He peered down at its screen, and he saw the time was 11:57 PM. He glared at Devon. "There's been no late word from Bogotá. I was hoping they would've already figured a quick way to receive the money undetected, but a solution wasn't meant to be."

Unemotional and calm, Devon said, "Cap, you made the right decision to abandon ship. The longer we wait, the more the odds will be against us."

An artery in Tony's neck pulsed.

* * *

MAY 17, 11:58 PM

From his position on the top deck, Ryder heard only the sounds of the ocean. The ship's engines had stopped running. He'd gotten used to the steady rumbling noises of the *Sea Trek*'s machinery combined with the sound of the ship's wake. The quiet ship was now at the mercy of the current.

The wind had kicked up, and Ryder heard waves splashing against the hull of the mammoth cruise ship. The deck seemed to roll under his feet in an ad hoc rhythm the ocean had created. He smelled a fresher, warmer wind. Was a storm brewing?

Ryder felt his senses go on high alert. Something was about to happen. His innards told him so. He stood and surveyed the deck to see if a pirate sentry was nearby. Holding his rifle down along his trouser leg, he ventured to the railing on the port side of the upper mid-deck. He peered down through the fog, which thinned every so often. As the fog grew wispier, he saw the conning tower of the narco sub inch upward. Each time the wind gusted and the fog grew thinner, the top of the submarine appeared more clearly through the thin veneer of mist. The blowing haze gave the sub a phantom-like appearance.

Ryder could see the shell door had been opened, and the black tarp had been removed from its doorway. Dim light outlined its ten-foot-square opening. Lit by moonlight, a man emerged from the submarine's hatchway and stood near the conning tower. "Toss me the monkey's fist."

"Okay," a voice replied from inside the shell door opening.

Three seconds later, Ryder saw a line with a big knot on its end, shaped like a ball of yarn, fly toward the sub. The man who stood on the submarine grabbed the knot end of the line and pulled it. As he did so, Ryder saw the line was attached to a thicker rope, which the submariner tied to his submersible.

During the next four minutes, men inside the shell doorway pulled the sub close to the side of the drifting *Sea Trek* and tied two more ropes to it. Ryder watched the submariner climb back down inside his small vessel. Ryder waited five minutes, but nothing more happened.

Because the pirates had unloaded the sub earlier, Ryder figured the one reason for them to tie it to the *Sea Trek* again was to evacuate high-ranking pirates. It had to be more comfortable to sail away in a sub than to swim for shore where FBI agents could be waiting.

The second rendezvous with the sub had taken place for a reason. Had the pirates received their ransom? How long would it be before buccaneers would leave the *Sea Trek*?

Because his leg was throbbing most of the time, Ryder moved back to his chair near the swimming pool to wait for an attack, though he believed one to be less likely, if the ransom had been paid.

FIFTY-ONE

THE PIRATES' deadline had passed eight minutes earlier. The FBI agent in charge of the Hostage Rescue Team, Duke Duncan, was disturbed. He stood at the head of the conference room's long table, around which his task force senior members sat. He stared blankly at the SAT phone he held in his palm. Tony had abruptly hung up in the middle of their last discussion.

Duke scanned the faces of the people sitting around the table. "Since negotiations have broken off, and Franco is crazy mad, I think he'll follow through with his threat to execute passengers. At the least, I believe he will wake them and use them as human shields." Duke's eyes focused on Rita Reynolds. "I've decided to execute Operation Sea Save at once."

His eyes shifted to his assistant. "Randy, are we ready? Any last-minute glitches?"

Randy glanced at his laptop computer. "The airborne teams are sitting in their copters. The rowboats have moved as close as they can under the fog."

"Contact the commanders. Order them to assault the ship after they agree on the soonest coordinated execution time."

"Yes, sir."

* * *

MAY 18, 12:12 AM

Ryder heard the distant sound of a helicopter approaching the *Sea Trek* from the southeast. He stood and peered at the dark sky over the shore, only just visible in the light of the full moon. He glimpsed downward across the bridge, through the smoky mist, at the ship's bow. He saw the fuzzy silhouette of a pirate aiming a shoulder-fired missile launcher at the oncoming copter.

Ryder dropped his cane. It clattered on the deck. A jolt of pain caused him to jar his left leg. Ryder's face felt hot. He raised his rifle and aimed at the thug. Another sharp pain yanked his arm aside. Ryder gritted his teeth. He got a new bead on the pirate. He began to squeeze the trigger.

A Stinger IR-guided, antiaircraft missile leaped from its launcher with a pop. Less than a second later, a V-shaped, whitish flame and gray smoke erupted from the flying projectile as it streaked toward the helicopter. A microsecond later, Ryder's M1 fired, and orange flame bounded from its barrel following its .30 caliber slug. He felt his weapon kick. Its heavy bullet smashed into Tex's back. The man's rocket launcher tumbled down into the water seventeen decks below.

* * *

MAY 18, 12:13 AM

Its two side doors removed, the FBI helicopter code-named Chopper One carried fourteen agents and two pilots as it flew toward the *Sea Trek*. A missile streaked toward them, its light-colored smoke trail behind it. The aircraft's copilot yelled, "Missile. Fire flares." Before he could utter anything more, the helicopter's automatic missile approach warning system spotted the incoming Stinger missile. The system jettisoned two swarms of hot-burning flares, one to the right side of the chopper and one to its left.

The pinkish-white, bright light of the magnesium-based flares resembled fireworks falling from both sides of the whirlybird. The older model Stinger locked onto the group of flares arching downward and away from the chopper's starboard side.

When the pilot saw the Stinger heading to his starboard, he sharply banked his helicopter to his port side. A half second later, the missile exploded amid the swarm of flares in a ball of orange flames and pitch-black smoke.

The seven agents on the port side of the flying machine peered down at the layer of fog below them through the aircraft's open doorway. On the chopper's starboard side, the men saw the full moon above them. They heard nothing. "What's going on?" one man muttered.

After the pilot righted his chopper, he pushed his microphone button. "Sea Save Command. This is Chopper One. A Stinger missile attacked. We deployed flares. The missile exploded to our starboard. We are not damaged."

"Chopper One, return to base." The Sea Save mission commander paused. "Chopper Two, also head back to base."

Both pilots replied, "Yes, sir."

Chopper One's copilot breathed a sigh of relief. It was lucky the missile had been fired at Chopper One's nose because its engine's hot exhaust had been harder for the missile to detect and lock on to.

The mission commander made another radio call. "This is Sea Save Command to all R-boats."

"This is R-boat One. Go ahead, Command." A loud bang interrupted Boat One's transmission.

* * *

RICK HAD SURVEYED the top decks of the *Sea Trek* in the minutes after he'd taken his post after sunset. He had seen two M60 machine gun placements, spotted the Claymore mines attached to the railings along Deck Four below him, and noticed two pirates armed with Stinger missiles. One was on the roof of the bridge at the bow of the ship, and the other was stationed on the helipad at the ship's stern.

Rick's skin felt extra chilly, though he wore a jacket over his steward's uniform. He guessed he was feeling colder than he should because he'd lost thirty pounds in the last month. Cancer was eating his body.

He held his rifle with his left hand. He was cold. He held his right hand inside his hip pocket to warm his fingers. The distant sound of a helicopter near the California shore grabbed his attention. He glanced southeast. At once, he concluded the FBI had begun its assault on the *Sea Trek*. He lifted his M1 rifle and held it with two hands in front of him. In his jacket pockets, he carried extra clips of eight rounds each for his weapon.

Rick was concealed in the dark shadows of the smoke-stack-like funnel of the ship. He continued to peer at the distant southeastern sky where the helicopter noise had originated, but he could not see an aircraft. When he noticed movement below him, he shifted his gaze to the helipad on the stern of the ship. He saw a pirate stationed there along the rail pick up a Stinger launcher from the deck, mist swirling around him. The buccaneer propped the weapon on his shoulder.

From the other end of the ship—at the bow—Rick heard a pop. As he turned around, he caught sight of a second pirate and the Stinger he'd launched, which was racing toward the helicopter approaching from shore. Flares erupted from both sides of the chopper like a Fourth of July pyrotechnics display. A shot rang out, and the Stinger shooter fell like a bag of rocks.

Ryder got him, Rick thought as he swiveled to face the helipad and the other buccaneer armed with another Stinger. Rick heard a second chopper coming from the northeast. Rick squeezed off two shots. The second pirate fell dead. Rick smelled the acrid odor of gun smoke. *Six shots left*, he thought.

A burst of three M60 machine gun slugs struck the funnel next to him. He dove to the deck a moment before the gunner unleashed another three-round burst of 7.62mm bullets, which flew over his head. Rick then fired three shots at the machine gun's muzzle flash. The shooter fell aside and squirmed in death throes on the jogging track, where he'd set up his gun on the port side of the ship.

Rick rose to his feet and ran to the starboard rail. He peered down into the haze along the side of the ship, lit by moonlight. He searched for a pirate standing by to set off the Claymore mines along Deck Four should the FBI or Coast Guard launch a waterborne assault. There was a thud below him. Rick spied a grappling hook, which had latched on to a rail. The feds had arrived.

A pirate emerged from the shadows. He held a device in his hand. There was a huge explosion of all the daisy-chained Claymore mines along the starboard side of the *Sea Trek*. Rick heard men's screams from the surface of the water. "Pull back," someone yelled from inside the blanket of thick fog. A second pirate manning an M60 machine gun on the bow of the ship began to shoot toward the screaming men. Rick figured they were on rowboats.

Three rapid shots sounded like they came from Ryder's M1 at midship. The second machine gun fell silent. *Excellent shooting, Ryder*, Rick thought.

Rick aimed at the pirate below him who'd detonated the Claymore mines. Rick fired twice as the man took a step. Hit in the shoulder, the buccaneer fell but held onto his AK-47. He raised it with one hand, its muzzle pointing at Rick. The weapon was on full automatic. The thug pulled the trigger. A hail of bullets zipped upward toward the top deck.

Rick was diving down. In mid-air, he felt like he'd been punched in the chest. He saw deep, dark nothingness. He died as he fell.

* * *

MAY 18, 12:13 AM

The commander of R-Boat One dropped his two-way FM radio after the deafening blast sounded and hurled hundreds of eighth-inch-diameter steel balls at his men and him. He felt pain in his right hand and left leg. He peered through the haze at his hand. He felt warm wetness. It was his red blood, its color dulled by the flat light of the swirling fog.

Willard had fallen next to him in the boat. His lifeless eyes stared upward into the mist. Noah, who'd tossed his grappling hook upward, floated nearby in the water, his corpse peppered with wounds.

Machine-gun bullets slapped the ocean's surface near the rowboat and spattered water. Slugs struck the boat. Boat One's men fired their automatic weapons in the direction of the machine-gun fire.

The boat commander picked up his radio with his left hand and depressed the push-to-talk button. "Sea Save Commander, this is Boat One, over."

"Go ahead, Boat One, over."

"We're taking heavy fire. Claymores and machine-gun fire. At least two dead. I'm wounded. There are more casualties. Over."

"This is Sea Save Commander to all boats. Pull back."

* * *

MAY 18, 12:17 AM

Ryder had lost his cane in the darkness before he'd fired at the second machine gun on the bow of the ship and killed its gunner. He leaned on his M1 rifle, its butt against the deck, moving painfully forward toward the flashes of a third machine gun. He wished to find a place where he could get a clean shot.

He saw bright flashes spitting from the machine gun's

muzzle. The weapon was on the roof of the bridge, the highest spot for a gun placement on the ship.

The pirate manning the machine gun kept firing toward the screams coming from men splashing in the water, some calling for their mothers. The cries chilled Ryder more than the brisk wind cutting into his face. He braced his weapon on a banister and aimed at the bright flashes of the third and last machine gun. He squeezed off two rounds. His rifle made a ping sound. His weapon needed to be reloaded.

As Ryder grabbed a clip of ammo from his pocket, the machine gunner blasted a burst of bullets in his direction. One round tore a path through the air within an inch of his left ear. The resulting loud sound—a sonic crack—deafened his ear. He jammed the new eight-round clip into his weapon.

He dove behind a steel bulkhead near the staircase and aimed toward the roof of the bridge. Another burst of 7.62mm rounds impacted the wall near him, throwing bits of lead in his direction. Three sand-sized fragments ripped his right jacket sleeve. He let out half a breath and depressed the trigger bit by bit. The weapon surprised him when it fired. The pirate at the third machine gun fell dead.

Though the noises of splashing and voices came from the water, Ryder heard no more shots. He reckoned the men in boats were busy saving the wounded who'd been scaling the starboard side of the *Sea Trek* when the Claymore mines had exploded in their faces.

Ryder worried Layla would be in harm's way. Leaning on his M1, he painfully limped toward midship to take the elevator down to Deck Two and the port shell door. He felt faint. He sucked cold air into his lungs in deep breaths as he proceeded. His leg hurt the same as it had after the pirate had first struck his left shin with the heavy, glass ashtray. Ryder clenched his teeth and fought to move forward as fast as he could.

FIFTY-TWO

AFTER TONY HEARD heavy gunfire and earsplitting explosions from the Claymore mines on the starboard side of the ship, he knew the FBI had attacked. He stood in the space inside the open port shell doorway. Both the narco submarine and the *Sea Trek* drifted with the current.

Tony grabbed his CB radio, pressed the transmit button, and spoke. "Quartermaster, order all the buccaneers and Pilot to finish abandoning ship as fast as they can."

The wind blew twenty miles per hour while the waves slapped the sides of the massive cruise ship and the smaller submersible. They both rocked in the turbulent ocean. Tony faced Gino, the captain of the narco sub. The submariner stood next to the open shell doorway.

Tony said, "We need to leave fast." He peered along the short passageway, where it joined the center passage which ran the length of the ship. "I'm going to get Heather."

Gino nodded, stepped through the ten-foot-square door-way, and climbed down the rope ladder to stand on top of his submarine. He fingered his knife. After Tony and the girl were aboard, Gino would cut the ropes securing his fiberglass vessel to the big ship. Meanwhile, he'd let pirates in scuba gear use his sub as an entry point into the sea.

Within thirty seconds, two pirates wearing all of their scuba equipment stepped toward the shell door and waved to Gino. He nodded, and the first buccaneer carefully stepped down the rope ladder through the mist carrying two sets of flippers. He got on top of the narco sub. The second man handed two DPVs down to the first. It wasn't long before the two divers entered the water and started toward shore. Others followed them.

* * *

MAY 18, 12:20 AM

The *Sea Trek*'s engines were silent, and the engine room was eerily quiet. After Jeff had heard the huge explosion of the Claymore mines, he had stepped outside of the engine room. The din of distant gunshots had greeted him. The sound of gunfire was echoing from the port shell doorway along the passageways. He figured pirate sentries on the top decks had sighted Ryder and Rick, and a firefight had begun. Jeff also concluded the Claymore explosion meant the FBI had assaulted the ship.

The signature boom of an exploding grenade told Jeff the fight was ongoing. He stepped back into the engine room and slipped his Ka-Bar combat knife from its scabbard under his shirt. He decided to take out the pirate who guarded the C-4 bombs.

Jeff formulated a plan as he neared the buccaneer guard. The pirate surely had heard the Claymores explode. Jeff decided to approach the man and tell him shots were being fired, too.

Jeff guessed the bushy-bearded guard who sported a ponytail would flee the engine room before the C-4 bombs exploded. Since Jeff resembled a young man without any fighting experience, he thought the buccaneer would underestimate him. But Jeff had one worry. Would the guard be suspicious because Jeff didn't work the third shift? He decided to risk it.

As he approached the hairy pirate, Jeff held his combat knife alongside his trouser leg, out of sight. He stopped two feet in front of the bearded man who was standing and alert.

The pirate stared at Jeff. The man seemed ready to abandon the engine room immediately, his AK-47 in front of him in both hands. Jeff leaned closer to the tough-looking man and said, "There's shooting."

The guard nodded, and his beard bounced. He glanced toward the door. He turned to leave. Jeff grabbed the man's ponytail. From the back of the pirate's neck to its front, Jeff's knife sliced his enemy's throat and jugular vein. The buccaneer fell forward. Blood pulsed onto the deck. He died in seconds.

Jeff wiped his knife on the ruffian's shirt. After sheathing the Ka-Bar, Jeff picked up the dead man's AK-47 rifle. Jeff recalled he'd seen wires leading outside and along the passageway toward the port shell door and the bombs' plunger.

Had Tokyo Joe booby-trapped the wires going to the plunger? Jeff hoped not. He took a deep breath and cut the wires with his knife. Now there was no chance a pirate could use the plunger to send a high-voltage surge to the blasting caps in the C-4 bombs in the engine room. Jeff figured the bad guys could still set off the bombs using a radio signal picked up on the top decks. From there, it would travel through the ship's telephone wires to the C-4 bombs.

Jeff debated whether or not he should cut the four sets of phone wires, if he could get to them. He dismissed doing it. Tokyo Joe had most likely booby-trapped those wires.

Jeff headed for the engine room exit. He would check on Layla in the closet near the port shell door.

* * *

MAY 18, 12:20 AM

Standing on the bridge of the Coast Guard cutter *San Diego* Lieutenant Commander Ralph Essex ended his satellite phone call with the FBI. He turned to Captain Chuck Stone. "Captain, FBI Agent in Charge Duke Duncan requests we aid the HRT. They've sustained heavy casualties. They've reported Claymore mine explosions, grenades, and machine-gun fire."

Stone said, "Since the shooting is over, per our long-range microphones and drone images of the upper decks, it'll be a rescue operation. Deploy four response boats. Make sure at least two medics are on each boat. Send explosives specialists, too."

"Yes, sir."

The cutter sailed toward the embattled *Sea Trek*.

* * *

MAY 18, 12:22 AM

Heather lay flat on the carpet in the deputy security chief's cabin on Deck Two, close to the passageway which led to the port shell doorway. After she'd heard explosions and gunfire, she had pounded on the cabin's door and yelled. No one had come to her aid.

She hoped the FBI or the Coast Guard had attacked. It crossed her mind Tony or one of his pirates could use her as a human shield.

The cabin door's lock clicked. The solid thud of a kick against wood made her roll away from the doorway as the door banged open.

Tony stared down at her. "Get up. We need to go."

Heather's hands shook. She pushed herself to a standing position. "Where are we going?"

"To a submarine. Cooperate, or you'll go down with the ship."

Heather felt faint. "It's sinking?"

Tony pulled a small orange box the size of a pack of cigarettes from his hip pocket. "I'm going to detonate the bombs."

Heather's stomach turned. She felt like puking. "I'm coming." She moved toward Tony.

Tony pocketed the orange radio transmitter and seized her arm. He dragged her through the doorway and drew one of his Glock-17 pistols.

Heather gulped in air and trotted in front of Tony as he pushed her along the passageway toward the port shell door and the narco submarine.

* * *

MAY 18, 12:25 AM

The sound of explosions and the firecracker-like reports of gunfire still fresh in her mind, Layla crouched in the janitor's closet. She'd cracked open the door to peer through the slim opening toward the shell door.

Her body shaking, she wondered why she hadn't listened to Ryder and stayed in Rick's cabin in relative safety. She watched as two pirates in scuba gear carrying small bullet-shaped machines and flippers scurried toward the open shell door. One by one, they got on top of the submarine and then entered the water.

Where were Ryder and Rick? She heard more shooting. Was the FBI aboard?

She wished to be strong. But tears rolled down her cheeks when she thought of the pain Ryder must be in. Could he survive the shooting? He had to be in tremendous pain.

Someone tapped on the closet door. "Layla, it's Jeff." Jeff stepped forward, hoping she'd see him through the narrow slit between the door and the doorframe. He held an AK-47 rifle.

* * *

MAY 18, 12:26 AM

Sixty feet from the port shell door, Tony guided Heather around a corner on Deck Two. Twenty-five feet away, a man held an AK-47 rifle and stood in front of a janitor's closet. Though Tony doubted the man was one of his crew, he wanted to be sure. Tony pushed Heather down onto the deck.

She closed her eyes and covered them with an arm.

Tony trained his Glock-17 at the thin man's back. He screamed, "You."

The young man turned, hesitated, and dove down to the deck.

Tony fired five times.

The young man lay silent and still. Blood leaked onto the floor. His AK-47 had fallen in front of him, and his blood pooled around it.

Why hadn't the stranger fired? Then it struck Tony. The thin man had been afraid of hitting Heather.

Heather uncovered her eyes. She screamed like a wounded cat and fainted.

Tony slapped her, and she came to. "Let's go, God damn it."

As the two of them neared the closet and Jeff's body, Tony heard whimpering from behind its door. He yanked it open and saw Layla on her knees. She wore a stewardess outfit. "You're back to stealing jewelry." He laughed.

Heather yelled, "Get to a lifeboat. He's got a remote bomb trigger."

Tony grabbed Heather's arm again. "Shut up." He glanced at Layla, took the orange plastic box from his pocket, and waved it. "She's right. Run for a lifeboat." He dragged Heather toward the submarine. He could feel the ocean rocking the *Sea Trek* more than it had since he'd been aboard the big ship. Cold air blew in through the open shell door, carrying with it a fine, chilly mist. The wind howled.

Layla quaked uncontrollably.

* * *

MAY 18, 12:30 AM

The janitor's closet door wide open, Layla watched as Tony and Heather neared the open shell door. The moonlight was bright, and she could see the fog swirling over the water and the submarine, creating smoky special effects like those in a theatrical production.

Layla debated whether or not to run for a lifeboat station. The bombs were not far away in the engine room. Where was Ryder?

She saw Tony force Heather down the rope ladder.

In seconds Heather stood on top of the narco sub near its conning tower, the top half of her body visible from Layla's position.

The submersible bobbed up and down on the rough waves. Periodically, the fog thinned when the wind cut clear pathways through the misty blanket. The air smelled stormy with the odor of rain. Lightning flashed, or was it something else? More fighting? Thunder roared a moment later. There was a slight odor of ozone.

Now Tony stood next to both Heather and a man near the sub's small conning tower while the submarine rocked wildly on the ocean's surface.

Gino cut the ropes which had tied his vessel to the *Sea Trek*. Moving at a slow clip against the waves, the sub then pulled away from the big ship.

As Layla ran toward the shell door, she slipped on the pool of blood surrounding Jeff's AK-47. Then she heard someone thumping the deck with something solid. She turned. Ryder struggled forward, leaning on the wooden stock of his M1 rifle. Each time he shuffled ahead, he brought the stock down on the deck with a thud. His face showed he suffered excruciating pain.

Next to the open shell door, Layla glanced to her right. Tony was still atop the narco sub, undulating on the rolling waves. He held the orange trigger box, and he smiled. The sub was twenty-five meters away from the ship.

Layla stared at Ryder and screamed, "He's going to blow up the ship."

Ryder peered at Jeff's body and then at Tony. "I'm gonna get that bastard." He stumbled and fell forward flat on the deck.

FIFTY-THREE

PILOT SAT in his olive-drab Vietnam War-era Huey helicopter on the *Sea Trek*'s helipad. The chopper's rotors were turning, and Pilot had left its side doors open in case he'd need to ditch the whirlybird in the water. His gray hair whipped in the wind, and fog swirled around the ancient flying machine. With his side vision, he caught sight of movement to his left when he was about to put on his helmet and liftoff.

Lit by the full moon, a man was running toward the helicopter through the fog. He was young, short, and skinny. Pilot recognized the nerdy man—Joe Clarke, a.k.a. Tokyo Joe, an electronics and computer expert, who was also a bomber for hire. Tokyo Joe smiled and pointed at the back seat behind Pilot.

Joe yelled over the sound of the blades whipping through the misty air, "Can I hitch a ride?"

Pilot nodded, and Tokyo Joe climbed into the rear, side-looking seat and buckled in. They were the only two people aboard the chopper.

Pilot switched the craft's dome light off and turned his gauge lights down to a dim setting. He donned his helmet, which included night vision goggles. With their aid, he could fly into the darkness and feel as safe as flying in daylight. He took off but kept the Huey low, less than ten feet above the rough ocean water. He headed southeast and zoomed into the fog bank leveling off fourteen feet higher than the top of the rough ocean water. He'd stay low to avoid radar.

As he came closer to shore, the blanket of fog grew taller, fifty feet thick. The cold wind and cloudy air whipped through the cockpit, chilling him to his fifty-five-year-old bones. He was sorry he would have to lose this old flying machine, his mechanical pet he'd named Fafnir after a mythical Scandinavian dragon. The chopper was unique enough that the authorities would surely find him if he decided to keep it instead of disposing of it.

In minutes, Pilot would be off the coast of Mexico. He sighed and turned the volume up on his headset, intending to enjoy his recording of Beethoven's Eroica Symphony for the last time, at least in this flying machine.

FIFTY-FOUR

GRIPPING HEATHER'S SHOULDER, Captain Gino Gonzales stood next to the open hatch on the deck of his vigorously rocking submarine. Below deck, Waylen piloted the craft.

Gino wondered why Tony had not yet pushed the button on the radio transmitter and detonated the engine room bombs.

Gino was shivering from both the cold wind and his fear. "God damn it, Tony, get below. We gotta crash-dive."

"No, I need to be above water to set off the bombs, and my guys in scuba suits are still too close."

"They started swimming a while ago."

Tony grimaced. He held the orange radio trigger and smashed down its button. There was no explosion on the *Sea Trek*. "Shit, the battery's dead." He tossed the orange transmitter into the water. His face showed worry in the pale glow of the full moon.

Gino had pulled Heather closer to the hatch. "Tony, we need to dive."

Tony unsnapped a pouch on his pistol belt to grab his backup radio transmitter. "I'll come down after I blow the ship to kingdom come." The sub was rocking furiously on the rough sea. Tony slipped sideways on the wet surface of the vessel and caught hold of a handle on the conning tower. He grabbed the second radio trigger and peered at the *Sea Trek* through the fog.

Suddenly, Heather kneed Gino. She leaped into the water and swam fast toward the *Sea Trek*'s port shell door.

Gino groaned and felt like throwing up. "Damn her." His face felt hot even in the cold wind and ocean spray.

* * *

MAY 18, 12:33 AM

Ryder pushed himself up after he'd stumbled and fallen on the deck. Shooting bursts of pain ran up his left shinbone and throughout his leg. He muscled forward toward the open shell door.

Layla stood near the doorway. She grasped Ryder's left arm while he used the butt of his rifle to support his left side. He peered out of the opening to his right. The sub was moving southwest at three knots against the windblown, choppy waves and the current. The gale was cutting swaths through the fog bank. Clear, mist-free patches appeared over the water.

Ryder could see Tony waving his orange remote bomb trigger as he argued with another man standing near the sub's conning tower. Heather's blond head was visible as she swam through the thinning fog toward him.

After she'd jumped, why hadn't the two men gone down the hatch and crash-dived the submarine? Ryder knew the answer. Radio signals couldn't go through the steel hull of a ship and wouldn't penetrate water, either. Tony would have been unable to detonate the bombs if he were underwater. Was he waiting for the sub to go a safe distance away before he set the bombs off?

Ryder raised his M1. He braced the rifle on the doorframe. As he aimed at Tony on the rocking submarine, more than fifty meters away, Ryder leaned on his left leg. A loud snap came from his shinbone. His vision went black. He thought he was plunging into a cool, dark void. There was no pain, just cold iciness.

His weapon tumbled into the ocean.

* * *

MAY 18, 12:34 AM

Three seconds after his left shinbone had snapped in half, Ryder came to. He gritted his teeth and pushed himself up to his right knee near the edge of the shell door opening. He realized how close he'd come to falling into the water. He heard footsteps. He turned at the same instant Layla hurled a doughnut-shaped life preserver on a line toward Heather as she swam against the waves.

Heather, a strong swimmer, had cut the distance between herself and the *Sea Trek* to fifteen meters. She took four strokes and grabbed the white life ring. Layla tied the life ring line to the left side of the shell door's rope ladder.

Heather was now only five meters from the door.

Layla stood and pulled out the Glock pistol she'd strapped to her stomach. From the right edge of the door, she fired wildly at Tony. Bullets hit the water far wide of her target.

Ryder yelled, "Layla, quick, git me the rocket launcher and a blue-tipped missile."

Layla set the smoking Glock on the deck and ran for the adjacent storage room, where the pirates kept the RPG-7 launcher and extra projectiles. Ryder could smell gun smoke.

Heather climbed the rope ladder, saw Ryder, and said, "I'll help." Dripping wet, she chased Layla.

Visible in the light of the full moon, the sub was at least a hundred meters away, making slow progress. All of a sudden, rain began to pelt the water. The wind howled. The misty fog grew thinner by the second. The sub violently rolled and bobbed up and down on six-foot waves.

Ryder yelled, "Hurry, Layla."

* * *

MAY 18, 12:36 AM

Ryder's left leg felt numb, as if he were losing circulation. Where was Layla? Would Tony push the detonate button before she brought Ryder the RPG launcher? Moving faster, the sub was now two hundred meters away. His left lower leg bent at an odd angle, Ryder felt faint.

Rapid footsteps sounded behind Ryder.

Layla slid to a stop and gave him the RPG-7 launcher, loaded with a blue-tipped projectile. There was useless Russian text on the weapon's side. But an adhesive label in English read, "Unscrew blue tip, cock hammer, shoot."

Ryder slid sideways to the center of the doorway, enabling him to aim to his right at the fiberglass sub. He unscrewed the blue tip and pulled back the six-shooter-like hammer. He yelled, "Don't stand behind me."

Layla and Heather moved to his right.

Ryder peered along the shoulder-fired weapon's antiaircraft-like iron sights. Pain pounded his leg. To correct for the wind, he aimed right of the submarine and upward. The *Sea Trek* and the sub bobbed on the rough waves. He squeezed the trigger.

The initial charge blew the 85mm rocket out of the tube. The rocket fired. It leaped forward at three hundred meters per second. The missile arced far left, pushed by the wind. The projectile missed the sub off its port side.

"Damn," Ryder said. "Hand me another rocket."

* * *

MAY 18, 12:37 AM

Tony saw the RPG round hit the water to his right.

Gino's head stuck out from the hatch. "The missile came close. Get down here, Tony."

Tony whispered into the wind, "Why did you leave me, Heather?" He took a deep breath and hovered his finger over the button on the orange trigger box. He visualized Heather's face. A tear rolled down his cheek, and it blew away in the gale. He wasn't sure whether or not he could press the button.

* * *

MAY 18, 12:38 AM

Heather gave Ryder a projectile.

Ryder heard the sound of helicopters in the distance. He slid the new projectile into the launcher's metal tube, unscrewed the blue cap, and cocked the hammer.

The sub was two hundred seventy meters away. Had Tony's radio trigger failed? Would the sub dive, or would Tony push the detonate button?

Ryder trusted his gut and aimed farther right and higher. He squeezed the trigger. The *Sea Trek* rose on a wave. The hammer struck the firing pin. It hit the primer at the tail of the rocket. The missile flew out of the tube, fired, and swooped left and downward. It struck the fiberglass sub. The sound of the explosion echoed across the water. An apricot ball of flame erupted. Its colors ranged from blackish to light orange.

Smoking pieces of the submarine littered the water's surface after the bulk of the vessel had sunk.

Great relief surged through Ryder's body. But severe pain shocked his left leg as if it had been struck by lightning. He dropped the RPG-7 launcher at his side. His chin quivered, but he resisted weeping. Instead, he felt a wave of sorrow mix with his relief.

The noise of boots pounding the deck came from behind Ryder. He turned. A man in fatigues aimed an automatic weapon at him. "FBI" was emblazoned on his field jacket.

Ryder said, "I'm Mr. Bear." He gestured at Layla. "She's Miss Bear." He glanced at Heather. "And there's Heather Falcon."

The FBI agent lowered his weapon. "You okay, Deputy Sheriff Ryder?"

"My left leg's broke. But I knocked out the narco sub with Franco on it." Ryder pointed to the blazing remnants of the fiberglass submersible boat. "He was gonna set off the engine room bombs with a radio signal."

"The bomb squad is in the engine room," the agent said. "Any pirates still around you know of?"

"I ain't sure, but some swam away in scuba suits."

"Let's get you to a hospital, Deputy."

Ryder gulped, nodded, and held back his tears, though his eyes glazed in the moonlight.

FIFTY-FIVE

TWO MEN SAT in a luxurious house on the outskirts of Bogotá, Colombia. They spoke in Spanish. The first man was eating a piece of toast with jelly on it. A glass of papaya juice sat on a fancy, oval breakfast table near him. His name was Ricardo Cortez, and he wore expensive but casual clothes. He turned to his companion, a stocky man with steel-gray, wiry hair, who held a cup of steaming coffee. "Jaime, you say Tony is dead. How?"

"An RPG round destroyed our submarine along with our fine friend, Gino Gonzales."

Ricardo sighed. "It's a pity about Gino. Still, our strategy worked. We moved forty-one tons of product in the last two days instead of nine tons. We made four times more American dollars than usual."

The older man asked, "What did it cost us to equip Tony?"

Ricardo studied the ceiling. "We paid five hundred thousand each to the seven guys who got away. We'll set up a legal defense fund for those arrested. The arms cost less than a million. The submarine was five million. We're still adding up the costs for the trucks and airplanes. Renting the chopper and paying Pilot, six hundred thousand. I'm glad he evaded capture. It's a miracle. He ditched the chopper and swam to shore, a feat for a man of his age. We'll buy him a replacement helicopter. He's a favorite of mine."

The older man nodded. He scribbled on a notepad.

"Yes, and we got rid of Tony, *el loco*." Ricardo sighed. "I shouldn't have sent Gino with the sub. He was a loyal man." Ricardo Cortez, the drug lord leader of *Los Hermanos* Drug Cartel, wiped away a rare tear trickling down his face.

FIFTY-SIX

A NURSE PUSHED Ryder's wheelchair to a patient pickup zone in front of San Diego Orthopedic Hospital while Layla carried his crutches.

A heavy-duty, black, electric sports utility vehicle with tinted windows stood at the curb. Ryder heard its locks snap open. FBI Agent Rita Reynolds exited the driver's side door and walked toward him and Layla.

Rita peered at the fiberglass cast on Ryder's left lower leg. "Thank God you're alive. And you're a hero." She turned to Layla. "You, too." She embraced Layla.

"I just wanted to survive." Layla glanced at Ryder. "The orthopedic trauma surgeon put in two screws."

"It don't hurt too bad," Ryder said. "The doc said it'd heal in a month to six weeks."

Rita opened the front passenger door. "Let's get in. I have a surprise for you both."

The nurse and Layla helped Ryder into the front seat. Rita and Layla stowed the crutches in the vehicle's cargo area.

As Ryder settled in the truck, he glimpsed backward and caught sight of long, blond hair and then a young woman's face. Heather sat in the back seat with a well-dressed, blue-eyed man. Ryder thought the fellow was in his late forties.

Heather smiled. She wore fresh, beautiful clothes and trendy red lipstick. Though she'd been through hell, she seemed calm and happy but tired. "Luke Ryder, this is my father, Howard."

Howard leaned over the front seat and offered his hand to Ryder. "Thank you and Layla for saving Heather's life," he said.

Ryder noticed the man was thin and bony, but athletic. Ryder said, "Heather helped, too, cuz she gave me the second RPG rocket in the nick of time. A second later, and Franco could've set off the bombs."

Heather smiled. "It's important for people to join forces in a crisis." She directed her attention to Layla, who was sitting next to her father. "You threw the life ring to me. The water was cold, and I was cramping. You saved me."

Layla demurely smiled.

Rita closed her driver's side door and glanced at Ryder. "Have they told you about the surprise?"

Ryder shook his head no.

Howard said, "I have a second home in the San Diego suburbs. If you and Layla would like to spend time there to rest and recuperate, my house is your house."

Layla said, "It's wonderful of you to share your home."

"It's nice of you, Howard," Ryder said. "Thank you."

Heather grinned. "Stay as long as you'd like—a month or two if you want." She turned to her father. "Daddy says our San Diego chauffeur and car will be at your disposal."

Howard cleared his throat. "Years ago, I had a skiing accident. There's a wheelchair at the house you can borrow. Maurice, our chauffeur, knows all the sights in and around San Diego as well as the best restaurants. Our housekeeper, Clara, is an excellent cook and will prepare your at-home meals."

Ryder smiled. "We missed Alaska, but at least after this nightmare, we can enjoy San Diego. Thanks."

"My pleasure, Luke and Layla."

Layla caught Howard's attention. "Is there any chance my young daughter, Angela, could stay with us here, too? She's still in Kentucky."

"Of course. I'll be glad to take care of Angela's travel."

Layla smiled. "Thank you, Howard. I miss Angela, and I'm sure she'll enjoy seeing the San Diego area with us."

"I'm happy to help." He glanced at Rita. "Are you going to go right to my place?"

"Yes."

Ryder admired the scenery as they drove and then asked, "Rita, can you tell me what happened to the *Sea Trek* after I was flown to the hospital?"

"Yes, but the Falcons must not repeat anything I say to the media or anyone else. Agreed?"

"Certainly," Howard said.

"Minutes after the medevac chopper flew you away, Luke, the bomb squad began to defuse the C-4 explosives. The rest of the Hostage Rescue Team searched the ship with the aid of the Coast Guard. They found no pirates except dead ones. The HRT assembled the passengers and crew at the lifeboat stations. We were about to evacuate the ship when the bomb squad reported they'd disabled all of the bombs. Then we brought a team of agents to the *Sea Trek* to debrief the passengers and crew."

Heather asked, "Will I be questioned, too?"

"I'll interview you because I've been in close contact with your dad throughout this crisis. I spoke with Layla when Luke was in the operating room." As Rita turned right, she glanced at Ryder. "I'll call you tomorrow for a debrief."

Ryder asked, "What about the pirates who swam for shore?"

"We caught four of them on the beach."

"A few could've left hours earlier," Ryder said. "Jeff Brooks told me the scuba gear was unguarded at times."

"You may be right. And one or two pirates must've flown away on the Huey helicopter. The Mexicans found it underwater near shore. Its doors were open. No bodies were found. I'm told the pilot must've autorotated the chopper's rotors and ditched it. For an autorotation, the pilot turns off the engine, but the blades keep turning. The chopper flutters down like a silver maple seed."

"What about Tokyo Joe?"

"We didn't catch him." Rita turned into a wide driveway and stopped in front of a large gate.

Howard pushed a button on a wireless control. A movable barrier swung open. "We're here. Welcome."

Ryder studied a mansion on the top of a hill. He fought to keep his weary eyes open. "It's beautiful."

Rita drove uphill along the winding driveway.

FIFTY-SEVEN

FOURTEEN MILES from the San Diego Orthopedic Hospital, Ryder and Layla slept in the master bedroom of Howard's coastal mansion. It sat on a hill overlooking the Pacific Ocean.

Ryder awoke in the early evening. Layla was in a deep sleep, her eyelids fluttering as she dreamed.

He wondered if he should take up Rita's offer of sessions with an FBI therapist to deal with the traumatic experiences he'd faced in recent weeks.

Ryder's brain raced through a series of flashbacks. He saw the murder suspect who'd died in a struggle with him at NASA the week before his vacation. Then he pictured the tall, dark pirate he'd killed who'd tried to rape Layla. Last of all, he envisioned the smoldering remnants of Gino's submarine.

Was Tony's mother still alive? If she were, would she grieve the death of her son? Of course. What had caused Tony to choose a life of crime? Would he otherwise have been an asset to humanity? He was, after all, intelligent, quick-thinking, and charismatic.

Ryder held back a tear when he recalled having launched

missiles at Tony and the narco sub. To try to think of something else, he eased back against the headboard of the California king bed. Daylight streamed through the wide, tall picture windows and vividly lit everything in the room. He looked outside.

The rain had ended and cleansed the air. The fog was gone, and the sun was as warm as a best friend. The nearby ocean was deep blue and matched the sky. Seagulls played in the wind as they soared and then descended to the surface of the sea.

Ryder felt like a king. There was no pain in his leg, thanks to his orthopedic trauma surgeon, who'd prescribed nonaddictive painkillers.

Ryder admired Layla as she slept. She was a slender ebony angel in her white cotton nightgown. Her deep-black afro hairdo was sexy.

Layla stirred, stretched, and yawned.

Ryder was embarrassed when he realized she'd noticed he was staring at her.

She smiled and asked, "Have a nice nap, dear?"

"Yes." Ryder shifted his left leg, which was elevated and cushioned on a fat pillow.

"Let me adjust your cushion." Layla got out of bed. She moved with the poise of a fashion model.

He felt the love she broadcast to him, but he casually said, "It was no vacation."

Layla sat next to him on the thick, plush mattress. "Yes, but I've learned what you do at work." She leaned against him. His crutches, which were propped against the side of the headboard, fell onto the carpet with a muted thud.

"And I learned you got a lotta spunk besides bein' a beauty."

Layla turned to him and gave him a long, French-style kiss. "Hon, you've relaxed. I believe it's because you've taken the special, new painkiller. It's working. But why not try a natural painkiller, too? The kind your body produces when you make love?"

Ryder hugged her gently. "The natural kind's habit-formin', but I don't mind."

She embraced him with passion, sealed herself against him, and pulled him down on top of her.

She was soft. He closed his eyes. He imagined he was in a forest glade in the sun, and they were lying on warm, soothing grass. He felt Layla relax beneath him. He again touched his lips with hers.

IF YOU LIKE THIS, YOU MAY ALSO ENJOY: THE FINGER TRAP

A TONY FLANER MYSTERY BOOK ONE
BY JOHNNY WORTHEN

When half measures don't get you the whole truth...

Tony Flaner is a part-time comedian and full-time commitment-phobe who has never been able to stick with anything in his life. After his fourteen-year marriage ends in divorce, Tony's life takes a dramatic turn when a drunken party ends in murder.

With his life on the line, he must uncover the identity of the mysterious girl who was murdered and how they ended up together in the first place. This undertaking is not just about clearing his name—Tony needs to prove to himself and everyone else that he can finish something for *once in his life.*

But when Tony discovers that his fate is intertwined with that of the mysterious girl he hardly knew—and that their lives are connected like a Chinese finger trap—he unknowingly embarks on a journey full of twists and turns around every corner.

Can Tony Flaner finish this one task and clear his name before he gets sent to prison for a murder he didn't commit?

AVAILABLE NOW

ABOUT THE AUTHOR

John G. Bluck was an Army journalist at Ft. Lewis, Washington, during the Vietnam War. Following his military service, he worked as a cameraman covering crime, sports, and politics—including Watergate for WMAL-TV (now WJLA-TV) in Washington, D.C. Later, he was a radio broadcast engineer at WMAL-AM/FM.

After that, John worked at NASA Lewis (now Glenn) Research Center in Cleveland, Ohio, where he produced numerous television documentaries. He transferred to NASA Ames Research Center at Moffett Field, California, where he became the Chief of Imaging Technology. He then became a NASA Ames public affairs officer.

John retired from NASA in 2008. Now residing in Livermore, California, he is a novelist and short story author.

Made in the USA
Middletown, DE
26 August 2023

37409690R00172